Praise for
Tell Me Pleasant Things about Immortality

"The stories in *Tell Me Pleasant Things about Immortality* will make you laugh, cry . . . and gasp. Here, Lindsay Wong has created an absurd symphony of tragedy and joy that leads Asian Canadian writing into uncharted and new, incredible directions. The horrible is hilarious, the tragic is titillating, the morbid is mirthful. In these stories you will find beauty, horror, pleasure, and play."
—JENNY HEIJUN WILLS, author of *Older Sister. Not Necessarily Related.*

"*Tell Me Pleasant Things about Immortality* is a truly original collection of short stories, a book that brims over with otherworldly creatures, disaster, humour, and the unassailable bonds of familial love and hate. Lindsay Wong asks us to accompany her characters as they fight, dream, and survive in worlds that are on the verge of collapsing. It's a wild ride and I loved every second of it."
—JEN SOOKFONG LEE, author of *Superfan* and *The Conjoined*

"From a hair-chomping grandma ghost to nine-tail fox demons who snack on frat boys, the women of *Tell Me Pleasant Things about Immortality* are moody, sharp-tongued, and subversive. With humour and mischief, Lindsay Wong spins horrifying tales across continents and centuries. These stories slither through uncanny worlds and dredge up deep feelings of alienation, longing, and shame. Eccentric and unforgettable."
—PIK-SHUEN FUNG, author of *Ghost Forest*

"Fans of the black humour of Lindsay Wong's debut memoir, *The Woo-Woo,* can celebrate. This is a dark, hilarious, and utterly brilliant collection that sees Wong unleashing her macabre imagination. Her doomed characters reflect the kaleidoscope of immigrant experiences; the stories skewer . . . stereotypes and deliver unique insights on intergenerational trauma and culture clash. A must-read!"
—JOANNA CHIU, author of *China Unbound,* winner of the Writers' Trust Shaughnessy Cohen Prize for Political Writing

"*Tell Me Pleasant Things About Immortality* is an engrossing, entertaining, and haunting feat. Lindsay Wong expertly braids fable and nightmare into the story arc, oscillating between shocking and twisted, and heartfelt and humorous. Family drama quickly turns to revenge and gore, as characters morph and grow to surprising ends. Packed with curses, ghosts, and death, this collection captures an unease rarely explored, yet certain to be richly valued by readers."
—DEREK MASCARENHAS, author of *Coconut Dreams*

"In this exhilarating collection, characters seek exuberance in hardship; they struggle to make the most of life, death, and everything in between. Wong writes against Asian immigrant stereotypes with a singular voice, seemingly freewheeling and maximalist but always in tight, expert control. Utterly unforgettable!"
—YZ CHIN, author of *Edge Case*

Tell Me Pleasant Things about Immortality

ALSO BY LINDSAY WONG

The Woo-Woo
My Summer of Love and Misfortune

Tell Me Pleasant Things about Immortality

Stories

Lindsay Wong

PENGUIN

an imprint of Penguin Canada, a division of Penguin Random House Canada Limited

Canada • USA • UK • Ireland • Australia • New Zealand • India • South Africa • China

First published 2023

www.penguinrandomhouse.ca

*Publisher's note: This book is a work of fiction. Names, characters, places and incidents
either are the product of the author's imagination or are used fictitiously, and any resemblance
to actual persons living or dead, events, or locales is entirely coincidental.*

LIBRARY AND ARCHIVES CANADA CATALOGUING IN PUBLICATION

Title: Tell me pleasant things about immortality : stories / Lindsay Wong.
Names: Wong, Lindsay, author.
Identifiers: Canadiana (print) 20210309121 | Canadiana (ebook) 20210309245 |
ISBN 9780735242364 (hardcover) | ISBN 9780735242371 (EPUB)
Classification: LCC PS8645.O46175 T45 2023 | DDC C813/.6—dc23

The following story was previously published in a different form: "Wreck Beach" was
published under the name Vanessa Li in *The Fiddlehead*, No. 253 (Autumn 2012).

Book design by Emma Dolan
Cover design by Emma Dolan
Cover image: (toadstools) © Anastasiia Cheprasova / iStock / Getty Images

Printed in Canada

10 9 8 7 6 5 4 3 2 1

Penguin
Random House
PENGUIN CANADA

*For my ancestors, who faced terrible and portentous horrors.
I've heard the stories about surviving famine and the Japanese
invasion of China and how starving villagers swapped
children to eat. Thanks for sparing Grandma.* 😁

CONTENTS

Happy Birthday!

"Very sorry-lah," Mr. Goh murmured, clanging his chopstick on a miniature porcelain bowl. "Attention, attention," he ding-ding-a-linged. "Important news, everyone."

Johnny sighed and forced more braised pork hoof into his mouth. He was in a shit mood. The chopstick was like a cymbal, clanging through his beatbox migraine, his stilted performance in a family sitcom. Having dinner with Mr. and Mrs. Goh was like watching an HD-3D laser projection of himself. He saw his vanity and snobbery in his toady mother; his bullish tendencies in his obese father. Johnny had become an immigration lawyer to spite them—it was one paycheque away from janitor. He watched his la-di-da mother smile at his father, who was turning sixty-five years old. Tonight, Mr. Goh was unusually quiet. Possibly even nervous. A splotch of white rice was glued to his cushy upper lip. The foundation he used to contour his apple-like cheeks was the wrong shade.

Johnny groaned as the chopstick smack-smacked the bowl. *Shit, I'm beginning to look a lot like Bah*, he thought, sucking in his fanny-pack gut. He was also wearing concealer—his wife said the mauve circles under his eyes made him look like he tried too hard. Johnny stabbed at an ogre-sized fish ball in his bowl.

"Sorry," his father said again. Rice sprayed from his mouth. "Don't want to ruin your good meal but this man that you're celebrating is a serial killer."

This was surely some seriously fucked-up joke, so Johnny smiled close-mouthed like he did in court. "Ha-ha!" he said because he was supposed to. He looked at his younger sister, college dropout Amy, for reinforcement, but she had begun shoving crabmeat into her maw.

"If Bah has a brain disease, this will be my last decent meal in a while," she muttered to no one.

"You're so goddamn selfish," Johnny retorted before he could stop himself. "Always thinking of yourself."

"Oh shut up, everyone," his mother said, still smiling. "Eat your supper, lóuhgùng, husband."

The greasy lemon chicken appeared yellow and globular under the bright lights of the dining room, the spindly crab legs looked sinister, and the grey abalone looked, well, undead. His stomach churned. He watched his father carefully. He had read in a British newspaper that a skewed, macabre sense of humour was a sign of early dementia. What was the punchline?

Mr. Goh frowned, and said in a shrill tone: "I'm not your husband. Sorry-lah." His wide eyes looked greasy and sad.

Mrs. Goh tittered in that way that irritable Chinese ladies at the Hong Kong Country Club in Deep Water Bay liked to do: her left hand smothering her puckered, processed face like a napkin. *Fucky-fuck, she looks like a powdered pig*, Johnny thought. *Hong Kong's Marie Antoinette. How did I not notice this before?*

"Who are you, then?" Mrs. Goh said in a we-won't-ever-have-sex kind of tone, which Johnny's wife had recently adopted.

"Bah's finally having that psychotic break," Amy announced, slopping her wine.

"Mimi," his father answered politely. "I'm Mimi. Sorry-lah, but your husband chopped me into itsy little bits."

They'd arrived early in the a.m. for their father's surprise sixty-fifth birthday dinner, flying into Hong Kong International from Vancouver (Johnny) and New York City (Amy). Both of them had flown business class, and then pointedly ignored the other while chugging down complimentary champagne as they waited to be picked up in the Cathay Pacific executive member lounge. They had frowned in unison when they saw their mother and her driver approaching, conscientiously straightened their luxury sportswear flight outfits, smoothed down their red-eye hair, and signalled for more flutes of champagne to be brought over. In the airport lounge, Johnny and Amy timidly shook hands with their mother because Mrs. Goh did not generally approve of affection, and so they had hugged their driver, Eddie or Freddie, instead.

Mrs. Goh had promised each of her children $5,000 U.S. if they showed up at their father's dinner, for a maximum of forty-eight hours and two other meals, preferably dim sum, and maybe a matinee of *The Magic Flute* with sloppy Cantonese subtitles. For any amount less, Johnny and Amy would not endure the trying familiarity of their parents' company. *Five grand is barely enough to cover a few fucking months of therapy*, Johnny thought.

"Your Bah's been acting strangely," Mrs. Goh said in the car, fidgeting with her pink Burberry handbag. She kept orange lipstick, pepper spray, and an oval compact of thick cream for yeast infections in the front zipper for emergencies. A fishy, coppery odour permeated the car, which she blamed on Eddie or Freddie.

"Mid-life crisis," Johnny remarked coolly, because he was thinking of having a more permanent affair with a very young co-ed himself. His banker wife, banal but comely-ish, thank god, did not get along with his parents, and she had not been invited to his father's party.

"He seemed jumbled this morning," Mrs. Goh was saying. "He screamed a little. Maybe coughed. Then he went into the bathroom."

"Then what?" Johnny said.

"We had breakfast. Eggs and congee. Oh, and then I almost forgot-lah!"

"Yes?" Johnny prodded his mother because his career had been built on asking timely questions.

"Toast with marmalade. He ate three slices. He never eats more than half of one-lah. He prefers salty."

Amy had been indifferent, saying that she thought that Mah, as usual, was being dramatic. "What's for dinner?" she asked, and then inquired about the $5,000.

"You shouldn't be so goddamn obvious about it," Johnny scolded, so their mother could hear.

"At least I'm not a fucking phony!" Amy shouted. Johnny's "fakeness" had become an international household argument, usually carried over three-page emails and scrambled texts.

"Both of you, shut up," Mrs. Goh said. She smacked her tongue as she reapplied her orange lipstick. "This smell is making me nauseous. You'll get your money at the end of the weekend-lah."

—

"You'll feel more like yourself once you have dessert-lah," Mrs. Goh cooed to her husband after his outburst/bad joke. "Of course you are my husband. Who else would you be-lah?"

Johnny knew that his mother would rather undergo liposuction without anaesthetic than argue in public with her husband. He smirked—his rich parents believed in fighting as much as they did in kindness. In their family, compassion was solely for the weak-minded and middle-class. Marriage, unfortunately, was an inborn duty, a well-schemed alliance to increase one's net worth and secure a long-lasting dynasty. Johnny's parents had gotten engaged on the second date, following recommendations from country club friends and a professional matchmaker, as did both their respective parents and grandparents. After college, Johnny, carrying on this tradition, had proposed to the Banker on his parents' detailed instructions, and she had agreed to the marriage because his family had a high ranking at the Hong Kong Country Club.

He was just as indifferent when he was accepted into a second-rate law school in Vancouver. Waving his acceptance letter at his wife when they were supposed to be on their honeymoon, Johnny had suggested that the Banker remain in Hong Kong. But his new wife had attached herself to him, like a fatty tumour, following him all the way to another continent. Why she had ever left Hong Kong was unfathomable to Johnny—he felt they would be on more amicable terms if they had a long-distance online relationship. He had dropped several passive-aggressive hints on voice mail, very aware that he was mimicking his mother's perpetually nagging, sing-songing tone: *Hong Kong is better for your complexion, dear. Aiya, so much rain in Vancouver makes many wrinkles appear.*

Mrs. Goh disappeared into the kitchen, returning with a beautiful mango pudding drowning in thick condensed milk, followed by a lofty two-tiered sponge cake with clouds of whipped cream and baubles of green tropical fruit. Whenever Amy and Johnny were visiting, she dismissed the housekeeper, chef, and servers, pretending that she was wholly responsible for the gargantuan feast. Not to mention, she didn't pay her staff well enough not to gossip openly about her children.

Feeling uneasy, Johnny severed the cake and the crayon-yellow pudding with a knife. They had dessert in the dishes used for their parents' second-rate guests. Even as children, they had never been allowed to touch the good plates, not even if one of them had gotten As at their fancy English-speaking-only private school. Hong Kong Academy was the most diffi-cult school on the island, reserved for gweilo foreigners, and the genetically prodigious children of dignitaries and mid-ranking aristocrats. Johnny had been upper-midpack (top fif-teen) in all of his classes; Amy had gotten expelled for having sex in the auditorium.

Amy shovelled in seconds and thirds of the yellow pudding. Johnny wished his mother would contemptuously tell her to Stop! like she did when they were children because Amy was obese by Hong Kong standards. His sister was pretty, but she always looked like she was twelve days constipated. Instead, Mrs. Goh was telling Amy about the new cake shop in Repulse Bay and some cousin's unfortunate match. "Married some schoolteacher!" she tut-tutted. "Doomed to work all her life. Just think, no more dinners at the Club, goodbye to her child-hood friends, just like that."

Amy finished her cake. "Mah, not everyone thinks that having to work for a living is unfortunate," she said.

"Well, *most* of us have jobs," Johnny said. "We finish college and don't live off Mah and Bah."

Mr. Goh coughed. "I really don't know what I have to do to get your attention," he said, "but your dad murdered me, you know?"

"Bullshit," Mrs. Goh said. She thunked her spoon on her placemat.

His father sighed. "I'm sorry, but please listen to me, okay?" He raised both hands, coquettish, like some young dancing girl at a nightclub. Johnny thought of the co-ed, his boss's daughter. "Are you okay?" she would always ask him in her schoolgirl Mandarin, her Q-tip eyebrows twitching with concern whenever she saw him at the office or when they walked down Robson Street together sipping lukewarm Starbucks lattes on their lunch breaks. Johnny wiped his mouth and burped. He flinched at the sound, a betrayal of his slowing digestive system and perhaps late-twenties metabolism. His father looked him in the eyeball, and seemed to mean what he was saying.

To his relief, Johnny's phone dinged with a reminder, allowing him to sever eye contact with his father. He squinted at the tiny screen. Groaned indelicately. He was supposed to email the Banker. He made sure to casually update her on his whereabouts and spending habits at least once a week, even though they shared a claustrophobic 550 sq. ft. two-bedroom condo on the stuffy west side of Vancouver. He lied more than half the time. At least now, he had an excuse to leave the table. *Why was I born in this miserable family?* he thought. *Why was Amy allowed to escape all family obligations? No one forced Amy to marry some piece-of-shit banker, lawyer, or doctor with unseemly wealth and connections. No one ever forced Amy to do anything.*

For the umpteenth time since they were children, Johnny wanted to strangle Amy for benefiting from their family's good name. He wanted to yell at his parents for not favouring him more, for not distinguishing him from feckless, ungrateful, wastrel Amy. Even her English name sounded unserious; three-quarters hippy, one-quarter unsanctimonious North American trailer trash. What were his parents even thinking when they chose that Western moniker? No one below the lowest of the upper-upper-middle classes in Asia was called Amy.

He reached for a toothpick to clean his front teeth. Swallowed his bitterness with a generous swig of warm cabernet sauvignon. He supposed he should excuse himself to the guest suite and compose his email to the Banker. Johnny usually wrote a quick list, like one he'd do for essential groceries.

He was about to excuse himself when the large pinewood dining room suddenly rumbled—a 7.5 magnitude earthquake! Johnny had only been in one small earthquake, when he was in the eighth grade and had disliked being forced to hide in a cramped space and count to 120. Then, to add to his burgeoning discomfort (*why couldn't they just finish eating dinner like normal people and immediately retire to their rooms, for fuck's sake!*), their father got out of his chair and did a stunning high kick in the air. Turned Radio City Rockette, he did, leaped right on the table, kicking a second-rate dish onto the white marble floor. He clapped his hands, twice. Mrs. Goh seemed unfazed. In the kitchen, the stainless steel refrigerator toppled over, followed by a top-of-the-line microwave. *BOOM!*

Johnny blinked.

Still no one said anything, so Mr. Goh swivelled his robust hips, thrusting his pelvis persistently, and all the windows and doors in the penthouse flew open. There was still no reaction from the family, and stunned, Johnny could feel himself becoming queasy, especially when the stilted paintings of English pastoral countryside and overpriced scrolls of fifteenth-century Chinese inks smashed one by one to the ground. He had always sneered at his mother's taste in art; she bid on whatever was hardest to acquire at Christie's once every three years. *Crash! Crash! Crash!* Mr. Goh whooped, and a few of the porcelain dishes cracked. Glass zoomed everywhere.

"Ouch!" Amy cried as a teeny piece of glass sliced her forearm.

"Serves you right!" Johnny crowed like a child because he couldn't help it. He was too afraid to look at his father directly.

"Gee, I don't know my own strength," Mr. Goh said, a fantastic gleam in his yellow, shifting eyes. Johnny's father's pupils used to be dog-shit brown.

Even Mr. Goh's features looked brighter, his skin tone changed from cosmetic beige to a grassy green, his lips reptilian, and icicles hung from his eyebrows. *Fucky-fuck*, Johnny thought, panicking, *is that mould growing on my father's nose?!*

Amy, who had finished three-quarters of the mango pudding, looked nauseous. "You are not my father," she yelled, backing away from Mr. Goh.

"Duh," the voice inside their father said, sounding pleased. "Watch this!"

In front of them, their dirty dinner chopsticks and teaspoons and miniature teacups levitated, falling back down and rising up again like hazy planets. Then they travelled side-ways, zigzagging, defying gravity. And then suddenly Bah's two-tiered birthday cake exploded. Johnny yelped as clumps of yellow-white sponge cake splattered everywhere, on everyone, like peed-on snow.

Mr. Goh cackled. The noise of a man who was possessed by a young girl of twenty or so.

"This is so not happening," Amy announced, wiping globs of cake from her eyes.

"Husband, you stop this right now," Mrs. Goh shouted, "and we won't talk about it ever again!"

Johnny had never seen his self-obsessed, puritanical parents bicker at the table or his proud venture capitalist father trans-formed. His mother's mouth was exposed in a squirrel-like squeak, and even Amy, who didn't care about anyone except herself, looked amazed. Johnny tried to compose his features into his pompous-lawyer face. *How is this even happening?* he thought. *Am I having some kind of psychotic break?*

But then Mrs. Goh's chair began to rise, like it was a stage prop attached to invisible cables. She herself began to spin and spin and she screamed and screamed upside down. Her beauti-ful black silk dress whooshed up, and Johnny pretended that he could not see her profuse varicose veins, which were like hateful calligraphy done by a child, etched all across her thighs. Poor Mrs. Goh rotated like an oversized, expensive garment inside an industrial-powered washing machine. Her chair landed on the white marble floor with a foul thump.

"Jesus Christ," Johnny said matter-of-factly.

"Got your attention now!" Mr. Goh shouted, an aha! moment illuminating his tin-coloured face. He appeared quite confident as he stood on the dining room table. Flashing his aluminum-coloured tongue, his father barked: "This is what's going to happen now, or I might have to kill somebody. Your Bah hated all your guts so much, told me all about you while he tied me up and threw me in his trunk. Selfish, all of you-lah.

"Now Johnny, you're gonna make a trust of ten trillion Hong Kong dollars and monthly payments to my baby girl and my middle sister, who is looking after her, all right? I want that in fancy lawyer writing."

Silence, so uncomfortable that to Johnny it felt like seventy-two-hour indigestion.

Blinking, he counted his breaths before realizing that he was hyperventilating. For once in his scrupulously cultivated personal life, Johnny had no semi-clever retort or half-formed argument. He moaned as he thought about his rapidly diminishing inheritance. Shouted: "Jesus fucking Christ!"

Then: "You mean a contract? Why can't you just find a notary public?" Then he added, in the collected, sympathetic voice he used for the internationally disenfranchised and also because he was planning on making partner at his firm in two years: "I heard they're very affordable, miss."

"Ten trillion dollars!" Mrs. Goh chimed in from mid-air, her legs flailing in a convulsive one-woman cancan. "Who the hell do you think you are?!"

Mr. Goh continued. "And I want little Amy to convince my sister to see the surgeon. She has an egg-sized tumour in her hooch and can live five or six more years if she gets it chopped, yeah? Otherwise, next month she's gonna kick the bucket while watching Korean soaps and my baby girl will be left all alone. Mostly, my sister just needs friends who aren't crackheads."

"How do I do that?" Amy asked.

"I don't know," the voice said. "Try Facebook. Send her a request."

No one said anything.

"You owe me!" the voice inside Mr. Goh whined, stamping his foot. "I was murdered in the prime of my life by your Bah. I was really hot!"

"No! No! No!" Mrs. Goh shouted, and Mr. Goh allowed her to float for a while.

An hour later, after six or seven cups of oolong tea and whiskey, they'd all been assembled in the LuxGlass elevator, except for Mrs. Goh, who was soaring in the penthouse like a squawking Canada goose and hadn't yet been permitted to downward glide. When they left her, Johnny's poor mother was eyeballing the ceiling for dust motes.

In the elevator, Mimi/Mr. Goh began to chatter, affable and easy. Two nights ago, before she woke up in her murderer's body, Mimi Lu, bendy exotic dancer, rated Stripper Supreme on Chinese Yelp, said that she was finishing her shift at Adam's Apple (3.5 stars) when Mr. Goh approached her in the parking lot and offered her $1,500 for sex, which was considered very cheap. When she asked for more money, he throttled her to death, smashed a few of her good teeth, and then dismembered her with an X-Acto knife.

"I don't believe you!" Amy screeched. When they were children and if/when Amy felt overwhelmed, she resorted to a feral tantrum, hissing and spitting. Her performance was like

The Exorcist but hamster-like, which the family liked to tease her about.

"Let Mimi talk," Johnny commanded, as if he were in a courtroom drama. The shock made him calmer, and if he blamed his sister, he could refocus his unresolved horror.

Their father, who was, yes, an asshole, could not be a serial killer. For Christ's sake, his Bah played squash, lovingly read Martha Stewart magazines, knew how to cook zesty Canto cuisine. But still, why was there a dead girl inside him? For fuck's sake, his Bah was possessed by a stripper.

The elevator dinged and they stomp-stomped downstairs into the underground parking lot of their childhood apartment building, Mr. Goh as their leader and Amy and Johnny flanking him according to birth order, polite and cattle-like. In the trunk of the car they found a portable picnic cooler for sandwiches and soft drinks. The smell from the car was pungent, much worse than this morning.

"Isn't that Eddie or Freddie's lunch box?" Johnny asked.

It wasn't. Mr. Goh hadn't had time to dispose of his work, apparently.

Inside the cooler, smack-dab in the interior, was the solo head of a once pretty girl, age fifteen or twenty-eight, it was hard to tell, with wide-set tabby eyes and gooey makeup. Her head was angled to the side, slushy neck cartilage and popping bones exposed. Johnny gagged. Amy barfed. Gold sparkles on the girl's beluga-blue lips were smeared in the cracks of her teeth. Johnny thought of the co-ed, wondering if this was what she'd look like with copious makeup. He thought of her in his boss's office, swivelling in her daddy's chair, in a UBC sweatshirt, typing her term papers, a cold sore on her unglossed lower lip.

Hastily, Johnny placed the lid back on the cooler. Amy asked Mr. Goh/Mimi where the rest of her was. She was apparently scattered throughout the city.

"They'll mistake my rotting body for restaurant leftovers," Mimi sighed. "Why, next Friday, a starving person will take a bite out of my leg-lah."

"This is like science fiction," Johnny murmured in Canto-English. "What should we do with your head?"

No one said anything.

They went back upstairs.

While she was suspended in the air, Mrs. Goh thought of many things, like whether she had been a blameless wife or an evenly keeled mother, or if she had donated enough to charity in the past year, because why else would her husband become so unrecognizable? They had been married for thirty-nine years, and he came highly recommended by Hong Kong's top financial consultants and doctors. Mr. and Mrs. Goh had honeymooned in Spain and Macau; travelled to Maui first-class every Christmas. She knew her mother-in-law well, a terrible woman but a formidable social climber. Was Mr. Goh a serial killer? God, she didn't know. He couldn't even keep track of his clothes or medical appointments—where would all the evidence go? Mrs. Goh handled all their household business transactions. She was certain that this would never have happened if they had produced more children. Had the nannies taken turns dropping

Johnny and Amy on their heads in some personal vendetta? Mrs. Goh knew she had never been a reasonable or remotely generous employer. But if she'd had a third child, a boy, and if he had become prime minister of a small but recognized country, her husband would not be punishing her right now.

Near the ceiling, Mrs. Goh discovered that if she kicked her legs a certain way, she could rotate almost ninety-five degrees.

Twenty-five minutes later, back inside the penthouse, Johnny began doodling terms for a contract on a napkin.

Amy shouted up to Mrs. Goh, asking if she was okay, and her mother nodded, panting.

"If we don't listen to you, what will you do to us?" Johnny asked the ghost inside his possessed father. His sweaty turkey-arms shook. He clutched his stomach as if he was trying to digest a plate of contaminated oysters. Wiping at his furrowed eyebrows with his sleeve, he grunted in aggravation as flecks of pyramid-coloured concealer came off. The last time he had been this ill was when he got engaged. His mother had ordered him via a three-way conference call to propose to the Banker. Later that week, the Banker had a prompt falling-out with his parents. But the $3,550,000 three-day wedding had already been paid for. Besides, there would have been cross-continental, transpacific talk if the event at the Shangri-La Hotel was cancelled.

Mimi/Mr. Goh giggled and said: "I'll tell your wife that you're planning on sleeping with a girl—your boss's daughter. Don't you wanna make partner?"

Johnny felt faint. *How had she known? Goddamnit! Could the dead see into his head?*

"Also," Mr. Goh/Mimi cried, "I might just throw your Mah out a window for fun-lah."

Mimi wiggled her shoulders suggestively, and Mrs. Goh began to twirl and spiral until her head, like a football, smacked the crown moulding. She shrieked in Cantonese: "Husband, was it just one lapse in judgment? For Christ sake, how many girls? Tell me *now*!"

Mr. Goh/Mimi beamed. He said: "Five and a half, not including the ones on family trips to Shanghai and L.A.!"

Mrs. Goh sobbed wildly as her head whacked the ceiling like a drum, *thumpity-thump-thump*.

"Shit," Amy said. Her face looked like an overripe avocado.

"Fucky-fuck," Johnny said.

Using his best defence voice—he was not a criminal lawyer, never had been—he weakly argued that five, which was less than six, didn't necessarily make Bah a serial killer.

Amy, who Googled it, said that the definition of a serial killer was three or more. "You can't argue with the internet," she said, and sent a friend request on Facebook to Mimi's middle sister, who was as pretty as Mimi had once been.

It was nearly dawn when Johnny finished the contract and scanned it over to his secretary to be spell-checked and mailed to a friend in California who dealt with trusts for rich Asians. While his mother floated, finally unconscious, Mimi/Mr. Goh went through Mrs. Goh's Burberry handbag and applied her orange lipstick, haphazardly, to his lips. Then the possessed man went through Mrs. Goh's closet and paraded around in her favourite dress, a plunging cream Valentino that he split over his corpulent hips. He tried on her Jimmy Choos too, not a prodigious fit, and asked Amy for fashion advice.

"I think jewel tones are more your palette," Amy replied, as she tried on her mother's second-best dress.

It seemed that Amy and Mimi arrived at a semi-truce while both trying on Mrs. Goh's best clothes. Johnny didn't understand how girls could fight and forgive within what felt like a heartbeat of inhuman seconds. He couldn't understand how Amy could seem so unbothered by these unwholesome circumstances. Johnny would need at least twelve Xanax to gush about this season's clothes and jewel-tone colours. Still, he wondered what his boss's girl would look like in his mother's $9,000 Valentino. Surely, with makeup, she was much prettier than him, Mimi, and the Banker combined.

When the sun crept through the wide kitchen windows, Mrs. Goh tumbled to the floor, squawking as she landed on her bum. The front of her coiffure was dishevelled and greasy, and there was a melon-sized welt on her forehead—wait, was that a toupée? Johnny was suddenly embarrassed for his mother—he had never seen her less than perfect, and she looked vulnerable, human even. She got up and glared at them all.

Johnny wondered if Mimi was losing her power at sunrise, and whether his father was somewhere still inside. *Forget Christmas and Chinese New Year*, he thought, panicking. *How will the estate be split up, now that Bah might not ever truly die?*

"Get me some tea, lady," Mr. Goh/Mimi said, and ordered the rest of the family to make her breakfast.

After they had eaten scrambled eggs cooked by Amy, sipped sweet milk tea with bourbon, and inhaled a few sawed-off pieces of tomatoes and sourdough bread, Eddie or Freddie was called to take Johnny and Amy to the airport. Johnny decided that he would email the Banker a brief but honest exposé that he did not want to be married to her anymore. He thought of the young co-ed squinting at her laptop, and swiftly banished the thought when Mimi/his father winked at him, her/his expression wicked but knowing.

I'm going to be celibate for the year, Johnny promised the spiteful ghost in his head. *I'll spend my time gambling in Macau instead.*

In reply, Mimi/Mr. Goh rolled his animal-coloured eyes, one pupil at a time.

"Your middle sister can have my five thousand dollars," Johnny quickly said to Mimi, hoping she'd stop reading his manic spurts of panic.

"Mine too," Amy blurted. She glanced at Johnny with a proud, almost untranslatable expression, and then, to his own chagrin, he snorted. Then laughed out loud. Not unkindly.

"This sibling rivalry is getting ridiculous," he muttered, finally wiping his eyes from exhaustion and near hysteria. "You need all the help you can get, Amy," he said. "I mean, what the hell will you do without any money?"

"I'll stay in Hong Kong for a bit. Maybe find a job, maybe marry a doctor." She reached for more bourbon and looked surprised that it was finished. "Some cardiologist, probably. I'd prefer a plastic surgeon, but I heard those are hard to find these days because everyone is marrying one for the free surgery." She puckered her mouth like a depressed goldfish.

Mimi/Mr. Goh chimed in. "Your parents would love all those complimentary face and butt lifts. And don't forget your

Mah has all those connections at the Club-lah. I'm sure she can find you a high-paid surgeon."

"That's true." Amy grinned, and Mimi/Mr. Goh smiled back at her eagerly. The new BFFs laughed in high-pitched sync. *Like teenage seagulls mating*, Johnny thought, horrified.

"I've always been jealous of you, doing whatever the hell you wanted." Johnny surprised himself by admitting this in a soft voice that he reserved for pets and tiny children. There were no secrets anymore, especially when a murdered stripper could access his private thoughts like an internet database.

"I know they're really hard on you," Amy said, hesitating. "I'm sorry I've been such an asshole."

Johnny nodded but did not say he was sorry. Instead, he promised that he would text her when he arrived at his next destination: a five-star casino resort in Macau.

In the penthouse, the light was preternaturally ghost white. Mrs. Goh watched her once beloved husband, who was now a stranger, sit, beaming, at his usual spot at the dining table, a newspaper in his steady, serial-killer hands. His eyes were less gold than they had been before, but more than half of his face had turned blueish, and his nose had been replaced by an unmistakable black hole. She turned away to politely shake hands goodbye with her children.

Cringing at his father's new face, Johnny quickly found his black Versace leather loafers at the entrance. When he looked back at his father again, he felt something matchy-matchy rattling around in his intestines. There was an ugly void inside his family where their souls, like a hearty blob of red bean pastry filling, should have been. He shivered again, wondering if he had been polite enough throughout Mimi's/his father's sixty-fifth birthday dinner.

"Fuckity-fuck-fuck-fuck," he said out loud, grimacing.

Does anyone who's anyone actually care if you're a serial killer these days? he asked himself as he walked, whistling self-consciously, down the luxurious yellow hallway.

Tell Me Pleasant Things about Immortality

The Si Chi Hua, Night-Blooming Deathlily or *Lilium mortiferum nocte florente*, according to ancient scholars, is the strangest plant in all of China. It blooms under the baldness of a full lunar moon and glows hot and silvery under the constellations of the Purple Forbidden Enclosure. If consumed in excessive quantities, it will grant eternal life or kill you.

People who seek immortality come to China to consume the plant. It's like gambling in Las Vegas—everyone loses. On the full moon, every twenty-nine or thirty-one days, I watch adults stretch their arms towards me, behaving like monstrous babies on grassy deathbeds. "Please hold me, ancient Auntie!" they implore, hiccuping blood. It doesn't matter what dialect they speak, northerner or southerner, rich or poor, these sad fools are always afraid. Their screaming mouths look like fluttering black bats as their pupils blot.

What can I say? Their neediness makes me uncomfortable. Ask anyone: hiccuping coppery-tasting fluid is a sad way to expire. As the oldest living woman in the world, I know all this first-hand. I am the only known survivor of the deathlily. The only one who ate enough flowers to achieve immortality.

Over the centuries, I have received a few million fan letters, heralding my fortitude and regal appearance. From a distance, I might pass as a kindly madam or a spinster goo-mah with tragedy in the cracked graffiti of her face. Kinder admirers tend to ignore my spotty moles, which could be mistaken for black-flies on a bruised apple. But I do have the fleshy belly of an aristocratic hag, and if you look closely, my eyeballs are red and sunken, like twinkling rat eyes or what *Vogue China* calls "unexcavated rubies."

But there has been something wrong with me lately. My skin has been peeling off in greyish clumps. And some of my fingers and toes have fallen off. I lost an ear when I was bathing in the stream last month. Either a fish nibbled it off or it must have floated away!

Soon, gone will be my arms and legs, and I will be grotty chunks of a still-alive corpse. A torso without a head. What will happen to me then? After centuries of semi-living, I question whether there is even an afterlife.

Lately, my feelings are getting worse, contiguous with the weather. I feel foul when the crazed monsoons attack my home in the mountain valley, and then frail and peculiar when the atmospheric pressure plunges into a vertiginous zephyr. I used to spend 90 percent of the time worrying about myself. Sometimes, I still do. Why, just yesterday, I lost a most favoured lateral incisor when nibbling on a little Mongolian pine nut—swallowed the damned tooth whole!

Pingwei, my manager and publicist, is alarmed by my morose mood. We are good business partners but better drinking friends. "Will you please, for the love of all things immortal, practise your goddamn smile?" he says.

In this century, out of all the publicists sent by the government, Pingwei is my favourite, and honestly, not terrible on the eyes. With his spiky purple hair of the young Beijing bourgeois, he exudes a greasy charisma even if he's wearing a neon orange biohazard suit and safety goggles. He worries about accidentally ingesting or touching the horrible plant whenever he flies to my home on Mount Phoenix. He's not really an idiot, you see; he has witnessed the thoughtlessness and ambition of those who want to live forever. It's better, we both think, to skydive flamboyantly through life and not seek enduring decrepitude.

Pingwei says I look excellent for 380 years old. When I was 370, he said the exact same thing, except that I had all my teeth and fingers and toes. What I would give to have another spindly finger again to luxuriously pick at the flaky dandruff on my scalp.

"Three hundred and seventy-six," I say irritably. "You didn't get me anything for my birthday."

"So what if you are missing a little bit of your nose?" he says, ignoring the part about my birthday.

"I look like a mummy in a museum," I argue, swirling my tenth huangjiu, a filthy yellow sake, a favourite indulgence of mine. A piece of eyebrow is floating in my glass like a writhing slug. "What will I do when I reach a millennium? I'll be a walking skeleton!"

"Shush," he clucks, pouring us more alcohol. "Think of how many people in the world are dying to be you, Shuchun. What you need is a new personality. It's a fact that happy people live longer than sad ones."

The moon is red and full and inflamed, which means that it is nearly time for another Death-Eating Flower Festival. As soon as the stars tumble lazily to the menacing tops of Phoenix Mountain, they will form a phalanx at the south-facing, queenly Baihua peak, before plummeting into the cruel Longmen Gully. Yellow starlight fuels the flowers' botanic presence, as if each lump of violent gas is a tumbling coin in a slot machine. Since 2001, the festival has relied on impressive falling stars to form its opening credits.

The bloom of the deathlily is a glittering and grotesque affair. Jungle-like vines churn, spraying smelly gold pus into the air like congratulatory streamers. Eerie white flowers uncurl up to fifty feet in the air. The film crews, especially *National Geographic*, can never get enough of this award-winning footage.

On cue, Pingwei preens at a podium and graciously welcomes the helicopters and private jets, which deliver important politicians, government officials, billionaires, celebrities, and reporters, all in biohazard suits. I stand beside him, in a delicate gown of pale cubic zirconia, waving and smiling—a deranged beauty queen. For effect, I wear a lethal crown of prickly death-lilies to cover the soggy patches of my scalp that are not quite peeling off. I blink back a drooping eyelid.

In the last century, it was easy to find the deathlily. Follow the messy, luscious tropaeolum until you reach the ailing silver-grey grass. Up until the late 1900s, there used to be mile-long pathways of bird, goat, and human skeletons extending from the quarter-acre patch, and the whole perimeter was crunchy and brittle, filled with exquisite little femurs and scapulas. Now, human rights and animal activist groups have rallied for the skeletons to be removed. And the Chinese government has commissioned a helpful sign for English-speaking tourist groups who hike up Mount Phoenix all year round.

CAREFUL DYING WITHIN 100 FEET.
EATING AT OWN RISK.
HAZARDOUS HEALTH IS A FLOWER!

The festival is less of a celebration and more of an international eating competition. In the seventeenth century, it used to be a means of punishment: adulterous young women and half virgins were forced to consume the plant; in the nineteenth and twentieth centuries, murderers and China's political enemies chewed themselves to death in front of a solemn audience of world leaders. In the 1960s, after I live-demonstrated to them that I could not die by any means, officials offered me a government job. I wore a pretty cheongsam and was paid a decent salary to pour cups of rice wine for President Truman and President Khrushchev, and afterwards to bury the sullen-faced dead. In the past decade or so, the deathlily has naturally become a televised game show, more exciting to watch than America's *Wheel of Fortune*.

For the chance to live forever, current participants must pay a nonrefundable fee of ten million yuan to the Chinese government. They must roughly consume twelve pounds of the flower's dense tissue, approximately six hundred petals. Eat enough deathlily and aging slows down, mortal illness subsides. Scientists have not exactly figured out how. Something to do with chemicals that toxify yet embalm soft, sticky organs. A superior kind of bio-organic formaldehyde.

Tonight's gamblers include a fading software billionaire from Japan, an incredibly vocal dying lady from America with a fancy lace hat and white opera gloves, nine excitable blue-eyed nuns with shaved heads and missing pinkies who call themselves Schwesternschaft des ewigen Heils—Sisterhood of Eternal Salvation. What they have in common is a pungent fear of not existing. There's nothing to lose if they're all bound for a sterile and claustrophobic freezer. Maybe it's better to bleed and hiccup violently to death in one evening as a reality TV star. Saves time and hospital bills. I, for one, used to want eternal death, but now I am not so greedy, and I prefer to be intact. Of course, there is also a bored socialite from Hong Kong, barely twenty years old, in expensive jeans and platform sneakers. He complains that our competitive-eating contest is an elaborate hoax. "No one really dies on reality TV!" he scoffs in his punk-sounding Cantonese. I suddenly want to watch him expire with blood on his inflamed lips and send him to the afterlife with a teasing wave.

But where is this airy viciousness from? Perhaps it's my own body, mutinying, from ligament to limb. Perhaps I am so used to living that it has become a nasty habit.

I pick at the shedding skin between my eyes, taking comfort in the fact that very soon everyone will start chewing and screaming. The first few bites of deathlily always taste a bit like burning hair. And then the mass dyings come, followed by the calm efficiency of the body disposal crew.

I never thought I'd find the deathlily, let alone eat it.

It was 1637, and I lived with my three sisters in Emperor Chongzhen's harem, until we lost his divine favour. My flighty oldest sister fell in love with a visiting Turkish nobleman, and as punishment, my sisters were all sentenced to a violent death.

I was supposed to die too, but Emperor Chongzhen gave me a choice. (I had always been his favourite.) I could either watch my family die or join them in the Heavenly Afterlife. I chose to live and watch their torment because I was afraid, and in those days, lingchi, death by gently slicing off a hundred pieces of flesh, was a favoured method of execution. That sounded unnecessarily painful. Emperor Wen had outlawed the cutting off of noses in the Han dynasty, so Chongzhen ordered my demure oldest sister's breasts to be chopped off instead.

Bleeding and barely conscious, she was hung in the purple courtyard to warn the other imperial concubines and wives from committing adultery. My second sister's baby was roasted in a clay oven and fed to her like strips of fatty duck. She stabbed herself in the stomach afterwards, quickly. The last sister, the prettiest one, was thrown off the yellow palace roof. Her neck snapped, the sound like a string breaking on a flimsy musical instrument.

After their executions, I curled up on a bamboo futon and begged for some common poison. I prayed to be struck down by the black plague. A palace guard took pity on me, and after I agreed to sleep with him, he smuggled me away.

In the filth-splattered village of Li Jiqian, I lacked domestic skills to make a living, and farmwork hurt my concubine fingers. I tried whoring at a backwater tavern, but the patrons smelled like chickens and cows. One night I entertained a group of shaggy-faced peasants who spoke of an uprising. I followed them to an underground meeting, where I caught the attention of the rebel Li Zicheng when I stood up and complained about the Emperor. Zicheng allowed me to camp among his men. I did not actually fight, but I lugged weapons and learned how to take care of horses and people, mostly beheading them when they were fatally injured. Lady Chop-Head, they called me, Shunu Zhan Tou. I felt as bold as Hua Mulan in the legends.

The grand Battle of Beijing in 1644 should have killed me. Maggots had ruined the army's rice supply and we were perpetually hungry. There's nothing like extreme starvation to make you philosophical and sulky about your past. It even caused a profound hallucination, because I glimpsed my three murdered sisters! The afterlife hadn't transformed them into hideous apparitions—dying just seemed to make them pale and dreary.

"Shuchun," they lectured, sounding exasperated, "stop feeling sorry for yourself. Hurry up and kill that bastard Emperor Chongzhen."

"You're giving me far too much responsibility," I complained.

My oldest sister, her head tilted at what looked like an uncomfortable forty-five-degree angle, slapped me, a vicious firecracker exploding near my ear. I thought that her ghostly hand would slice through me, but my skin singed for days.

I was relieved to see my sisters, even though they were dead and capable of hurting me.

Unrequited family love is a burden.

To punish myself for living, I leaped in front of unwieldy arrows, men with broad, jagged swords—anything to quickly die. With determination, I pushed my way through carnage, but all I received was six broken ribs and a messy spear wound in my left shoulder blade, which did not get infected as I had hoped. Surely I was cursed: I could not die.

Our rebel group defeated the Chongzhen dynasty. The Emperor sobbed and begged unceremoniously before committing suicide. His death made me feel better for a while. Li Zicheng, who was once the village shepherd, blacksmith, and mail courier, was declared the Dashing King of the Shun dynasty. Squat and inbred, he was not the most handsome of heroes. But he let me hang the Emperor's head from the largest palace window, like a fleshy lantern, where the royal pigeons happily pecked out Chongzhen's eyeballs.

I said no when Zicheng asked me to be his Second Wife. His First Wife was the formidable Lady Gao Guiying, a peasant commander, but he admired how capable I was at beheading men and beasts. I argued that it would be tragic if his newest bride died of suicide because I still wanted to die.

"Oh, Shuchun," he protested. "Once you become accustomed to palace life, you will no doubt change your mind."

"You presume far too much," I teased. But after he asked another three times, I said yes. To be honest, I was happy to soak my feet and rid myself of fleas in a weekly bath of fresh mint and lotus leaves. Palace life meant less vermin and lice, no more itchy skin. A softer complexion.

In the first lunar months that we were together, Zicheng spent his mornings marshalling officials to govern the districts, while I sat under a blood-red pavilion in the hibiscus gardens, pretending to listen to courtiers' grievances. Our afternoons unfolded on expensive silk daybeds, surrounded by comely women, men, and unending tamarind wine. We were treated to troupes of sweet-throated singers and long-necked dancers from every province in China. We feasted on the hot organs of freshly maimed goose, peacocks, and grimacing stags. We were almost happy.

Zicheng could have had his own dynasty, but he became preoccupied with achieving eternal life.

"Isn't ruling all of China enough?" I asked him one night in our gilded canopied bed. He was translating some thick ancient book that reeked of disease. Zicheng consulted scholars, magicians, priests, and fortune tellers until he found a lunatic folklorist who told him about the mountain and the legendary flower of eternal life.

"The flower could kill you," Zicheng warned, gesturing at a hand-drawn map. As he talked about his legacy, a bit of spittle landed on my cheek, and I sighed with consternation. "No one has ever survived," he exclaimed. "Except of course, I will." Despite enjoying bathing and eating regularly, I still wished to die. So I tagged along with him.

The crew has finished filming the flower blooming opening sequence, which will premiere on Food Network around the world. Refreshments for excited spectators are arranged on silk tablecloths under a bright orange canopy with the Chinese pictograms for luck (运气) and long life (长寿). They used to serve warm brains still inside living, chittering monkeys until PETA threatened to boycott our culinary event. Tonight's apologetic-looking escargots and eyeball-sized tomatoes stuffed with croutons and white cheese are not offensive. When no one is looking, to rid the scent of decay emanating from my skin, I douse myself violently with Chanel No. 5.

The loud American lady with the fancy hat grabs my right arm, as though stalking indelicate prey. She should be with the other contestants in the medical tent, overdosing on last-minute appetite-enhancing drugs, painkillers, and shots of adrenaline. I want to curl up in my little campsite by the dribbling stream, a short walk from here, where I usually hide out in between shots. But this woman grips my elbow harder. For a dying woman, she certainly has the strength of someone who feels entitled to live.

"What's the secret?" she drawls, in deliberate, drawn-out English. I picked up the language from a visiting delegation of British ambassadors in 1793, but I rarely speak it. False lashes droop off her red eyes like batwings. The woman must be in her early seventies, judging by her diaphanous skin. Stomach cancer, by the bayou of blood she spits out. I stingily give her three months.

"Tell me how you survived!" she pleads. "I can pay you whatever sum of money you want! I only have one child and he doesn't deserve to inherit!"

She is using a sob story on me that she has used on TV, although she has forgotten that she said that she had two children before. She thinks that I will be sympathetic, but I became the oldest woman in the world by being selfish.

I pretend that I don't understand what she is saying and look away. "I must have the stomach muscles of a cow!" is my standard quip when magazines ask me how I devoured so many deathlilies. But this woman won't appreciate the humour. I wait for Pingwei to usher me away or for one of the crew to stop her. Previous contestants and enterprising fans have all tried to bribe me—a Hollywood actress offered to give up her flamboyant new Porsche and her crying newborn. And once, a prince promised me a palace that nudged the sun.

I don't know the answer. Truthfully, I have no patience for the snivelling and geriatric who have lived long and fleshy lives yet are too cowardly to die. They are not plagued by becoming a very literal definition of a talking, walking corpse. It's not as if these cowards are flaking apart like an eight-day-old pastry. Every time I move my neck, I have to constantly check if my remaining ear is still attached to my head. I cannot rub my sleep-speckled eyes! I dare not comb my snarled hair or change my clothes too often in case I pull off my puckering epidermis, which bulges ungracefully. I am jealous that these paying contestants get to expire in one literal piece. Buddha, I wish that I had a whole body in this age when women are allowed to enjoy sex! Yet it amuses me that there's practically a name for an illness for everything nowadays, from foul manners to nervousness. In 1644, we just quarantined anyone who was hopelessly sick. Sometimes, the most helpful treatment was to chop their head off, a most effective lobotomy for anyone with mental illness or relentless stomach pain.

"You are an abomination! A freak!" the woman suddenly cries, snapping my arm so violently that she actually breaks most of my forearm off, which has grown soft with spectacular rot.

Nervously, I burp. She has not noticed that she is carrying my arm like the stalk of a wilting plant, the oyster-coloured fingers of my right hand drooping. If she is not careful, the bones will disintegrate.

Screaming profanity is what always happens when I deny

people the answer to what they believe is eternal life—if I had a response, don't they think I would share it for a palace and a new car? Everlasting life doesn't exist, lady.

Pingwei and the security guards arrive just as the woman realizes what she is clutching, and screams. The sound chills my undead insides, cuts into the whirling night of mosquitoes and celebrity chatter. A string quartet thrums.

Anxious, I hiccup again, and try to smile gratefully at security, who move to calm the woman. But she flings my arm on the ground. What a nasty old bat! She looks faint. I feel an eruption of hiccups marooned inside my chest. I belch. A gooey tonsil splashes on the grass. Followed by what looks like clumps of wet dirt.

"You have just defiled a national Chinese treasure," Pingwei scolds the American woman in his ungainly English. His expression is unreadable, the lenses of his safety goggles illuminated by the hot, declining stars crashing above us. "Her arm is at least worth 80,764,000 yuan. Will you be paying cash or credit?"

Everyone wants to know how I survived, but even I do not know what happened after I swallowed the deathlilies. Zicheng and I rode for thirty days until we found Phoenix Mountain. The locals had warned us not to digest any of the natural scenery. We did not listen and decided to have a moonlit picnic.

"You were a decent Second Wife," Zicheng said, chewing on a petal.

I kept eating until I collapsed from the inferno in my gastrointestinal tract.

When I woke up, the Shun dynasty was over. Later, I would find out that sixty years had passed. Zicheng was dead—his skeleton was nearby, his hands positioned in a parody of difficult indigestion. I was severely disappointed. Because I was very much alive. The skulls of tiny animals that had pecked at my mephitic skin were scattered around me.

Staring at my reflection in a shallow creek, I saw that the transformation did not make me hideous or beautiful. Rather, immortality made me dowdy. My knee-length black hair, which made me a passable beauty in court, had become dry, like scorched grass, and my skin was coarse and pale. I looked like my sisters' ghosts.

My walk became a lurch, as if my joints and muscles had been replaced by bamboo. I thought that I had turned into a tree. I acquired a lisp—the flowers' acidity burned a button-sized hole in my cheek where the breeze blew through and the occasional insect laid eggs. I sounded like a Siberian chipmunk.

Inside, I felt impatient and mean. I've never told anyone that the deathlily transformed me into something undead and uncanny. People only want to hear pleasant things about immortality.

For the next decade or so, I did my very best to drown myself. I sank into the cooling sands of the Yongding River, stones bulging in the pockets of my billowing hanfu. I watched nervous grey tilapia swim for months, which was amusing after I got over the disappointment of not dying. The water was unpolluted and refreshing in those days, and as furious crabs with spindly little antennas pinched my toes, I prayed that my sisters' deaths had not been too painful. Although I hoped that my oldest sister, the one who had slapped me, had suffered a little for her transgressions with that Turkish nobleman. I wanted my sisters to visit again, yet even ghosts are afraid of the walking dead.

When I was feeling better, I tried to throw myself off a promising precipice. But I just bounced off the jagged rocks. A congenial hanging with well-made rope made my neck sore. Arsenic gave me a rashy, inflated tongue that did not fit in my mouth for days. I bleated like an aggrieved sheep for weeks after a gallon of delicious strychnine.

There was something quite wrong with me.

Grudgingly, I climbed back up Phoenix Mountain, waited until the Flowering Full Moon, and tried to gobble as many plants as I could. If immortality could be given, surely it could be taken away? In my haste, my gluttony gave me violent, inconsolable hiccups, which have lasted for a good part of these centuries. I have been eating white starchy deathlilies on my mountain well before the Chinese government declared me a national treasure in 1991.

Intermission. The young Hong Kong socialite takes his first bite of flower and concedes a loss after his lower lip melts off. They carry him off-screen on a stretcher even though there's nothing wrong with his legs. The German nuns are fabulous at dying; they seem to enjoy the pain. The Japanese billionaire, cub-like, is still munching away.

Pingwei says we've got to find me a replacement arm or a long-sleeved jacket. I can't go on television looking like a peasant who had a conspicuous accident with her farming equipment. But, he concedes, every reality tv mascot should be known for setting trends. The oldest woman in the world only requires one arm! We must be brave and forward-thinking in this new millennium as China is destined to become a world leader for the disenfranchised.

To be truthful, I am fed up with Pingwei and the annual death-eating competition. His optimism gives me a toothache. Can't he see that I am dying in the most literal sense? Mostly, I think, I am tired of being mistaken for an elegant dowager with a toothy and saccharine smile. I was an imperial courtesan of the Emperor. I was essential to the rebels' cause, for Buddha's sake! I chopped off heads without flinching! Now I am a useless figurehead for a brand of eternal life, which has become thrilling twenty-first-century entertainment.

What this TV network needs is a one-armed striptease. My last hurrah!

I push my way past Pingwei and onto the stage where presidents' wives sip pink champagne. I am an ancient goo-mah who may not be very strong, but I have nothing to lose.

I pull off a high-heeled shoe, and a bunion/big toe flies off. Don't really need it anymore!

I struggle to unzip the side of my dress but it snags at my waist; some of the cubic zirconia embeds in my torso.

A security guard grabs my shoulder, but it crumbles like hollow ice. Whirling around, I decide to kiss him as if I weren't his ancient ancestor or grandmother. My dry tongue snaps off inside his mouth like a cracker. I feel the guard's shock as he lurches back, spitting me out and yelling that he can't afford to

pay the government for a replacement. There is more screaming and roaring as I crash into a table with champagne flutes
and ulcerous-red roses. Pingwei glowers at me, but I'm sure our
network ratings will be higher than last year.

Someone accidentally pushes me from behind. Head tum-
bles off. End music.

The Chinese government, I think, has put what's left of me in
an industrial-sized freezer, and for a long time I see nothing but
its white insides. Then a specialty restoration crew replaces what
little skin I have with shiny plastic. I cannot move, so I patiently
wait until I am fitted with immaculate and chattering false
teeth. It's telling when they do not replace my tongue with a
plastic replica. A black wig made of real human hair is screwed
onto my scalp. Then I am buttered (quite literally, with a palette
knife) with an orange chemical glaze, which makes me glossy
and new. No one talks to me or asks me how I am feeling.

I am strung up and arranged in what looks to be a very tor-
tuous position—hands raised high above my head as if I am
about to do a dazzling twirl; my facial expression feels like a
grimace.

I am the star in my own exhibit at the National Museum of
China. Tiny clay pots of ink and burnt oracle bones from the
wrong dynasty are my co-stars.

This is my suffering for choosing self-preservation instead
of family and a premature death.

I would give nearly anything to be able to scratch this rough
itch on my buttocks.

I don't sleep anymore, but I have a dream about my three sisters. We are tiptoeing and pirouetting on the shimmering waves of the South China Sea. We are pretty and whole. The landscape cuts to night, and I begin to sink. The ocean rises and falls with such maddening unpredictability as my sisters drift away. I tell them to wait for me, but no matter how much I scream or swim, the thick, brackish water overcomes me.

When I wake, I feel a dab on my cheek, like a brushstroke of paint, cool and light, which must be condensation from the museum's glass case. An uncontrollable ocean swells deep within me. The glass box is freezing, air-conditioned, and I wish they'd dress me in warmer clothing.

I shiver inwardly, violently, as a tourist snaps a photo.

The Ugliest Girls

In my village of Beiji, in the coldest, whitest corner of Heilongjiang Province, my harelip has always been fierce and unapologetic, my eyes like misshapen mouse turds. My long, uneven braids dangle like parasites; my mouth pinched like a rotted lotus flower. I have been crowned with the dried leaves of red Manchurian ash trees twice—the dishonour of being one of my village's ugliest girls.

My mother and her midwife screamed in astonishment after she birthed me, and my father attempted to snap my newborn neck in the blue Daxing'anling woods. Afflicted with pity or guilt, he changed his mind.

"Why didn't you just eat me when I was born?" I asked my mother, who was rolling dumpling dough on our rickety kitchen table. "The Tsungs ate their ugly newborn last week."

"Your father and I were not starving then," she said, wiping flour off her grey chang'ao.

"The Yangs are rich and they ate three girls before one was acceptable looking," I insisted.

"Well," my mother said, "I guess your father and I lost our appetites when you were born. That's why we eat our meals separately and you eat alone in the barn."

As one of the ugliest, most misshapen girls in my village, I had been told that I had no future. The brothels did not want me, and even blind men shuddered at the thought of my deformities. It was commonly known that the ugliest girls of the north were worse than average snaggle-toothed girls with bad skin. That ugliness could be passed around like venereal diseases. *You should not sleep with an ugly girl, but you may eat her* was the saying in all our villages.

Being ugly was our curse, and perhaps being cooked in a stew when the chickens and pigs and sheep had been eaten was an ugly girl's fate. It all depended on the state of the winter harvests and our families' unpredictable appetite for kindness.

After a long, harsh winter which turned our lips blue, the ugly girls and I were preparing to be eaten when government representatives arrived swiftly on strong white horses, clutching imperial red scrolls from the Emperor Tongzhi himself.

An esteemed-looking man, as thin and elite as a calligraphy brush, bowed as he entered the courtyard of our siheyuan. He wore a changpao of blood-orange silk. "Is this the residence of an ugly girl?" he demanded.

My parents, sensing opportunity, bowed quickly and ushered the Emperor's representative inside our threadbare ancestral home.

As my mother poured oily green tea for us, the Representative recited in an official-sounding voice: "There are respectable bachelors across the ocean, in a faraway place called Gold Mountain. Perhaps you've heard stories of such a dwelling in the West, paved with riches? Our benevolent Emperor has sent China's finest sons to acquire this gold and build a vast colony. What our wealthy bachelors require now are proper wives. You will be paid handsomely if you sell your ugly daughter across the sea in service of China."

Trying not to look too eager, my mother offered him a generous slice of day-old mung-bean cake, while my father nudged me to hide my monstrous face in case my presence offended the Representative.

But he did not seem disgusted because he asked my father if he could have a closer look at me.

At the Representative's request, I showed him my coarse hands and yellow donkey teeth. He nodded his approval at my flea-eaten skin, even though he was careful not to get too close. My parents clutched each other like prized meat.

The Representative looked pleased. "You are doing China a wonderful and patriotic duty," he said to me, smiling with a blank, superior benevolence. "You will be going to a land full of ghosts—gwei—but you will repopulate for the sake of our beloved Emperor, won't you?"

I was stunned. I had never imagined anything for myself. I nodded with what I hoped was acceptable politeness. I felt numb and tongue-tied in his presence. Would I have a future in this land full of frightening ghosts? Would I still be the ugliest thing?

The Representative sipped our proffered tea and bit into our stale cake. My stomach lurched, hopeful. I wondered if it was possible that a stranger with money and genteel manners might actually want me.

My beaming father signed the offered scroll, marking an eager but determined X where his name should be, and in return, received three months' wages. It was a large enough sum, able to feed my mother and him on a steady diet of eggs, poultry, and sour vegetables. The Representative chatted easily with my father while my mother helped me pack my only two ruqun in a burlap sack. She wrapped a homespun veil over my head to hide my hideousness.

"Keep your face covered when you meet your new husband," she said, not bothering to pretend that she was sad. My father tried his best to look regretful. He clutched the satchel of coins to his chest, as if praying.

"Farewell, Chicken-Face," my mother called as I accompanied the Representative outside. "May your daughters be more fortunate-looking than you."

As I followed the Representative to the borders of my snow-ravaged village, my pale lips stopped shivering. My complexion lost its icy hue. Dusty roads I walked, while the Representative rode beside me on his sturdy white horse. When my stubby legs tired, I was allowed to sit on the edge of the road and wet my harelip with a thimble of sour millet wine.

I thought I had escaped a grisly fate.

For seven days, the Representative and his colleagues gathered other ugly girls. We were forbidden to speak, but each of us, whenever we caught each other's eye, felt a sting of excitement. A tiny flicker of upward movement in our crooked lips. Did we dare fully smile? It was said that smiling was for average-looking girls, so that they might one day become pretty. We had no hope of becoming beautiful, but perhaps slightly below average was something we could aspire to.

As one hideous herd, we made our way to the blustery port off the southeastern coast of Guangdong Province. Farmers gawked. Townspeople glared. Rough sailors were too unhinged to whistle. I had never seen white gushing waters or such stately merchant ships before. Up in the highest hills of my village, the lakes and rivers were always frozen. Up north, ice clung to our eyebrows like frozen seagull droppings, but on the coast, the sun made us giddy. Even the most hideous of us glowed like wolves after an intense feeding.

The ugly girls of the southeastern coast, the ones that we collected last, were burned blotchy red from the harsh sun and resembled the overcooked entrails of pheasants. The girls of the highest north, like me, looked as if we had frostbite, with our stumpy appendages. Who was uglier? None of the Representatives could agree.

At the loading docks off the gusty coast, the Representatives ushered all the ugly girls onto a cargo ship called *The Crooked-Nose Maiden*. "The Emperor thanks you for your sacrifice," they repeated solemnly as we boarded.

The voyage was long and hard and uneventful. Huddled together below deck like seasick monsters, we quaked from the unending damp. We were fed crusts of mouldy bread, and for days we had nothing to drink except our own urine, which was sour like fermented alcohol. In the cramped space, we argued about who was the most miserable. "My legs are mouldy," a girl called Snake-Skin, from the eastern seaboard, boasted. "My stomach is constipated," Onion-Head, of a wealthy vegetable county, bragged repeatedly.

"Chicken-Face, do you think we'll be pretty in Gold Mountain?" a young girl called No-Nose, from the rice paddies of Jiangsu Province, asked. In addition to missing her nose, she was short and had the face of a Shar-Pei. I was confused when she had latched on to me because I had never had a friend or confidante.

"Ugly is ugly," I said, swigging my pee and choking, "but just think about how ugly our future husbands must be to have been sent so far away. Perhaps they were also the ugliest men in their districts."

For months, discomforted with seasickness, we nibbled on our bread crusts and dreamed, uneasy. If we asked too many questions or complained, the Representatives told us that we should be grateful. They assured us that we would be assigned high-ranking husbands. For once, we ugly girls would hold value, some spectre of purpose. The ghostly beating inside my chest picked up.

When we docked, rough men with moon-coloured faces seized us like dumbfounded cattle, blindfolding us. The ugly girls who protested were slapped hard across their cheeks. A terrible taste, like soured goat milk, rose in my throat as we were forced down flights of creaky stairs. Darkness trickled under the rough cloth that covered our eyes. We each held tightly to the shoulder of the ugly girl in front of us. Some of us stumbled. Some of us were sure-footed as reindeer. The stairs creaked in complaint of our herd's weight. I remembered: the stench of wet, mouldy laundry as we descended lower, lower, lower. *A terrible thing has happened here*, I decided, and then was shocked by my own admission.

When we were permitted to take off our blindfolds, I saw that we had been taken to a dank, rectangular cellar. A windowless holding space forged of shit-coloured bricks and red lumber, one that was hardly any different than the ship's cargo space. My heart plummeted. *Another prison not even fit for livestock*, I thought. Some of us ugly girls began to wail. "Chicken-Face, I want to go home," No-Nose whimpered, and I patted her uselessly on the head, twice. I had no idea how to comfort another human being, and so I treated her like a baby cow that would soon be put to slaughter.

Like a heavy shroud, our terror tightened around our chests. I wondered if we would be kept in the gloom for some nefarious purpose. I blinked as dozens of blood-red lanterns on the wall blazed as if by magic. A spidery-looking madam with burnt skin and clawed hands appeared. She wore an elegant icicle-white cheongsam and creaky wooden slippers. Her hair was shiny and black, piled and twisted around a luminous gold phoenix crown. The left side of her face had been brutally smashed. Her large lower teeth protruded over her worm-grey lips. The ugly woman surveyed us like a cruel governess.

"Where are our husbands?" an ugly girl asked, and the woman laughed. Not unkindly. It was a straightforward sound. A sound that a goose made in the throes of passionate mating.

"I'm your madam, the Lady Xiwangmu of Gold Mountain, and I own you," she said in a clipped accent, showing us that she was neither high class nor poor. It was an odd dialect that I could not exactly place. "This is my abode," she continued. "You have successfully crossed the vast ocean to Gold Mountain, and it is your service to me which funds our empire. Don't think that your sacrifice is not noted."

I do not know why none of us tried to run. Perhaps we were stunned; perhaps we wanted to trust her; perhaps our bodies were too weak. The madam looked like one of us, and we thought that she could perhaps be an Ugly Sister. We stared at our new madam, confusion distorting our unfortunate features. Some of us, exhausted from our months of voyage, no longer clinging to a spiderweb of hope, stumbled to our knees. Some of the ugly girls wept, but the crying did not last. There were simply no tears left.

A night or day passed, and we were told to strip to our underthings and lie down on coarse mats. If we wanted food, we'd do as we were told, and do it promptly. The madam's personal sentries were hellish visions, with clay-coloured faces and mangled snouts for mouths and noses. *How did she create such monsters?* I wondered, and finally understood that our ugly madam was a witch.

"What do ugly girls have that beautiful ones do not?" the madam asked. Smiling strangely, she answered her own peculiar question: "You have layers and layers of sadness and pain; your emotions are rich and extremely delicious. Exactly what wealthy socialites want. Your ugly memories will fund export, travel, and war for the Emperor Tongzhi. Ugly girls must serve your country's economy."

In that moment, it felt like ghostly fingers were reaching out from the frozen blue trees of Beiji and pinching my heart. I felt an unquantifiable despair. I knew that bearing a strong resemblance to a lowly farm animal was a curse, but I had never suspected that my ugliness would be inherently useful.

"What does this mean?" No-Nose asked. She turned her hideous face towards me. "Are our husbands coming later?"

"It means that we are to be used and thrown away," I said bitterly. "We have travelled far away for nothing."

"I don't understand," No-Nose said, her voice like a child's. And I remembered that she was one.

"Quiet," the madam said, pointing sharply at her. "During your service to the Emperor, you will not speak." And so it was. The last words I thought we would ever utter.

"Open wide, my ugly girls, my beautiful chickens, my money-making cows," the madam commanded in a soothing voice. At first I refused to open my mouth, but a sentry pried my jaws wide with a pair of rusted tongs. As I gagged, he stuffed a blood-red leech, the size of a baby's fist, into my mouth. The worm writhed in anticipation and made a squelching noise as it latched onto my flesh. My eyes watered. My breathing shallowed with dull, insectoid fear. I reached for No-Nose's hand. She lay beside me, and her pale fingers felt like the stubby tops of potatoes peeking through the first spring frost in Beiji.

One by one, the ugly girls opened wide and gave a leech our tongues for fodder. We were told to think of our deepest, most private memories, the ones that we had swallowed in desperation. "Your everyday sadness is exquisite," the madam cooed. "But your thwarted desires and lifelong disappointments are coveted delicacies for our discriminating buyers." As the leech writhed and yipped noisily inside my mouth, I remembered the promise I'd made to myself. No one would ever know my deepest shame.

Snake-Skin was the first one of us to choke on her leech. She could not control her violent gag reflex, while Dung-Breath died during a fit of hiccups when the leech bit a vein. Crab-Fingers was ticklish and giggled every time her leech twitched. During the first day, three of my ugly sisters died, clutching at their throats.

"It happens to the very best of us," the madam said in a reassuring tone. She patted each of the dying girls on their hideous shoulders and thanked them for their patriotic duty to the empire. To the rest of us, she said, "Give us your sad memories, my ugly girls. Start at the very beginning of your pain. Your first loves, your losses, your shame."

When my leech clamped down even harder, I relented. I gave my leech all my sadness from being born unfortunate-looking. The dishonour that I had placed upon my mother. The burden of my heart-heavy father, who could not sell me for cheap fodder. The leech, gurgling with infant-like pleasure, swelled to the size of a small red turnip. My cheeks bulged. Engorged with my unwanted emotions, my leech let out a heinous shriek to let everyone know it was done feasting.

Smacking like an overfed man, the leech was plucked out of my mouth and placed in a glass vial. The madam explained that it would be cooked, dusted with copious amounts of sugar, and sold to the rich, who would pay handsomely to experience our divine suffering. To be enjoyed on one's tongue like an extraordinary treat, savoured slowly. Bitterness was sweet; sadness was hearty. A vivid unpleasant memory with scenes of brutal violence could be enjoyed as a scrumptious three-course meal.

"A horrible memory can earn up to one hundred gold pieces," the madam said excitedly, and I could tell she had no soul. "Best of all, each ugly girl contains fifty or sixty bad memories."

Time bled viciously as the leeches sucked on our secrets and our deformed feelings. Feverish and nauseous, I learned it was better to quickly give in. If I kept my mind blank, the leech would bite harder, its teeth injecting a violent poison that blistered my gums. Inside my mouth, the blood-red leech became a piece of flaming coal.

Still, I promised myself that no one would learn my hideous secret.

After we fed the leeches, we were allowed to inhale a bowl of paste-like gruel and drink a cup of water. Some of the ugly girls were too shell-shocked to put food into their mouths. Others had lost too much blood. A few of us faded from hallucinatory fever. Their bodies, still breathing, were tossed into a brick oven.

"Why is this happening to us, Chicken-Face?" No-Nose whispered. I urged her to drink a mouthful of water. She side-glanced around to make sure that the sentries weren't watching; we'd be beaten below the neck and denied our meal if they caught us conversing. Her tongue was so swollen and purple that it could not fit inside her crooked mouth. She rasped in terror, "What have we done to deserve this fate?"

"We were born ugly and female," I tried to say, but my mouth was too damaged to shape the words.

—

A boy would have brought honour to our poor northern family. He'd inherit our ancestral siheyuan and the tiny field where we grew a patch of white potatoes and raised a few limping chickens and reindeer. A boy would help my father with the farm chores and the momentous task of ice cropping in the early spring. Perhaps it was my misfortune that my father had a random change of heart in the bluest part of the Daxing'anling woods. My mother had instructed him to sell my corpse at the market. Girls, especially ugly ones, would fill one labourer's stomach and last two to three good meals if she was big-boned. But he could not bring himself to kill me. He could have easily smashed my face in with a medium-sized rock and dug a snowy grave if he did not wish to feed me to starving villagers. Instead, he carried me home and forbade my mother to harm me. My parents prayed to Buddha and accidentally had my ugly twin sisters.

My mother took charge after my father failed to kill me. I was alive because my father was too weak and water-hearted. When I was old enough, I walked with her to the market, carrying a heavy burlap sack. As my mother haggled with a smiling couple, I looked inside the sack and saw my dead baby sisters. I recognized my own snarling harelip on theirs. My mother traded the twins for the six-day-old head of a half-frozen deer. For supper, I was allowed to chew on the animal's uncooked eyeballs, which tasted of rotted leaves.

When my infant brother was born, I was assigned to his care. In exchange for my life, I was to be his devoted nursemaid. I was forced to sing lullabies and chew his meals for him, spitting the mush back out, spoon-feeding him.

When he was three years old, I took him outside to play. In truth, I was jealous of him. My brother, who was not ugly, but soft and round like the insides of a winter melon, was their favourite. He was lovingly given wooden figurines of our heavenly anointed Emperor. He was bestowed with fresh meat. He would take over our farm when he turned fifteen. Despite his princely air, he was colic and shit constantly.

While the snow tumbled from the cobalt skies, I charged across the icy lake, calling for him to chase me. I ran, uninhibited, and the veil that covered my deformed face blew off in the wind. I took it as a symbol, an omnipotent emblem of my independence and a future without a weak boy sibling. As I grinned, I heard a crack, followed by a sickly yell. By some unholy instinct, I knew then that my puny brother disappeared below the ice.

I did not turn around. I did not return to the lake. Instead, I went for a long walk in the lush blue forests, humming oddly to myself. I wish I could say that I had been overwhelmed by shock, but I remained unmoved.

After, my mother tore out my wind-tangled hair and beat me. For days, she and my father wept, immobilized by grief. My mother asked me: "Why do the ugly never voluntarily die?"

Shrugging, I responded: "Perhaps the beautiful die first? How should I know?"

There would be no mourning period until late spring. We had to wait for the ice to thaw so we could find his frozen body in the lake.

—

The madam would certainly revel in the fact that I was a jealous murderer of my kin.

On the ninth day, the leech's sharp incisors pried at the edges of my most prized memory. I felt a vicious sensation inside my skull, then a crashing noise like a wood saw harvesting thick blocks of ice from our village's frozen river, flashes of iridescent white and blue.

Quickly, I forced myself to think of other fragments of despair. Below deck aboard a wet, crowded ship. The rot of seasickness. Gangrene. And finally, my disappointment in finding out that I would never be given a husband, title, and warm bed made of fine goose feathers.

These memories were not satisfying enough. In frustration, the leech's teeth latched harder onto my tongue, but I refused to give in. This went on for days until the madam declared this particular leech defective.

A fortnight passed. No-Nose, Fox-Ears, Ox-Teeth, and I were invited to a grand gala dinner upstairs. We were the healthier of the uglier girls—all four of us could still stand up without clutching a walking stick. Emaciated, with urine-coloured skin and scraggly nails, we now resembled skeletal monsters. The madam allowed us to splash our faces with day-old water and change into ill-fitting ball gowns. My grey garment, with lacy bell-shaped sleeves, bore a splotchy brown stain in the back, and I wondered if its previous owner had met an unseemly fate. *Was it murder or menstrual?* I quietly asked Guanyin, goddess of women and compassion, even though I knew the answer. *Please, please,* I prayed anyway, *let it be the latter.*

I checked the other girls' poufed skirts, which could clothe half a dozen starved village girls. None of them had ugly stains, though No-Nose's dress was roughly torn at the shoulder.

"Let us swap, sister," I told her, even though I knew she did not want to. No-Nose's gown, yellow like cat piss, would look far better on me.

After we had dressed, the madam, smiling, clucked at our appearance and painted our ghost-white faces with cosmetics. She announced that we would soon meet the mayor of Gold Mountain, his fine corpulent friends, and their aristocratic ladies. For fifteen gold pieces, five medium-length pubic hairs, a finger, or a year off their lives, the guests paid the pricey admission to the madam's fine banquet. As ugly girls, we were the main attraction. To be served after a scrumptious ten-course dinner. Paraded in, gawked at, after the doll-pink bon-bons were served and the expensive bourbon was poured. Each guest would place a leech or five inside our hideous mouths, whatever could fit. One by one, we would be drained of our remaining memories and emotions. A renowned chef and confectionery maker would transform these leeches into sweets, so that the white devils could enjoy the fattened leeches for their amusement.

It hardly mattered that our tongues were too damaged by the foul leeches to elocute. We ugly girls embraced one another, scratched our lice-infested scalps, and noiselessly wailed. We knew it was the end. Why were they not feeding us one good supper before our bodies disintegrated?

We were led upstairs to a cavernous ornamental ballroom, as looming and imposing as the White Horse Temple, which the village elders spoke of during our solstice celebrations.

Luxurious blood-red carpets complemented glittering silver lights and moon-white statues of screaming lionesses. I shivered at the lifelikeness of their maws. Herded to the centre of the cave-like space, we trembled like baby chickens.

Looking around us, we saw glittering creatures with the starchy pallor of death on their faces. We shuddered, wondering if the mayor and his fancy guests were actually, in fact, month-dead cadavers. Surely no living thing could be leached of so much colour.

One of the mayor's friends was shouting, spit droplets foaming white on his inky beard, while a tall, bejewelled woman with shiny gloves laughed beside him. A sea of rouged lips, babbling away in foreign tongues. Enthusiastic applause resounded, and at first I thought it was for us, but then the madam smiled with shrewd grace. She bowed knowingly at the rich lords and ladies, as if she were a purveyor of fine, robust cattle.

When our names were called, I lay beside the other ugly girls on a blood-coloured silk chaise, the nicest and softest that I had ever seen. I pretended I was a well-loved courtesan in the highest courts of the Emperor Tongzhi who was simply taking a nap. *Soon*, I thought, shutting my eyes, *soon, soon, soon, it will be over.*

A sharp voice chattered above me and a gloved hand pinched my cheek. I opened my eyes. The voice belonged to a young woman in a magnificent pink dress that resembled an enormous circus tent. Wild feathers adorned her buoyant red hair, and her face was powdered white like a six-day-old corpse. Her plucked eyebrows arched and her soured cupid's mouth

puckered. She clapped her hands with child-like glee. I stiff-
ened as the madam told the sentry that the woman wished to
purchase at least fifty leeches. She wanted to see how many
could be placed inside my mouth at once.

The red-head woman had a blond horse-faced friend who
picked her long nose excitedly as she spoke. Tittering, the
blond woman tugged at my lice-infested hair. She turned to
No-Nose and viciously kicked her with a white lacy slipper.
Wincing, my ugly sister doubled over. "I think it's only the
ugly and poor girls who feel," No-Nose muttered, surprising
me with her wise-sounding words. "No one rich has ever been
called ugly, at least to their face." I hardly recognized No-Nose,
once the naive girl on the boat. Torment and daily bloodletting
had aged my only friend at least twenty years.

Before the woman could hurt her again, I spoke out of turn,
my lips clumsy from lack of conversation. I blurted: "Would
you like to try a leech on you, my lady? You'll feel so unbur-
dened and much lighter."

Our madam blanched and glared at me with murderous
intent. The rooster-haired woman seemed to insist that our
madam translate what I had said. She gestured at me, frowned,
held out her elegant coin purse with expectation. Jabbed at
me with her moon-white gloved finger. The madam hesitated,
then gestured to the sentry to bring her a gold tray of fresh
squealing leeches.

A blood-red leech was placed on the eager tongue of the
rich young woman, but it would not latch. Despite the coax-
ing and cheering from her insatiable friends. Despite reposi-
tioning her pointy devil's tongue. And so, another leech was

dropped inside her mouth, and yet this leech, grumbling, also found her memories quite displeasing.

"She does not have any horrendous memories," the madam said to us ugly girls, smiling almost apologetically. "It feeds only on those who have suffered plainly."

Astonished, I stared at the woman who lacked a single bad memory. To my eyes, she was neither ugly nor beautiful. She was only cruel, in her childish delight and bubbling curiosity. She caught me staring, and patted my arm.

Because they had paid handsomely with coin, hairs, fingers, or years to fund the madam's potions, the guests held us ugly girls down, and then with gleeful excitement, they laid the leeches onto our quivering tongues. The red-haired woman stuffed three red leeches past my mangled harelip.

For fear of choking, I dared not scream when I felt the leeches' teeth tugging hungrily at my deepest memory. As my vision flickered, I heard the guests' jabbering voices and squeals of unreserved mirth. *How dare they find pleasure in my agony!* I thought. In the joyous din, I heard Fox-Ears scream.

Vertigo descended. Darkness, like a flock of black grouse, flew across my dying vision. My thoughts swam like frogs in water. As if soothing an abscessed molar with snow, I dreamt up another life. Chicken-Face, twice crowned the divinely beautiful girl of Beiji. Chicken-Face, chosen on behalf of the honourable Emperor Tongzhi. Chicken-Face, a haughty tree princess who lived deep inside the blue woods. A beloved woodcutter's daughter turned rich and fearless aristocrat.

The leeches stopped their noisy feasting.

Lying seemed to confuse them. Falsehoods hurt them. They could not digest a combination of my complicated tall tales. Each one shrivelled like an autumn leaf.

And so I quickly thought up only untrue memories, of eating fine-grained rice, of changing into a heavy gold-spun qi pao in the late morning and a horde of servants who peeled my unblemished fruit. I thought of the delicious comfort of bathing in rosewater under the warm afternoon sun, of combing my tangled hair with a proper ivory comb, touching myself with sweet, hideous pleasure. My face flushed. The leeches screamed in absolute disgust.

The red-haired woman cried out in disappointment, as if she had never been denied a wish. Roused by the noise, I propped myself up, willing my shaking legs to stand.

Staggering towards the partygoers in their finery, hands outstretched like claws, I roared at my ugly sisters. "Think of only lies! Think of how pretty we were once in China! We were once all princesses, empresses, or queens! Think about how we were so absurdly happy."

I hoped that each one of my sisters heard me in their weakened, dying states.

Perhaps it was only my frenzied imagination. Perhaps it was a semblance of power that causes one to think they are capable of mighty things. But I could feel the architecture of the dark room shifting. Its wooden bones screeched. The air turned electric blue. The guests shouted, confused.

The madam's face loomed, an ancient and terrible mask.

In that moment, I envisioned my baby brother's death. I saw his scared face and then his tiny hands flailing in the wind-chilled air, still clutching his stupid wooden emperor figurine.

Then silence, so impalpable, that it stung my ice-filled eyes.

Brother killer, I thought. *Oh, I am a brother killer.* To think I could escape my past just like I could hack off a useless, frost-bitten limb.

Gritting my teeth, I lunged at the madam's witchy visage, and we plunged to the burgundy floor as one blurred monstrosity. Her lopsided pupils expanded like two dirty yellow moons, revealing her hideous surprise. Elbowing her ghastly face, I used my hands to pull the half-squealing leeches that clung to my chin and shoved the creatures down her puckered throat.

"Help me!" the madam half gurgled, half shrilled.

Her guests looked on with overt disappointment, but no one moved to save such an ugly thing.

Sinking Houses

There's a mushy hole in my husband's stomach where the chandelier skewered him, and his arms are twisted over his head, paralyzed in a lazy arabesque. His legs look flimsy, crushed beneath the serrated glass. A stiff marionette femur pokes through his pyjama pants, jutting through the effusive print of a smiley, self-effacing pineapple. My husband doesn't look dead. He's pale like a museum-mounted skull except for a few sprightly pieces of hair. I bend close, tap his forehead. His eyes snap open; they are vampire-yellow and wild.

I throw a woolly rug over him, mostly so I don't have to look at the hole. He moans that he is too warm and wants me to open a window.

"What have you done?" he rasps in Mandarin.

"What do you mean?" I shoot back.

"You've just ruined a really expensive rug!"

This is what I get for agreeing to marry an older man from an international dating site—ingratitude and paroxysmal blame-mongering. After a month of instant messaging I said "Fine!," which has apparently cemented my reputation as a pushover.

My new husband (Mr. Lim, 62 years, 5'5, Likes Badminton, Thai Food, Aerobics) has the disposition of a fatherly leprechaun. We met in person just three days ago on his cracked pink front porch in Nebraska City. The sky was black and thick like rot, even though it was barely noon.

I clasp his icy hand like I would a squirming child's, and I try not to stare where his belly should be. The hole is oozing and making the rug soggy. I won't tell him that the stain looks permanent. My new husband may be bossy and cheap, but he is sometimes kind. He held me when I cried, which was/is often the past three days. He is the only person in this town who speaks any Mandarin. I suspect that I won't have anyone to talk to if/when he dies.

"You brought the apocalypse to America," Mr. Lim accused me prior to the light fixture harpooning him as if he were some luckless sea mammal. We were drinking a bottle of rice wine in our pyjamas. We had almost reached a 911 operator. But then the basement caved in, followed by some of the tiled roof, which shed apart like fish scales. It wasn't at all dramatic, so we laughed. Then the light fixture, a monstrous horned thing, impaled him. Mr. Lim is now pinned down by crystal shards and faux-decadent metal in what was once the living room. He looks a little regal, like a surly king flattened by a throne.

Yesterday, when the internet was still working and we had running water and electricity, the earth swallowed at least six identical subdivisions and one town in dull neighbouring Iowa. My husband, who translates the news for me, said it was no big loss to anyone. "The houses on our street are bigger and built better for families," Mr. Lim had proclaimed, right before we looked out the living room window and the neighbour's house shuddered horribly and then sank within two minutes. Then he added, gesturing and sighing: "Their house was much nicer than ours, but that couple had such an ugly baby."

"Well," I said after an ice age of silence, too many shifty-eyed glances, "should we open the canned peaches?"

I almost like the gigantic gap in the ceiling. It provides us with an invigorating aerial view. Half of the sun seems to have combusted: fingers of orange blaze across the gloomy stratosphere. The sky appears to be on fire.

"You have to get me to a hospital," Mr. Lim suddenly sputters, and I remember that I am still married. A little red stains his front teeth like hot sauce.

"How?"

"There's a wheelbarrow in the garage."

I don't know how to tell him this is dying-old-man idiocy.

The walls of the house shake again. The last shudder was just a joke. A voluptuous vase with plastic roses bounces to the floor. A chintzy armchair collides into a wall. *BAM!* Another hole, south exterior facing. There goes a clicking clock. I don't think the house will last through the night. I want to ask Mr. Lim how much he paid for the rental deposit, and whether we will get some of it back if we survive. I want to know about things like life insurance policy and the petty legal definition of "natural disaster" in America. We haven't even talked about funeral arrangements.

Suddenly the floor tilts and we tumble. I smash my head, fracture the flat, fleshy rivulet between my eyes on the edge of an old coffee table. *Crack.*

In the place where I grew up, my father was half-possessed, a parasitic man who had crept up from the infected earth. How else to explain how he got inside and clung to our lives like plastic wrap? How he brought the invading dark into our living space when I thought we were safe? Sensing him, my mother would push me away, but there was nowhere to go. We shared a cramped studio apartment in the bloated Qingpu district of Shanghai with my dead-eyed grandparents. I slept under the kitchen table on a foldable chuáng diàn. Whenever he came home from the piers, I crawled under flimsy sun-yellow covers. I was small, and afraid of one man's earthquake.

My parents fought every day, except on weekends. That was their break. He would hold my mother down, flatten her like a blanket, and she would tear out his pomaded hair like weeds.

My grandparents would promptly avert their eyes and turn the CD player on, which played warbling singers who spoke-sung the folksy love songs of the 1930s. Piano accompaniment rose to conceal the bone-breaking noise. *Zai na yaoyuan de difang. In that place wholly faraway. In a faraway fairyland. In that distant place in a land far far away.*

I wake up under rubbish, or what was once the outdated living room. I'm disgusted by the home decor and shove a chintzy orange dining room chair out of the way. I am certainly not dead, but I don't feel thankful. It would be easy to curl up and wait for the ceiling to crush me, but I have only just arrived in this strange, sinking land. If you ask me, it doesn't make sense that a flat country with acres of pale yellow space can't support itself, but maybe the land is too soft. Perhaps the few dirty-pink farmhouses were an eyesore, which explains why the earth is swallowing itself. On the hour-long cab ride from the airport, I had gawked at my new country, wondering why anyone would want to own so much dying grass.

Being one of the last few people alive is not at all like winning a national lottery—it's actually quite stressful. What should I do? Should I tidy up in case any reporters appear? Am I supposed to behave/dress in a survivalist way, and do manners count in a large-scale emergency? As a new immigrant, I feel somewhat obligated to continue on (until I find someone else to do the dirty work) for the evolutionary sake of humankind.

My mouth tastes bloody. I must have swallowed a molar or three from smashing my head. I might need the calcium for later on—is one medium-sized human tooth equivalent to one glass of fresh unpasteurized milk? Then again, this is a major apocalypse, so I doubt anyone will notice my lack of teeth. If I had lost an incisor before, I'd probably want to kill myself for becoming less attractive. Funny how tragedy can severely inflate one's self-worth.

I am thinking mostly of myself. It might not be true what my grandparents have always insisted: marriage does not make a person any less self-involved.

Shit.

Mr. Lim is quite dead beside me, still tangled up in that lovely rug. His eyes are white and glassy. His mouth gapes in mid-complaint. There is no modest-sized rental home anymore. I am surrounded by wreckage, remnants of a life that I could/should have had. On the first night I arrived, Mr. Lim had trumpeted farts on an air mattress beside me—he let me have the queen-sized bed. I was repulsed, then grateful for his chaste sleeping habits.

Ravenous, I search frantically for the last of the canned peaches. No luck.

I can't find a wheelbarrow so I use my feet to soccer-roll Mr. Lim from under the rubble to the front yard. Pits appear where boxy houses, straggly trees, and mailboxes once sprouted from well-kept lawns. Not to mention the grassy and paved roads that have melted into gravelly quicksand. All I have to do is push Mr. Lim into a pit with my bare feet. I think about leaving him the rug, but at the last second, before he sinks into what was once his/our front yard, I unroll it from his still-bleeding torso. Then I wrap it around my shoulders, like a cape. I also yank off his fluffy white slippers, which have somehow managed to remain clean in this unprecedented catastrophe.

"Sorry," I say as the sand slowly devours him while he's face down. "I hope you don't think this is my fault. Thank you for the hospitality and slippers."

Doing my duty as the sole survivor, I follow a road that appears intact. Even though there is no wind, I imagine my makeshift cape billowing behind me, the internet-order bride as superhero! The end of the world is very dry—it's horrible for my sensitive, flaking skin. Using a tennis racquet that I find on the road, I poke the dusty earth before I step over it. Mr. Lim's fluffy white slippers become less white.

I alternate between hopping and trudging down the road. I fall asleep for an hour or two in a ditch on the side of a potholed highway. I wake up with some of my hair on fire and scream-holler until I remember that I am a widow now, which means that it's universally plausible that I could be the next of kin to die. Don't spouses usually follow the other's lead? So I quickly dunk my scalp in a pond of cool, chunky mud. As a result, my head is a little patchy, itchy, and filthy on one side. I will not make the mistake of napping again, so I continue on, using my tennis racquet to swat at burning sparks (like I'm playing Ping-Pong)! The tiny fires fly at me nonstop, like burning moths from crispy trees.

The next day, cirrocumulus clouds drop from the sky with a BOOM! You'd think that falling clouds would be soft and fluffy, but a particularly pleasant-looking one upends a commercial truck, and another flattens a herd of cows into white and black pudding.

No one else seems to be alive.

Perhaps I am walking in the wrong direction. I don't exactly know what I'm supposed to do during an apocalypse. I don't know if I'm supposed to find shelter or take on the role of mysterious backpacker, trekking cross-country with indeterminate purpose. I wish I had a map.

I bypass a coppice of twisted, bony trees that look like skeletons in prayer. A dog missing its back legs spins on the ground, furious, its front paws kicking in a semicircle. I can't bear to look at it, and wish somebody (not me!) would put it out of its misery.

As I plod on, little sparks of sunshine detonate impatiently above me, and I recall an ancient myth about the falling sky and the plummeting earth. In the myth, a man called Qi believes the world will fall apart like an enigmatic jigsaw puzzle, but his friend says: *The sky is all air, nothing but air. As you inhale and exhale, you breathe air into the sky all day long which holds it up.* When Qi asks about the earth, his friend says that as long as there are people to trample the ground into pathways of refined dirt, the ground will not shatter.

But I have not seen a single person for miles, which explains why the sky is falling and the earth is collapsing.

My mother wore wet burgundy lipstick, the colour of rotten apples and primeval scabs—undeniably rich and dirty. The colour made her teeth look like choppy boulders, a cheerless, uneven grey. I always thought she was colour-blind. I have inherited her arched eyebrows and fat, puckering lips, which make me look like a fierce tropical fish. At cosmetic counters in department stores, I have tried to find her peculiar shade of spiritless gore, but the samples are always uncomplicated and blasé.

My parents liked wreckage. My father would bite my mother while she kicked and screamed. My mother would claw at his skin, and he would tirelessly weep. When it was dark out, they would clean themselves up and go out in their very best clothes for dancing and drinks. My mother did not ever leave the apartment without her lipstick on. She was superstitious that way. She believed that red was blood, and blood was propitious, and she could use impulsive cosmetic fixes to conceal all broken or unseemly things. Sometimes she'd take me to the drugstore down the street and she'd slip lipstick and containers of cerulean eyeshadow into my coat pockets. Then we'd sip green milk tea at an internet café, and she'd paint me like a clown with our stolen cosmetics, before taking me to stare at the queenly lionesses at the Shanghai Zoo. "We do what we must to survive," she said. "Whatever happens, don't hate me too much, please."

The farmhouse is shielded by a muddy brown hill and seems to have been untouched by the earthquakes. Gusts slice half-heartedly in the air. I wonder if they could be dying easterlies. What kinds of winds does Nebraska City have, anyway? Falling chunks of sky have not yet crushed the farmhouse to bits. Old and rickety, it smells like the insides of a fusty refrigerator. Laundry is abandoned on the floor, a few cracked dishes. I replace my bloody pyjamas with someone's pink buttoned shirt that sags to my knees, and tug on old socks that reek of ancient car grease.

No one is home, they're probably dead, so I help myself to the pantry: an unsystematic treasure chest of jars. Red and orange fruit preserves, like the ones the flight attendants had served with squares of cardboard bread on the connecting flight from Shanghai to Omaha. Gassy from escalating anxiety, I had declined the snack, forcing myself to stare at an in-flight movie and mouth the Mandarin subtitles. I crack a jar open on the counter and shape out the insides into my hands, slurping like an animal. I am undoubtedly saved.

It shouldn't surprise me that this swill is the most disgusting non-food I've ever tasted. But I am so hungry and thirsty! Thank Buddha, there's half a bottle with wishy-washy liquid. Yellow apples steeping in homemade bleach: a sharp, fruity alcohol. I swallow it without fussing. Mr. Lim kept a cheap bottle of clear rice wine in every drawer and closet, a staple of any Chinese bachelor, imported through the internet. If you drank two to three cupfuls every night like he did, or replaced a meal with a bottle like my father, you'd discover a simple, anaesthetizing antidote for everything from heartburn to heartache.

Here is a joke: How many drinks are appropriate for a girl's first apocalypse?

When my mother finally fled to her cousin's house in America, my grandfather accused her of being unladylike. He blamed her for my father's conduct. In that tiny apartment in Shanghai, our family had become a dizzying compass of rage. A sinking unit, our force so strong we could drown continents.

When my mother left, I was eleven. Every two or five or six years—she displayed a staggering indifference to time—she mailed me postcards from America, false, motherly aphorisms from her travels. The last one came three years ago from a mailbox in San Francisco: *My darling, I hope you have taken after me in your looks. It would be unfortunate if you resembled your father.* Another postcard was from New York City, with no return address: *If you go outside with wet hair, you will catch tuberculosis.* And from a hotel in Las Vegas, unsigned: *To avoid heatstroke, sweetheart, you must drink lots of hot tea to cool down the body.*

In a faraway place lives a good girl. In that place wholly faraway. In a faraway fairyland.

—

I have a tendency to find myself in dysfunctional households.

Perhaps I wear its scent, like a high-end perfume, imprinted on my pores. Damage must be an obscene homing beacon.

When I wake up, a cool-tipped hammer is jammed against my temple, and a woman's bray fills the room. She's with a man, her husband maybe, or a temporary end-of-the-world lover. Both are large and robust, a churchgoing, bespectacled people from a formerly soft tribe. But they look unneighbourly, as if they have seen too much death in the past seventy-two hours to be hospitable. The woman has a torn lip, and the man has patchy burn marks on his ears where he must have caught fire. His glasses are also missing a lens. I see clouds of discomfiting double—I must be incredibly drunk!

I cannot understand these troubled people. They yell too quickly, unlike the basic English language conversation recordings I downloaded and lazily listened to before I arrived, where the hosts are always so infuriatingly patient. The only English words I can remember are "Thank you!" and "No thank you!" and "Please!" I force myself to remember the various social scenarios on my phone: shopping for a pair of elastic-waisted pants, shopping for lactose-free milk, shopping for souvenirs for all my friends back home (I listened to that lesson twice, even though I don't have any friends). Mild niceties can only get you so far in a foreign land. It's becoming very apparent that they won't remedy a hostage situation, especially when the woman ties me up with a beige spiralling telephone cord, wrapping it around me like I am prized rotisserie meat. She does all this while digging the hammer into my skull.

"No, thank you!" I blurt out, my voice jittery with fear, afraid that she will bash out my brains while she forces me to sprawl face down on the linoleum floor. My captor is dangerous. A gifted multi-tasker!

The woman jabbers to the man, so he tears off some toilet paper and stuffs it into my mouth. I gag a little. The wad is dense, like a sanitary napkin. She doesn't have to muffle me— I can't talk back, and who would I even call to for help, if I were capable of blubbering their nonsensical language?

This is like a pantomime. White woman screams. Asian woman, on impulse, forgets about toilet paper in her mouth, tries to screams back, and gags.

Screaming from white woman only stops when she hands Asian woman a framed photograph, practically shoves it in her face. The photo shows her happy and buoyant in an opalescent dress that makes her look like a pre-apocalyptic cloud. Hard to imagine clouds ever being elegant and debutante-soft. The strange white woman is kissing the same strange white man— their wedding photo.

A deep, sinking shame envelops Asian woman.

This is the couple's home, and she is an intruder, an incompetent immigrant, and a thief.

My parents met at a party through a mutual acquaintance whom they both couldn't remember. My father was in the People's Liberation Army Navy, and my mother was a child seamstress who sewed zippers onto oily mass-produced nylon jackets. They married without fuss because my mother was fifteen and pregnant with me. After my father was kicked out of the navy for disorderly conduct, they moved into my grandparents' one-room apartment. My father broke his commanding officer's nose and crushed his jaw with his shoe. He prized violence, and it suited him.

Mr. Lim and I didn't want a wedding reception. We had agreed that our marriage would be like a business transaction. In his email, he wrote that he owned a thrift shop in Nebraska City, where he sold and resold old and new clothing. For three dollars you could get a shopping bag full of pants and shirts and pretty floral dresses, although he warned me that the people in America were unusually large, and that I would not find my size.

He was lonely, had lived in Zhujiajiao almost a decade before, and wanted a wife. He had promised that he would help me find my mother. For years, I had daydreamed about our reunion, and I thought that I would either confront or embrace her depending how I felt that day. *We will hire a private detective*, Mr. Lim wrote, and sent a money order for $1,000 (real American dollars) in good faith. America had always looked so infinitesimal in the movies. I had Googled pictures of Nebraska City: wide, spacious land that looked like stacks of porous yellow cake, whereas Shanghai was cramped and messy, like a smorgasbord of leftover banquet food. I sensed a cruelty in the polluted drinking water, in the pouring monsoon rains. But on the day that I left Shanghai, the sky was blue and optimistic as the plane rocketed off the tarmac towards a floating Western continent where people seemed to discover bliss.

Two repellent truths: My father was convinced that he loved me. My mother was not sure how she felt about me, which is why she left.

Photographs are hanging askew on the farmhouse's poultry-tinted walls and pinned to the old refrigerator with magnets of the American states. The man and woman are/were avid collectors of jovial people. Grinning relatives or squinty, laughing friends, who must be very glad that they have not survived. It is a general rule that happy people do not thrive in apocalypses. No one, not even the universe, will suffer a false-faced, shit-eating optimist.

When a large quake blasts through the house, an oversized frame on the living room wall smashes to the linoleum floor. Flying glass from the Palladian windows slices our faces. The front door cracks off its hinges, and foul-smelling fumes *whoooooooooosh* inside. The house reverberates and hums. It's like being inside a sad, roaring microwave.

The woman sobs. She clutches the wrecked photograph of a boy and a girl who look identical, no older than six. Her hands are sliced badly. I wonder how her children died. I think they were lucky to have a caring mother like her.

I imagine the boy and girl playing outside on a beautiful painted swing set bolted among green, hunchbacked trees, before the grumbling earth swallowed them up.

—

Once, after my father smashed my mother's nose in, she crumpled to the floor and did not move for three days. He broke all the mouse-sized bones in her face. Her eye was a swollen hard-boiled egg. She told me she saw planetary rims, star-stressed floaters. Afterwards, I remember her lipstick on my father's face, on the solar tips of his yellowing teeth, a global smear on his cheek. I remember how, afterwards, he pulled me into a hug. "Don't worry, little one," he said to me, holding me under the kitchen table. I smelt the formaldehyde residue of sour rice wine emanating from his dry lips. Little tessellations of sweat on his skin.

I remember fat, quivering cherry blossoms unfurling against the window.

The one-lens man has a soft spot for me. I can tell that he is trying to be gentle, as if chittering to a house pet or a dumbfounded child. He talks to me for hours, such nonsense. Grief is an ostentatious language invented by wild mammals. It would be more practical and time-worthy if he just taught me some standard go-to English. He must be incredibly lonely, speaking to a house-crashing, pantry-thieving woman who cannot understand him. The man never gazes at his wife, a feral-eyed ostrich from primal times. He stares at his wobbly knees when she addresses him. I almost pity them. When he talks to me, I automatically say "Thank you," which seems to amuse him.

I am so hungry that my stomach spasms. During mealtime, the man removes the bunched-up toilet paper from my mouth and feeds me. Five spoonfuls of sweet, seedy fruit phlegm per day. He counts it, and sometimes gives me a dreadful sixth. The goop, which must be pig food, gives me terrible indigestion and causes my remaining teeth to ache. It's enough to make me wish that I had knocked out all my teeth at Mr. Lim's. It would have prevented cavities. At least my captors are letting me live.

Water is scarce, so we have nearly cleaned out a month's supply of liquor. When I get two spaced-out bathroom breaks, squatting limply, on a spread of newspaper on the floor, I try my best not to faint. My bird-like legs cannot sustain my weight. The smell is excruciating—it almost makes my captors want to let me go. Almost makes me want to give up on food and surviving. But suddenly I ache for chewy red bean cakes and spicy barbecued duck, even Mr. Lim's unending chow mein that we ate for three days straight. I convince myself that I love the uncomplicated anticipation of a good meal too much to give up and pass away.

One night, after my feeding, the woman seizes my hair and yanks it until I can feel my scalp tear. Perhaps it is garish satisfaction, this human ability to injure another. When she finally stops, I like to think she glimpses the same loss inside me.

I cry, but I don't mourn my life in China.

At dusk, when the sun's inferno abates, the woman leaves the house and brings back end-of-the-world treasures: a crown of paper flowers, a piece of charred cat. A child's candy-blue shoelace that she ties around her bread-like neck like a noose. When she carries back a thermos filled with water, which she sieves for minuscule rocks, it gives me hope that the world is not over yet.

I hope that she chokes on a pebble.

There is not much to do when you are tied to a chair during an apocalypse. Time seems irrelevant; it moves too slowly, dribbling consciously like a pus-infused wound, and then much too quickly, when something inevitably catches fire or explodes.

The man and I often wail together. He shows me wallet-sized pictures of his children, and I nod. I pretend that he is exceptionally kind and grin at him, toothless. Or that he is my new husband and we are facing the apocalypse together. *The next one will be much better,* I tell him in my childish fantasies. *Only people we dislike will die.*

As if to destroy my daydream of nuptial apocalyptic bliss, the farmhouse will pulsate with terrestrial groans, mechanical screechings, and I wonder if/when the house will collapse. I feel myself sinking in these moments. A typhoon waylaid in the throat.

The man and woman argue too much. I begin to wonder if they are debating how/when to kill me. I wish they would hurry up. Truthfully, I cannot subsist on this terrible substance any longer.

If we are the last three remaining survivors in Nebraska City, then humankind is un-ironically doomed.

Days/sleeps/hours later, when the woman leaves on one of her foraging excavations, the man unexpectedly kisses me. I seize up as he grabs me like a can of fish. I am trying my best to quietly expire, tied to a kitchen chair with a telephone cord, but he must find my semi-comatose state attractive. The man's lips taste like dry apples and extinction. His hands are charred like overdone meat. We both smell like prehistoric mammals. I stare at his pebbly teeth and my stomach heaves. He unties me and I try to run. I do not get very far before he clubs me on the back of the skull with a fist. Then he sits on top of me and turns me inside out.

My father cried when she left us. He stayed in the apartment for weeks, drinking syrupy baijiu and punching himself in the face until his smooth features transformed into a red-and-purple mask, the hue of a bubonic plague.

"Lift up your dress, little one," my father said, and I did what I was told, while the mosquitoes whined through the night and my grandparents, who watched over us like our dead, peeping ancestors, did nothing—except turn the music back on. *In a faraway place lives a good girl. In a faraway place lives a good girl.* In my memory, the CD player is stuck on repeat.

My grandfather says that I am my mother's daughter. A week after my father died (a heart attack in the street), I dropped out of the prestigious Fudan University and announced that I was going to America. I was going to find my mother. I was going to ask her why she didn't take me with her, but mostly, why she sent those postcards if she was going to bother to write anything at all. I wish she had been more or less cruel.

One morning when the woman is away, I suddenly, brazenly, kiss the man as soon as he plucks the soggy toilet paper from my mouth. "Ahhhhh," I say, like I am having a root canal at the dentist. "Ahhhhh," he says, when I kiss him. This is the first time that I seem willing. His hands stay floppily, unsure, like two undead salmon, at his thighs. This is my chance! I taste longing and a wet, discomfiting sickness. I'm sure that he wants to have one great tragic love affair before the world triumphantly finishes us off. I wait for him to untie the telephone cord that mummifies me, and he helps me stand, awkward, while reaching for his pants. Our kiss fogs the solo lens of his skewed, broken glasses. Sweetly, tenderly, almost like love.

The dilapidated farmhouse wobbles. I feel myself splitting and cracking, just like the flowery baroque wallpaper on these sinking walls. A part of me is upstairs in the past, hovering on trembling foundations. I am divided, but in this moment, I want to live. So quickly, unexpectedly, I wrap the telephone cord around the man's throat and squeeze. Then I bite the triangle of his nose as hard as I can. He scream-wheezes while I bite down and squeeze again. Blood oozes onto my tongue, and it's sweet and spicy at the same time, reminding me of peppery hoisin sauce and all the meals that I haven't eaten in a long time.

I spit out his nose. I won't say that I am not tempted to swallow a piece. I need the protein. Alarm seems to reanimate the man's zombified face, making him almost young again. Loss of a prominent facial feature will transform anyone. Furiously, monstrously, I grab the telephone and pummel him, not once but six times between the eyes until I see the shock splutter out of his round, blinking eyeballs like unsteady lights before a blackout. He falls.

—

I have stolen a half-dozen jars of this fruit yuck. I have taken a few kitchen knives, a clay mug to collect falling water—all this I carry in a cloth shopping bag. Of course, I take my blood-stained rug, which I wrap over my shoulders. Poor Mr. Lim. Poor everyone! I will follow the dipping road, continue past the farmhouse. I feel like I have enough food/optimism to last until tomorrow.

As I plod to the back porch of the sinking house, where the grass has been fried urine yellow, I pass two tiny, grotesque scarecrows propped up like sacrificial offerings on the remains of a white picket fence. The corpses have faces like melted candy, children only a few weeks ago, charred beyond synaptic recognition. From the photograph, I know they are the twins.

Mr. Lim wanted a baby girl because he said that boys were foolish and overrated. We were going to try in two years, when I was twenty-three. A swollen belly wouldn't have been the worst fate.

I find the largest sinkhole and drag the twins over. The ground eats them headfirst and spits out what I think is a bone at first but is just a white, indigestible child's slipper.

The sky seems to be dipping lower, almost at a forty-five-degree angle. Maybe the world is leisurely flipping over.

"This is a terrible mistake," my grandfather said to me when I told him that I was leaving. "You can't run away from what you deserve. You can't abandon fate. The world will make you fall on your face if you try to escape. And if that doesn't work, it will find a way to break both of your legs. What will you do then? Crawl on your stomach?"

I am suddenly determined to find my runaway mother. If she's anything like me, I doubt that she's dead. An apocalypse won't/can't kill her. I must be very hard to kill, a trait of endurance inherited from my dysfunctional people.

A cracking sound stills me, and I gasp as frozen rain, in the shape of pink marbles, spits down. I taste some of it on my tongue. It refuses to melt, so I bite into one very slowly. Crunch. I'm almost disappointed that frozen apocalyptic rain isn't delicious. I surprise myself by giggling.

I recall a memory that I've held closest to me. I was maybe nine. A chilly, rain-flecked autumn afternoon together at Fuxing Park. Laughing in her shrill bird-like pitch, my mother grabbed my hands and spun me around and around. Inquisitive bystanders stopped to look. We were dressed like oversized porcelain dolls, clad in white atrocities with absurd swathes of cheap spiderweb lace, but I liked how the wind picked up our skirts and showed off our bare legs. "Faster," I said, "faster," and she spun me around and around, like we two were the earth, alone. As we whirled under towers of green horse chestnut trees, the staring people became shapeless blurs. Until slowly, one at a time, they slipped off our own private planet, leaving my mother and me, unperturbed.

Wreck Beach

I t must have been the crows that first discovered the pancake stretch of beach so concealed it was like origami, creased under the coppice of black evergreens. Seven kilometres of zombie-coloured sand that extended along a dusky blue tide, you had to nose-dive down a feral rabbit hole to find it. Because Wreck Beach, heavily canopied by conifers, was like being exiled to some yummy Jungian dream. It was a wild slog to the periphery of Vancouver, from our city of pure glass. If Portland had its cults and vampires, Vancouver was known for its downpour of drizzling mystical energy, its nasal-voiced psychics and ziplock baggies of fat, magicky mushrooms. We said the crows had found this shred of coastline, but it was called Wreck Beach because everyone said we'd wreck it by 2025, litter mounded to the grisly skyline.

To get to Wreck Beach, it was 594 steps down a jagged sliding incline, a muddy slant that had you panting and gasping for ragged evergreen air, the sweet saltiness of the Pacific Ocean snuffed up your nostrils like magic fairy dust. Trail 6: a sluggish trek that took around forty-five minutes to get to Wreck, and if you felt faint going down and woozy going back up, there was a friend usually accommodating enough to slap you. Besides, if you blacked out, you'd wake up with the crows flapping, tearing bits from your clothes, your snarled wet hair. Wasn't that motivation enough?

But before Wreck Beach became our favourite public nudie beach, my great-uncle, who had come with the other Chinese in 1881 to build the continental railroad, once camped out on the marshy land. When it wasn't too wet and sloshy in July, he slumbered under an orange tarp tied to some trees. He hated the boarding houses in Chinatown where you shared a bunk and snored toes-to-head with another man, so he sank into his gritty blanket of soaking sand. I imagined the cawing black crows, glass stones for eyeballs, pecking at his little bald head. One night, a funny-looking man who had the hooked beak of a crow came to him and challenged him to a game of dice. If he won, he'd have unlimited riches, women, and opium and be allowed to return to his village in China, but if he lost, he forfeited his ancestors. My great-uncle, drunk on cheap gin, laughed and lost his dice roll. He disappeared, and some of the family thought he crawled into the water and never floated back. But others believed he became a bird-man, that our family was all descended from the birds and we'd join them when the man with the beak collected our souls.

It was Find-Daddy Night, which meant Mom had time off from her waitressing job at the Happy Smile, a greasy spoon where the forks were rusted from month-old egg crud. We lived and worked in the blue-collar bits of East Van, which boasted crooked houses and storefronts with words like *cunt* and *whore* graffitied in Chinese by sloppy hoodlums.

Just nine blocks away from the greasy spoon, we rented a place above a strip of Asian delis and a bar where the patrons (the deli owners) pitter-pattered home around 2 a.m., so the apartment stairs stank of sour alcohol and cat piss. For months, peanut carcasses steeped in wetness that wasn't water. No elevator, so you had to pull yourself up eleven flights, the ammonia-like stink burning your lungs.

Find-Daddy Night made my mother excited, and before she stocked her purse with extra undies and socks for me, she'd scour our one-bedroom with bug spray, squash the scuttling roaches on her way down. "Look look," she said, stomping with glee in her yellow rainboots like a child in a sludge puddle, "look how fast they run. They're smarter than mouse. Are you smarter than mouse? No, you just stand there and not move so your heart so bad. No exercise, come on. That's why P.E. teacher give you a C. C for crappy heart haha."

Really, Mom was so excited to see Dr. Yu, and she said my heart was destined for her big marriage plan. There'd be red rose petal hearts all over the wedding cake. And if she bought him enough sweet-and-sour pork from the Happy Smile, he might fall desperately and urgently in love with her.

"How do you know he's going to marry you?" I asked her, watching her pin up her black hair with the grey sinewy strands. She was forty-eight, and Dr. Yu looked much younger than her.

"Because it's your father's fault that you have a curse," she announced. "And don't you want a doctor for a new daddy, not a bird?"

You see, Find-Daddy Night meant wooing Dr. Yu or some other poor Chinese cardiologist that she wailed at in the harassed bluntness of our dialect. My bad heart was her excuse.

Other mothers and daughters went shopping and primped themselves in the changing room mirror, but we went to Find-Daddy Night at the hospital.

On the bus ride there, she swabbed expired powder on my cheeks to make me look pasty. It might have been the beginning of cherry blossom season in May, but vicious hail droplets splattered across our grey-hued city. I shivered under my oversized men's hoodie while she hollered at me to stop moving. My mother, who was bony-thin, spread wide brushstrokes of rouge on her own cheeks so she'd look healthy when the doctors talked to her. When she had no money for drugstore lipstick, she bit her lips to make them red.

In all honesty, my mother looked ancient and tired and famished, and even her hospital clothes—black skirt and low-cut champagne blouse—looked shabby. If I saw her on the street pushing a shopping cart with all her things, I might have mistaken her for one of our city's multiplying homeless.

"Show them what you really are, that you're a really cursed girl. Your daddy disappear and so will you!"

"I'll try," I promised her, because I just wanted to please her, because I pitied her.

"Good girl," she said, and slipped five bucks into my palm. That was all she could afford.

At Vancouver General, we sat, straight-faced with purpose, in the waiting room. Even though I was fifteen, I wore one of my floral nightdresses (the one with diluted pink roses) and Hello Kitty slippers. My mother forced me to change out of my red

Converses when we checked in. I scowled at the spotty lino-leum under my feet.

We were greeted by her special friend Darryl, who grabbed her ass and then reached for my hand. I yanked it away. I won-dered how the triage nurses saw us. Mom, with her curls and her frantic, jumpy eyes, playing the part of doting mother. Darryl, a manager at Value Village, who was white and skinny with a lumpy head. Then Cousin Zhou Tau, Billy to me, who kept guffawing at my nightgown. He was in grade 12 and was sleeping over tonight because his mom worked late shift at the restaurant and he was always in some shit. As kids, we had played Barbies before lighting the neighbours' lawns on fire. But lately, when Billy dropped me off at the Asian mall, where I stuffed chocolate bars and pretty underwear into my bag, he'd forget to pick me up. At the hospital he didn't even look at me; he just kept snickering.

"You okay, kid?" Darryl asked me. He was harmless, really, just liked to touch your shoulder too much when he was talking—probably some kind of white person tic. "Your mom says you're unwell again? Want a hug? No, I think you need one. No, I insist, kiddo."

Mom had befriended Darryl because he worked at Value Village, where he bought my matching hospital outfits with his senior employee discount. We had been doing Find-Daddy Night since I was seven, when my father suddenly vanished. Despite the passage of time, the changing hospital staff, the new doctors, my outfits were always the same. It helped that I had the gangly body of a prepubescent boy, perpetually weigh-ing eighty pounds, and could still fit into the XXL sizes in the children's section. If Darryl didn't bring home pyjamas with Donald Duck faces, I'm sure my mom would stop talking to him. It was important for me to look like a serious patient. My clothes were second-hand but good-quality cotton, discarded by rich people, the kind that had nurses rubbing your shoulders, bringing you grape popsicles. The kind of outfit that said you required attention immediately.

After all, Mom's English sucked and I couldn't imagine what she and Darryl had to talk about. Darryl's voice was a shaky murmur, and whenever Billy slept over, we heard them in my mother's room, headboard smashing and their pitchy voices moaning in sick, tumultuous octaves. She kicked him out of the apartment when he spoke of things too sentimental, like a future with her, vacations on Denman Island, a possible baby brother for me.

Once Darryl caught me ripping a round metal tag from a bra I had stolen from Walmart. It was embarrassing when you flashed your loose second-hand bras from Value Village in the girls' change room before Phys Ed. But I didn't know that if you yanked off the anti-theft device, purple dye would sting your fingers, stain your new push-up bra. I didn't know I'd have an allergic reaction, my hands inflamed like mitts. Darryl threatened to call the cops, but in the end he accompanied me to the walk-in clinic. I suppose he meant kindly, but how could you like a shrimpy man who asked you to massage his forehead?

In the emergency room, there'd always be a long lineup and your spot was determined by how fast the nurses thought you'd die. A kid with bloodied teeth came in with an old lady. He howled and blubbered blood so the triage nurse gave him a plastic dish. He was not a priority. Mom lied and said I was fading, vanishing, disappearing.

It was so exciting, she said, having nurses fawn over us. Besides, I needed a strong father figure, and wasn't Dr. Yu paternal enough? You couldn't count on some white foreigner, some gweilo like Darryl, to stick around.

While we waited, Darryl would always make me and Billy whisper the Narcotics Anonymous prayer with him, and I pretended to, because otherwise he'd want a hug. We clasped hands, and Darryl snapped his eyes shut with theatrical zeal.

"God," I whispered in Cantonese, "grant me the serenity to accept that my mother has truly shitty taste in men, the courage to change our mediocre fate, and the wisdom to never date an idiot gweilo who is stingy with rides."

After Darryl was done reciting, he'd moan delicately, and hum a little.

"Tell them you are not a good girl," Mom would whisper to me in Cantonese again and again, because she hated waiting, and this was a clue for me to start screaming and clutch my chest spectacularly. "You need to get rid of family curse," Mom urged me, and I would crumple and flail my arms and legs like I was some half-hearted victim in *The Exorcist*, while Billy sniggered. Later, I would invite Billy up to the old fold-out couch that I slept on, and wrap myself around him.

"Is she going to disappear?" Mom wailed at every medical professional, and everyone thought she was such a brave but sad immigrant mother. "Stap-haney, my girl, very, very curse."

"Roll a little bit more, aiya," Mom admonished. "How come you insist on wearing underwear with big hole? I've seen you in nice underwear. You're not so helpful in getting us Dr. Yu."

Disgusted by my performance, she'd stand up, open her mouth, and scream for help—deserving an Oscar for best supporting actress. "PLEASE! MY DAUGHTER! SOMEONE PLEASE HELP US!"

Slogging home at 5 a.m. on the bus (Darryl never offered us a ride), Mom went straight to the restaurant, where she would whip off her hospital clothes and change back into her polyester waitress uniform. Billy and I watched television and smoked a little baggie of bad weed that probably came from the swirling blades of someone's lawnmower.

Halfway through a show about rich white people, Billy's tongue was jammed down my throat, his hand clawing my thighs and leaving tender rashes, but I was just so happy I wasn't so lonely anymore. The messed-up thing was, we were bound by a dark family history, vanished fathers, and a nonpermutable fear that we were unlovable. Paranoia drew us towards one another, until I told myself that I didn't know where I or Billy began. Whenever I saw my cousin, I saw my own childhood tragedies. When we were naked and transcendent together, I was only fucking myself. Left alone in my shared misery, I was fierce, if not frenetic.

It really wasn't true that Chinese kids were good at school. I cheated, and my cousin and his friends cheated by copying each other's answers.

After school, all the Chinese kids, mostly Billy's friends, hung out at Wreck. None of us were friends because we liked each other. We were the poorer Chinese, not like those rich ones who had come from Beijing with money and cars and maids—the kind that white Vancouverites liked, boosting up the economy.

It was warm enough to strip down to your underwear, or if you were the bolder sort, you flaunted it all, even if you were a boy-chested girl or just another hairless boy with guinea-pig-sized balls. It didn't really matter anyway—everyone else was naked and it was only polite you joined those with jiggling flesh. Sometimes we saw our teachers, the cool young science one who grinned at us, and we waved back, horrified by his briar patch of pubic hair.

It always seemed like it was crow season at Wreck Beach. The birds watched us, wheedling our group for bread crusts and potato chips, pimpling our bare legs and asses with their surly beaks if we didn't comply. One crow kept cawing and circling, although we had fed it a potato chip. It came close to my hand, nipping, berserk, gasping and staggering around before dropping dead. We may have talked like we had assimilated, but we still believed the crows could give you shit luck. Since we were old enough to speak, my mom had told us again and again about how any of the crows could be our missing fathers. Gently, I nudged the crow away with my flip-flop.

"Ummmm, I have something exciting to tell you, Staph," said Fiona, who called herself Fokfok. She was Billy's some-times girlfriend, a buttery-looking Taiwanese with bleached hair and a squashed nose. I didn't really like her, and she always stared at me with aloofness whenever we were having dinner at Billy's house, her chopsticks digging hard into the burnt barbecue pork.

Not wanting to look eager, I shrugged and looked at the dead crow.

"Garry Chan told me he wants to fuck you," she declared, while we lay on the sand.

I groaned. Garry Chan, the smartest kid in Billy's year, who had won a scholarship to the University of Toronto and was probably going to be a doctor.

He may have been smart, but he was seriously deformed. He looked like someone had splattered acid on his ear so that it had melted into the right side of his face. The left side of his face was smooth, but the right side was red and mottled and looked perpetually angry, like my hands when I stole the bra. The rumour was that he had been tortured in a refugee camp.

If I was being honest, I had no valid excuse to be cruel to Garry. It wasn't his fault that he was the ugliest of our flock. My only defence was that our superstitious parents had taught us that how we looked dictated our lives. How rich or poor you'd be depended on how tight the gaps in your fingers were. I had no lifelines on my palms, a significant hole in my heart which meant bad fung, wind that went through me and made me flaky. Being nasty to Garry meant that I could feel better about myself, even if it was only temporary.

At school, white kids referred to Garry as the Phantom of the Opera and told him to wear a mask. But it was the Chinese kids who froze him out. We whispered bitingly behind his back and never invited him to our parties at Wreck. Everyone except Billy, who wore too-tight jeans with his hip bones jutting out, his red streaks, and his class-clown swagger. Billy, my dear cousin, sometimes nice to Garry when we weren't.

"Hey, hey," Billy always said, "he's not a bad guy."

"You should go to the grade 12 dinner and dance with him," Fokfok crowed at me. "He's gonna ask you. You'll be Frankenstein's date."

"Shut up," I told Fokfok, who grinned, so I flung wet sand at her face.

Beside us, more birds choked and dropped dead. It must have been some weird strand of avian flu that didn't affect humans. Caw, caw, caw. Another crow was trying to nibble on my fingers, and I wanted it to peck out Fokfok's eyes, but then it suddenly dropped dead too, its glassy eyeball staring at me.

I had a sister once, and she was also called Staphanie. My parents didn't know how to spell Stephanie so they spelled it like they pronounced it: Stap-haney. My mother screaming our name across the bus stops to the elementary schoolyard where she sometimes dropped off a McDonald's Happy Meal. Staphanie Number Two, I imagined my father would whisper, in an unhappy baritone because I couldn't imagine what he looked like.

I knew why I had been born with a hole in my heart, a fissure the size of a splinter. There needed to be room for my sister's spirit. Staphanie, I found her laminated death certificate in a shoebox under my mother's bed—a funereal shrine of cardboard and plastic. Staphanie, I was told she was better than me, and supposedly luckier because she had big Buddha lobes and an impossibly high forehead for a baby. I had been told she suddenly died in her slumber, her sweet burble of sleep. Had she been suffocated by our mother's histrionic fussing?

Had she been stolen away by a hungry bird? In Chinese mythology, crows caused personal misfortune; if they entered your house, someone would die. There was some mythology about them being the naughty adolescent sons of the sun god Dijun, transformed carcasses that the great archer Hou Yi had shot down. When the crows crossed the murky Pacific, flying over their remaining brother, the last waking sun, a blackness would eclipse the city, before the crows camped out on power lines that zigzagged across our urban terrain.

"Who was the creepy bird-man that tricked my great-uncle?" I had asked my mother one day, and she'd shrugged. Had she slapped her thighs in disbelief when my father told her about the bargain Great-Uncle made with a demon?

So much guesswork in our ancestral migration. Secrets, undignified, woven into a patchwork history.

What was certain was our abundant sorrow, and the crows breathed and fed on it when they watched us, my mother and me at the bus stop in front of our building, our arms anchored down by groceries in plastic bags.

"Husband?" my mother said to the crows, sometimes offering them day-old Chinese buns in a gesture of appeasement. "Is that you?"

"Staphanie, you look whiter than usual. Aiya! You are disappear!"

She was worried about me, my mother said in her accented English, glancing sideways at Dr. Yu. It was Find-Daddy Night once again, and I was annoyed at her because I was impatient to meet up with Billy after I was finished being pricked for blood tests. I hadn't seen my cousin since he last came with us to the hospital with Darryl, two weeks earlier. After school, I had messaged my cousin sixteen times until he agreed to spend a fraction of his night with me.

"Are you sure you're feeling that sick?" Dr. Yu asked me. "We could always do another biopsy."

Amplified by his stethoscope, I imagined my heart sounded like a garden hose whooshing. The right atrium, palpitating, *lub-dub, dub-dub lub.* The left atrium, stretching and budding and contorting—a meaty fist squeezing.

"You feel rotten inside, aren't you?" Mom asked, urgency in her voice.

"Sometimes," I muttered, and then she gave me her tiny pissed-off look.

"Tell Dr. Yu how you want to be good girl, okay-lah?"

The waves smashed the shore in sync to my off-colour heart-beat, and Billy worked my polka-dotted summer dress over my head. I felt instantaneous relief when my too-cool-for-me cousin, shrugging, had finally showed up an hour later than the agreed-upon time. And I was semi-reassured when he moved his warm, smirking mouth against me. But he was fumbling, rushing, put off.

Our mothers were at work, and Billy, setting a timer on his phone for our rendezvous, said he didn't want to spend a full night with me and sleep over at the apartment. His dry mouth pressed on the flat of my stomach, teeth scratching the feathery hairs of you-know-where. It was so dark that no one was out here, the waves slapping the greying sand, and I thought about why the crows returned. What was it about the west coast that seduced you, that made you want to come back to the wilderness that circled the city?

The birds of our city, swooping over black square dumpsters and pecking at the patches of hurled vomit on the sidewalks. Some twenty thousand crows came to Vancouver each year to roost, flying in squat, undulating queues. They were perpetually hungry, foraging, doing anything to survive. The crows mocked the cooing hustle of baby pigeons, pilfered bread crusts, shredded candy wrappers. They smelled our insecurities, our damp, swampy fears, because they were migrants like us, ravenous but unmerciful scavengers. I had seen five crows peck to death a grey-eyed pigeon with a diseased claw, but the only difference between them and us was that we couldn't leave if we wanted to.

Sensing that Billy was in a strange mood, I joked that our relationship was the result of our Chinese culture being so repressed. Not to mention, his girlfriend Fokfok resembled some hybrid of a herd animal, part cow, part sheep. Pinching my inner thigh hard, Billy told me to Shut It. I felt tears burning through my eyelids, so I babbled instead about how the Chinese newspaper recently said that East Asians had the most incest of all the racial groups in North America, and it was probably true. Billy wasn't listening, so I continued a monologue in my head.

I was sure both our mothers knew what we did, but it was okay as long as we didn't have babies. It was hard being an immigrant. Mom had her Dr. Yu, and I had Billy. After all, my cousin and I had bonded as snot-faced toddlers because our fathers disappeared one day. All their clothes, keys, shoes, wallets, and phones remained, and no one knew where they had gone off to. Mom kept screeching that my father had transformed into a piss-yellow-eyed crow on the way to work, while Billy's mom went to the bathroom for five minutes before discovering her husband's clothes, underwear, and fuzzy socks on the couch, as if he had stripped and suddenly ran off. A shoe-sized hole in the living room window screen. The instant noodles and egg-battered Spam on the stove were still hot, the television blaring *The Price Is Right*. No one had seen a naked man running around the city. My father did not show up at the tuna processing factory, where he worked six nights a week, ever again. The police could not find our fathers; no one could.

"Can you do me a favour?" Billy suddenly said when he was finished.

"What?"

"Can you go to the year-end dance with Garry?"

It was the halfway point of drizzly May, still chilly like the insides of a supermarket freezer, and Billy and his friends were graduating.

"Why?"

"I owe him a favour."

I got up, naked, my hair whipping across my neck, and plunged into the icy water. I thought about catching pneumonia, about dying that instant. As I somersaulted and flopped backwards over a booming wave, Billy took a picture of me on his phone.

"Do it again," he said, snickering. "But more graceful."

In middle school, Billy got arrested for terrorizing neighbourhood girls. You didn't need to walk more than a block from our school before you saw these girls, who were desperate to be full-grown women. You recognized them because you probably swapped lip gloss and strains of mono once in the bathroom, but most of them skipped their classes and hung out at the McDonald's by Science World on Main Street. A month before Halloween, Billy paid Garry fifty bucks to chase these high-heeled wannabes with an X-Acto knife. The girls probably thought it was Jack the Ripper back from the dead.

I thought that Billy wanted to borrow Garry for another stupid stunt.

As I quaked in the night-cold, I felt something, perhaps a shadow-man, blur into my peripheral vision, tickling my skin into itsy-bitsy bumps. Something cruel guffawed in my eardrums. *Staphanie*, the voice mocked. *He doesn't love youuuuuuuuuu*. I spun my head around, but there were only some crows.

"Did you see that?" I asked.

"Don't change the subject. So, Garry? What's it gonna be, S.? Do you want me to leave you?"

The timer on his phone buzzed loudly. Billy was gone before I could respond.

The grade 12 dinner and dance was where the white and Chinese kids kind of got along. They took saccharine photographs with their arms wrapped around each other's waists. If I didn't know any better, I'd think we were all friends. It was so dim inside the Best Western that served us pink, rubbery chicken and mashed potatoes, I barely saw anyone's made-up faces. Some of the white parents who didn't work in the evenings went to the dance as chaperones, cheering on their gyrating offspring. Garry was in the dance mob, waving at me, while Billy whirled Fokfok around the room. When the DJ played Bollywood and Chinese pop, the idiot kids dry-humped like monkeys, accidentally ripping the hems of their pageant gowns, their poufed $1,000 dresses. *What privilege*, I thought, eyeing the pink, blue, and yellow tulle, *to dress up like a gourmet cupcake and not worry that someone will take a giant bite out of you.* My $4.99 black velvet dress from Value Village (with Darryl's discount) was too bulky for me, the straps slouching off my shoulders. As the music pulsed louder, Billy and Fokfok became a pixelated blur. I watched, unable to tell which arm or mouth or leg belonged to whom, until Garry, shouting my name, stumbled towards me.

I pretended not to hear him. I snatched a few sparkly purses left out on the upholstered dining chairs and escaped to the women's bathroom. I ran my hands over the linen handkerchiefs folded in the square baskets and marvelled at the patchwork of gold-and-white tiles on the wall. I locked myself in a stall and went through the stolen purses, stuffing fifties and twenties into my shoplifted Walmart bra. I found Yves Saint Laurent lipstick in proud harlot red, wrote B + S 4EVR all over the door until I finished the entire tube. With someone's compact mirror, I studied my features, and wondered why Billy preferred Fokfok over me. How was she better? I wasn't beautiful, but surely I didn't look like a melted block of unsalted butter?

Around midnight, Fokfok came in and knocked on my stall, and said a bunch of us were going to have a bonfire at Wreck. Under the door, I saw that one of her open-toed sandals was missing a silver bow, and I felt better about myself.

She said: Garry was really sad I had behaved this way; he thought I was a better person than that. I clucked in annoyance, not bothering to hide how I felt.

An hour later, we got off the bus that took us outside of the city. Fokfok marched ahead with Billy, who was carrying beer in a plastic bag, and I followed with Garry. Fokfok and I carried our heels in our hands as we made our way barefoot down the ragged slope of Wreck.

"What are your plans for graduation in two years?" Garry asked, but I pretended I couldn't hear. "Do you think you'll be going to the University of Toronto too?"

"Too?" I said.

"Yeah," he said, "like Billy. I helped him with his essays, you know."

My teeth ached; my stomach clenched. Billy was leaving, and we had never talked about it. For the first time in my fifteen years, I actually felt as if my heart would implode. Did Fokfok know? Obviously. Those times she had stared at me, turning up her stupid bovine nose. Did I expect him to stay in Vancouver forever? I guess we weren't mated for life.

There comes a time in every girl's life when she regrets something, when she says or does something criminal and reckless.

Somewhere in the middle of Trail 6, we'd hear Billy's body tumble and crash into the sand and thicket of trees.

Fokfok screeched "Murderer!" in both English and Mandarin.

After he bounced down 221 steps, I thought he'd be dead. Immediately.

About a month ago, a baby pigeon thunked into our apartment window. Apparently, a flock of crows was chasing it and the pigeon tried to fly through the glass. Mom told me to quickly fetch it, because squab was a delicacy. I ran out of the apartment, picked up the mangled lump by one fragile claw. It snapped off and I couldn't find the leg again, so I picked it up by the other claw and cupped my hand underneath it in case I lost that leg too. Mom plucked off its feathers, chopped off its beak, fried the bald bird in a pan with soy sauce, and halved it.

Then, like we did ever since I was little, she would chew the meat, spit it back out, and expect me to eat her mush. "My baby bird Staphanie," she cooed at me. "I am helping you, making you strong so you will not leave me like Daddy-Daddy."

This time, I refused. I was no longer an infant, no longer her compliant creature. I would not accept her half-chewed sacrifice. She wanted me to carry her love, her heavy burden. A mealtime ritual between mother and daughter, meant to be a wounding. A clipping of my wings. To spite her, I grabbed my own half of the tasty pigeon and ate it with greed, filthy brown sauce dripping down my chin and onto my hands.

Tears dripped from my mother's saggy brown eyes. "You want bad life? Look what happen to Daddy-Daddy. He fly off and disappear into air."

—

I wasn't sure I did it. It was all a big headachy blur. I thought I heard feral roaring in my ears. *He does not love you.* I thought I heard the crows scream. *He does not want you.* But the guilty party had to be me, because Fokfok was screeching in both languages and Garry had yelled "FUCK!" I was very quiet and then I found myself sitting on a step, and then I heard them crashing down the stairs, screaming "Billy, Billy, ohmygod!"

Gradually, I pulled myself up, and leisurely hopped down every step.

"You fucking bitch," Fokfok said when I finally got to the landing where Billy was lying unconscious. "We have to call 911. Fuck, there's no reception here. I have to go back up!"

"He can't feel a thing," I explained to Garry, who pulled off his jacket and waved it like a lasso, scaring off one or two birds as Billy lay contorted in a funny heap. "He's still unconscious," I said. "Save your energy and wait until he wakes up." I decided I'd let the birds peck Billy because he deserved it.

Garry sat down beside me, and as if we were on an above-average date, we watched the birds nip Billy. We couldn't see him anymore because there were so many birds, they looked like a cozy black tarp covering him. I thought about how nice it was, the bloated white moon and all the birds and how I liked not seeing Billy anymore. How the salty wind was whipping my dress. Afterwards, Garry got a bit antsy and tried to scare the birds with a stick, and I sat there and watched for a while.

"I think they're eating him," Garry said. "What the fuck do we do?"

The birds were forming an organized circle and maybe a hundred began to peck his skin and hair, slamming their beaks in sync, leaving gouges of oozing red and black on his face. Some of them began to peck Garry too, and he screamed and slapped them a bit. I watched, but didn't help. Instead, I cleanly bit off a hangnail on my thumb.

I remembered that Billy had been carrying beer. I popped open a can, offered one to Garry, who seemed shocked by my nonchalance. I shrugged when he declined and began drinking alone. "Why waste?" I said, and finished a six-pack and belched with astonishing force when the helicopter paramedics arrived.

It took them four hours to get to Wreck Beach.

By then, Billy's body was completely gone. Garry sobbed wildly, Fokfok accused me of murdering and burying him in the earthy bush. No bones, no tattered bird-ripped clothes— what could I say? Billy was missing. The birds had covered him up, maybe whisked him away, maybe devoured him completely. Garry and I reported this to the paramedics, but there was no suggestion of blood or bone shards. Was this a prank call? We had been drinking, right? What kind of drugs had we been taking? They transported us to the hospital where the police were called and additional emergency response teams rushed to Wreck. Billy's mother was notified at the restaurant— Where the hell was Billy? she shouted. Witnesses saw him leaving the dance with us.

—

That night, I was also sorry to say my mother would try to propose to Dr. Yu, bringing him five cartons of Chinese takeout and a specially scribed fortune cookie.

She was bridal that night, all pink and white in her tight floral dress and white stiletto sandals. A quick detour to borrow plastic flowers from someone's sick room. My mother had her hair piled up, had her makeup polished up at a department store counter, maybe looking five years younger.

"Wait here," Dr. Yu said when she got down and grabbed his knees, then gripped his ankles, and he gave a repugnant little laugh before he yelled for hospital security, and my mother began to truly flap and scream like a headless chicken when they escorted her to the psych ward for evaluation. "Please marry us, Dr. Yu," she yelped, and it was really quite sad.

I was proud of her. I was sad for her. I was in mourning, for Billy, for my mother, and for myself.

In my mother's mind, I imagine it went quite differently: he'd fall in love with this wild, sexy apparition in pink and white, and maybe thank her profusely for all that free Chinese takeout. Maybe she imagined their medical courtship, the times he leaned in too close to talk about my health, his hand touching her hollow shoulder. Always that practised doctor's hand that told people it'd be okay, that he could replace my father's, who had no hands because he was a bird.

Afterwards it was said that all the triage nurses cried for her, because they knew her so well, and thought that the stress of having a sick girl had been too much on a single working-class mother. And afterwards, Darryl came by the hospital to recite Narcotics Anonymous for us, and I let him hug me. He swung his arm over my shoulders and the police said I could wait at home until they had more questions. Darryl dropped me at the bus stop, and it'd be a long ride home to the apartment that would still smell of lemon-scented bug spray.

Long into the night, Billy came to my window. I shivered when I looked at him. His arms were plastered with wiry black feathers and there was clotting blood on his warped beak, but his eyes were brown and jarringly human. He was flying on aerial stilts, his deformed bird feet hunched over my windowsill. I would never let him in, no matter how viciously he pecked at the glass, no matter how unhappily he cawed. I stared at him, mouthed Too Bad, and then I shut the blinds because now I knew he'd never leave me. He'd revisit Vancouver each year to roost and he'd think of me. But near sunrise, I still heard his uneasy caterwauling outside, so I tried to find a paperweight that could sink my cousin mid-flight. *Billy-Billy*, I thought. *I'm so sorry-sorry.*

I'm not sorry to say that I missed.

Each time he cawed tenderly, I threw a rock, beer bottle, and once, my shoe.

Let me be clear: I was red-eyed with exhaustion, which could explain my poor aim. But what I felt most was an insidious loss. My heart was damaged, but not removed.

The Noodley Delight

In our living room, Grandmama Wu has yet to become a ghost or zombie.

"Shithead," she shouts, waving a mouldy arm at me. "Asshole!"

A ghost, I feel, wouldn't be able to call her oldest grandkid so many horrendous names. A zombie would probably just devour her grandchildren without parental consent. My little brother, Ernie, whose cranium is gargantuan like a GMO watermelon on account of him having too much brain sap, tries to hug her and she lets him. She bends her head, nibbles on Ernie's greasy hair like a bunny. Spits out dandruff.

"Delicious," she announces, and lets out a wet, unholy belch.

"What should I do?" I ask Mom and Dad, who shrug and say it's my fault that Grandmama died in the first place. They're too excited about the inheritance to care about anything else.

The funeral was only a week ago, and the old harpy is already back, still dressed in her nicest dress, something pink and shoplifted from the Salvation Army.

Death has not altered her much. Grandmama's face is IKEA-furniture orange and there's morgue makeup melting off her cheeks. Also, her hands are slowly disappearing. They flicker like bad TV.

"Just because I'm dead," she shouts at me, "doesn't mean you don't still work for me, asshole!"

Grandmama Wu owns the third-best noodle shop in the Asian food court in Crystal Mall, Burnaby, in the province of a Billion Chinese. The Asian mall is a wicked version of mainland China meets Los Angeles, bright and gaudy. Only incendiary assholes, like gangsters and my grandmama, open businesses here.

Six days a week, for $7.20/hour, I work at the Noodley Delight, mopping the floor, counting inventory, and scooping noodles and lukewarm chicken gizzards into Styrofoam bowls for hungry customers. I ring up the cash register and only over-charge a little.

Grandmama Wu's shop is rated only Number 3 because a few years ago, some dude choked to death on her giant rice noodles, right in front of our stand. Death has been horrible for the Noodley Delight's ratings on Yelp. We've had to serve smaller-cut noodles and put up a disclaimer that says EAT YOUR OWN FAULT. We've lost other customers because our black sesame vermicelli looks like pubic hair. This grosses out the non-Chinese and everyone born in a first-world country between the ages of thirteen and sixty-five.

Bowing at our formerly dead grandmama, my mom and dad rush out to see the lawyer about their inheritance. I always feared that money would allow them to ditch us like assholes. They never seemed to like me or my brother much. What this also means is that me and Ernie are stuck with our formerly dead grandmama, who insists on us going to the Asian mall. We groan because it is a forty-minute bus ride, and Grand-mama will probably put us to work on our day off. Apparently, some habits, like family members, do not die.

I change out of my polka-dotted pyjamas into a soft, flowy skirt. Grandmama stalks me down the hallway to my bedroom, gagging at my outfit, her eyes twitching like spazzy Christmas decorations.

"Boy don't wear dress," she snaps in her wild animal Mandarin. "Kyle, get me purse. Ernie, find me walking shoe. The one your mother chose for the funeral are shit."

This wouldn't happen if we had cremated her.

The B41 bus is super late, plus Grandmama Wu is scaring people: hollering and smacking her purse at anyone who looks rich. Her Communist upbringing in mainland China means that she can't abide showy wealth. I suggest a taxi but Grandmama looks horrified. Ernie is covering his nose. Grandmama smells like fermented fish.

"Fucky-fuck," she growls, and I apologize to a girl in a pink J.Crew scarf who has been whacked by Grandmama twice.

"Stage four dementia," I explain.

"I'm so sorry," the girl says, staring at us, alarmed.

Grandmama Wu laughs at this pitiful exchange and calls me a bitchy-bitch.

But before I can roll my eyes and sigh all passive-aggressive-like, Ernie says that he has to go to the bathroom and wants to stop at McDonald's. The bus doesn't seem to be coming any time soon, and the lineup of people keep gawking at us. Grandmama snaps at him to shit on the sidewalk, canine style, but relents when she glimpses his distressed gape. Ernie is the only person we both tolerate and like—the only person we both 150 percent appreciate.

"I buy you overprice Happy Meal because you are boy," she says to Ernie, shoving me out of the way.

—

Just before she died, Grandmama Wu caught me pocketing tens and twenties from the cash register. Each week, I'd take a little because the M&M-sized candies of estrogen and antiandrogens and progestogens combined cost more than my scholarship for first-year university.

"Thief!" she screamed, grabbing a chopping knife. "Asshole!" Then the old gorgon lunged.

She skated on some spilled noodles on the floor, pivoted right, left, sideways, then *kabam!*

Was it karma? Bad luck? Fate?

Grandmama Wu cracked her head on the counter like a walnut. A lot of blood and brains leaked out for such a scab of a hag.

It was like 90 percent my fault that she died. At her funeral, I wore a second-hand suit from the thrift store because wearing a dress felt unseemly.

"Murdered," the pastor sermonized. "Her family was gunned down by the mafia and she grew up on the streets."

"She was a prostitute for one or two weeks," my dad said, sniffling. My mom wasn't that sad.

Then, finally, it was me and Ernie's turn to say bye-bye to Grandmama in her open casket from Costco. I bowed three times to show old-school respect, clasping my hands together, trying to look genuinely remorseful. Ernie whimpered and shut his eyes.

I patted him on the back and said: "No worries, little bro, we won't ever have to see her again. Promise."

—

At McDonald's, I buy us lumpy strawberry sundaes, and Grandmama Wu eats the spoon. Then she swallows the plastic cup with the ice cream in a rapid, frightening gulp.

"Kyle, is the reason no one loves you anymore 'cuz you want to be a girl?" Ernie asks, radioactive-red syrup mosaicking his teeth.

"No way, dude," I lie. Don't want my little bro to know.

"In China, all poor girl are prostitute," Grandmama declares unhappily, a piece of plastic embedded in her lower lip. "Why you want to be one, hey?"

Angry, I mimic her trippy Chinglish tone: "This is Canada, not China, hey?"

For a second, her pupils glow corpsy white and she gnashes her seafood-coloured lips at me. She hisses. For a second, I think Grandmama will eat me. But then her entire image fritzes, and she looks at me with shame. Like sorrow clogs her sleeping heart. Like she was once a person with hope, in her more youthful days. It's hard to imagine but maybe she was optimistic and pretty once.

I think that we could be having a grandma-grandkid bonding moment. But then Grandmama recovers and whacks me over the head with her boxy purse.

"Idiot," she snarls. "I'm dead, which mean I can read your fucking brain."

The driver kicks us off the bus for cussing too much, but mostly, I think, for smelling like rotten fish, so we walk to the Asian mall. This is a huge mistake, because we spot Ernie's school pals, the ones who call him Mutant Shithead. Last week, a kid smashed a beer bottle near his ear. Now, these high-schoolers follow and taunt us, singsonging and chingchonging, the usual racist bullshit. The language of our colonizers never evolves. Grabbing Ernie's sticky hand, we stumble over my skirt. Grandmama rolls her butter-tinted eyes at us and announces that her grandchildren are wimps.

White dudes corner us, T. rex–like, into a dead-end street.

Ernie's face is grey, mollusc-looking. My heart is raging, a paroxysmal hard-on.

I leap in front of my little bro just as one of the dudes mauls his fist into my teeth. Shouting, I go down hard and then he pummels Ernie in the eyes.

I crawl towards him, but another dude stomps me down. Crushes my index finger badly.

Poor Ernie's screaming, all curled up. It kills me to see my baby brother this way.

Ernie's sobbing makes Grandmama Wu so animated that she, scowling, leaps behind his attacker and pulls him into a furious headlock. Death has apparently turned her into an indomitable sumo wrestler. I yelp as she, grinning with false caramel-yellow teeth, takes a massive bite of the asshole's hair. He screams as she tears more salmon-pink scalp with her dentures. Then she swallows and smacks the bully like he is a busted ATM machine. She shoves him to the sidewalk and struts towards the other dudes, but they run away, pissing their baggy below-the-butt-crack pants.

"I used to fuck boy like you on street," she shouts, hiking up her pink funeral dress.

Ernie claps proudly. "My grandmama is a zombomb-bie!" he hollers at his bullies, spitting a lot of blood.

"That was freaking awesome!" I yell, a little shell-shocked.

Grandmama Wu hmmphs and we stop at a barbershop and buy a bag of freshly shorn hair off the floor so she can eat. "Yum," she says, sucking on strands of stringy bleached hair like gourmet candy.

At the Noodley Delight, I fix Ernie a lychee bubble tea with extra pearls and clean his face with a paper towel.

"You did good," I tell him. We high-five. Fist-bump.

Then me and Ernie stuff our faces with week-old rice noodles. Grandmama Wu always lets us gulp as many noodles as we want but not the gizzards 'cuz MEAT NOT CHEAP!!! (there's a sign on the refrigerator door to remind us). Me and Ernie sit on stumpy plastic stools and slurp, competing to see who can chomp the loudest. The noodles look like bloated slugs, unholy and unappetizing, just like us.

Grandmama Wu joins in, munching assorted hair from her plastic bag. She wins the prize for Most Disgusting. Grandmama looks as undelightful as she will ever be.

"Why you want to be prostitute for?" she repeats. Her eyes twitch as she clutches her tiny chest. "When I was growing up, all girl want to be a man. Why the opposite? What's wrong with you?"

Separated by the twenty-first century, life, and death, not to mention clashing cultures and West Coast slang, could she ever understand?

Already, she is fading and her legs are almost gone.

Already, she is a pale ghost of her former self.

I'd been worried that she would never leave us alone, but her disappearance is a bit gutting. Ernie frowns and asks where all her body parts are going. Grinning wickedly, Grandmama announces that the afterlife has the wildest mah-jong orgies and the best drugs. To my horror, she vomits up a greasy hairball the size of a full-grown Chihuahua.

"Hey fucker," Grandmama says to me in farewell, "take care of your brother!" Then she vanishes with her bag of hair, leaving behind a huge tarry stain on the Noodley Delight's floor.

The Basket-Swimmers

My mother floats through choppy waters like a dead thing. Under the violet sky, in southern China, where the Heavenly Enclosures form an esplanade of timid constellations, my mother barely moves—treading water, a woven basket on her head. "Frozen by moonshine," my father once declared. One arm dipping into filthy mud water, the other balancing her bamboo basket, she is a trembling splash of starlight.

If you look closely, though, her arm is curved and spotted, her grandmother-fingers webbed like an arthritic toad's. The moonlight makes her crocodilian features look unpleasant.

My mother is the best basket-swimmer in the green village of Houtouwan, a lonely fishing hamlet on Shengshan Island. Half mermaid, half fish and amphibian, she leads the other basket-swimmers with her easy arms and sturgeon's kick. Every blood dawn, my mother and her colony of sisters and aunties and cousins join the other twenty or thirty basket-swimmers transporting sweet guava, segmented legs of purple starfish, or wizened oysters to market. The Lán yǒngzhě swim for six miles, a synchronized group of fallen stars, until someone collapses.

Her people, a weightless nation, spend their lives as half-drowned water mules.

—

Unlike my mother, I am most afraid of water and make excuses not to go in, blaming stomach cramps or wild tropical fevers. In the water, my skin does not change colours and my toenails curl slightly.

Everyone in our village expects me to be as skilled a swimmer as my mother because it is our only way of survival. In Houtouwan, girls must swim or sell their bodies.

"Oh, Lileng," my female relations hiss and sigh when I tell them that I have severe stomach pains for the sixth or seventh time. Then I show them my molars, which are beige and small and square, not jagged and snaggle-toothed like theirs. My eyes are also shit brown, but my relations' corneas turn from the deepest black to iridescent, expanding and diminishing with the setting of the blood sun.

"You need to learn to swim before your thirteenth birthday," my mother says, joining our huddled ranks. The other basket-swimmers bow their scaly heads. Suddenly, my mother bends over and bites my neck. Dark red blood dribbles down her lip and chin. I flinch. Growling with unrestrained disappointment, she scratches herself—her blood is bluish brown. She pushes me to the ground.

There is an immense outpouring of love between my mother and me, except that she is often proud and flower-hearted. Sometimes I worry that she does not fully love me, especially when I cannot turn into a frog-girl and swim.

I stay face down on the pier while the basket-swimmers collect their goods and jump into the swirling river.

—

I am still twelve summers old when she seduces him. At first, I think that the soldier could be my new father. That this is a romantic love story in the making. A tale that travelling minstrels will sing in the courts of noblemen and perform gaily at mid-autumn festivals. The young soldier's face is fresh and smooth like an underwater stone.

You see, when the Japanese soldiers invade our village, my mother knows she has to fall in love with one of them, and he has to become obsessed with her. When he sees my mother swim for the first time, the young soldier becomes mercurial, like the unfurling water in the Qiantang River.

"I do not know if she is human," he murmurs, frowning slightly.

When my mother swims, I wonder if the soldier realizes that her slender legs sometimes turn into tentacles, or if he thinks that she could be an odd water nymph. Maybe he doesn't notice her dirty yellow teeth or how she can stay underwater longer than normal women. The other villages in the province of Zhejiang know the tales: Houtouwan belongs to the peculiar, green-looking women who crawled out from beneath the earth. In the sixth century of the Chen emperors, a red tsunami and an eastern apocalypse swallowed our island, burying our ancestors among thousands of dying frogs. On full moons, none of us can speak. We can only moan and croak from fear and grief.

But the Japanese soldiers do not believe these myths, and tell themselves homesickness and war have made them hallucinate—the female villagers of Houtouwan have strangely textured skin, not fish scales. Perhaps they even have an advanced form of never-recorded leprosy.

"He is a little more handsome than your father," my mother declares when the young Japanese soldier brings us a basket of week-old tropical fruit. Unfazed by the spiked thorns, we peel a black durian together, and my mother gives me an eighth of the milky flesh. She swallows the remainder of the fruit without chewing and burps. *Ribbit!*

At first, my mother insists that the soldier is nothing but a means for our protection. But then he woos her with foreign gifts—starchy white powders and clay pots of rouge from Shanghai. We do not know what these sticky paints are for, and we try to eat the contents. The soldier laughs, not unkindly, and he shows my mother how to pucker her earth-stained lips so she can smear colour on them. I wish that I was as pretty and mud-splattered as my mother, but the cosmetics make her vainer.

Like all great love stories, this one begins and ends with a murder.

At the riverbank, I catch a frog, cupping its twitching head between my soft human palms.

If I were a real basket-swimmer, would my mother be proud to call me her own?

During the blue monsoon rains of the summer, I had hidden in our hut and refused to bathe in the river. My mother was impatient; she did not understand this foolishness.

"Lileng," she had snapped, her eyes turning yellow then burgundy then black as river rock. "Water is our blood."

But my skin is pale and soft like flour. I have ten and a half fingers, twenty-three toes. Far fewer than my mother.

In my daydreams and nightmares, the wild currents of the Qiantang gush out of my nose and ears as I soundlessly holler. Sometimes I worry about falling in, being swept away by its night-coloured tides.

I know that I cannot ever become a basket-swimmer.

"Why am I not like you?" I ask my prisoner. I watch the frog struggle. I press my palms together tightly. Its heartbeat spasms once, twice, like a war drum ceding defeat in the distance.

That night, watching from the corner of our hut, the young soldier embraces my mother on her bamboo mat, rubs her sinewy muscles, and kisses her webbed feet. I am slightly embarrassed because my mother never made these harsh, underwater noises with my father. He vanished one morning, then sent word a year later that he had eloped with his first cousin, a pig farmer from a neighbouring village. He claimed that our clan had bewitched him.

"You're exquisite, my water lily," the soldier breathes to my mother, who smiles with her two hundred teeth. In his dim-witted love state, he cannot see the seaweed shade of my mother's skin and bulbous lips.

My girl-cousins rarely talk about how our fathers and uncles and brothers sometimes hold our mothers down, and how they weep and scream.

Whenever good-looking men visit our village, our mothers bring them home. My girl-cousins and I had giggled as our mothers touched themselves in sweet, excitable bliss, smiling as they shucked off their hemp dresses and wiggling their hips like they were children learning to swim. We fell asleep listening to their unearthly moans, as the sun, slowly, burned the wet dirt crisp. We helped dig holes in the ground while our mothers birthed their giant speckled eggs. Then under the half moon, we dug up our tiny hatched sisters.

That first night, the soldier holds my mother tightly as he falls asleep, snoring like a munitions factory in providential Nanjing. I am slightly hopeful that he will stay with us.

If the soldier becomes my father and protector, I could remain safely on land, in our hut all day, devouring exotic fruits and wearing rouge like a haughty courtesan in the Emperor's court. I could learn to sing and dance and play a dizi made of the finest bamboo. My mother and I would never have to swim again. In the darkness of the hut, I examine my single-jointed fingers, and if I look closely, my hands are almost pure and translucent.

My mother and the other basket-swimmers are shedding. Multi-coloured fish scales fall constantly from their arms and legs and backsides. The process is painful, I think, because no one is in a pleasant mood.

"Sweep up the scales in the hut," my mother snaps at me as she scratches at her scalp. Clumps of hair fall from the slanted ridges of her forehead. "Use them to feed your new cousins. Pray that they will become proper basket-swimmers and not hopeless like you."

I am careful not to slip on her fallen scales, especially since her hurled words wound me more than a little.

—

The Execution will be held during the Hungry Ghost Festival. The Japanese soldier confesses that the killing will take place in five bold moons—when the villagers worship our dead ancestors, piling black glutinous rice cakes and mountains of sunset-coloured oranges on our doorsteps. The soldier, his brain damaged by love after a fortnight spent with my mother, decides that he can no longer murder for his country.

"We could run away," he says.

"Where would we go?" my mother asks. A smile transforms her sly reptilian face.

"South Korea," he says. "We could become chicken farmers."

"How would we get there?" My mother's third eyelids click as she teases.

"We would have to swim to the border," the soldier says. He grips her webbed hands as though she is made of the finest jade.

"But what about my Lileng? She cannot swim."

"Running away from a war means that sacrifices must be made," he says. "We would leave her behind."

I blink back hot, dense tears. I know what would happen if my mother were to orphan me. My mother's people would sell me to the brutish mercenaries of the white Chengshan Mountains. I would be lucky to survive until my sixteenth year.

My mother says, her syllables snake-ish: "Tell your commanding officer to cancel the Execution."

The soldier's handsome face stiffens. My mother whispers into his pink ear, and her charred, fork-shaped tongue flicks over his eyelids. I've seen her eat a man's eyeball or two. Apparently, they are soft and delicious.

The soldier sits up from the bamboo mat and leaves. But I notice that he does not promise.

I must bury hundreds of my dead sisters.

The gargantuan eggs my mother has laid will not hatch in the soggy autumn ground. The ones that do hatch are half-formed and semi-motionless. Some of them blink three orange-lidded eyes before they gasp and die. One of my half sisters lives for less than a fortnight, and then she expires, softly ribbiting in my palms. Her tiny human legs are tangled in brown knots. I bury her with the frog that I have killed.

My mother screams and threatens me, but she does not weep. All basket-swimmers claim to be incapable of tears. At first, I thought that it was because frogs and fish do not have feelings, but my mother's people secretly cry during births and deaths. Stoicism is a highly valued trait. To openly mourn or love is to garner unwanted attention.

"You've brought your curse to our village," she accuses me. "How can you be mine?"

We are lined up by the piers at gunpoint, first-light burning our faces. The basket-swimmers rely on boiling sunlight to warm their frozen blood. The sun does nothing for me, except prove that I am not one of them.

My mother and I had not seen the soldier since he left our hut a week ago. He stands in front of us now, freshly shaven and uniformed like the rest of his troop. He looks like a beautiful boy of no more than nineteen summers. He clutches his weapon proudly. I stare at him, but he does not look our way. I wonder if my mother's siren-like powers are fading, if she is somehow becoming ordinary. If her ability weakens and she diminishes, which of the basket-swimmers would replace her?

We are ordered to jump into the swirling water. The soldiers will shoot us with their machine guns as though we are an unlucky flock of pheasants for their hunting games. Those of us who survive will make it to market. Those of us who die will be kept as trophies.

The young soldier, eyes averted, drops his weapon. "I cannot," he says.

In response, my mother and the other basket-swimmers let out harsh croaks of hope. Their ribbiting is rich like a classical opera, but is soon interrupted by guttural screams. The commanding officer slams the young soldier across his handsome face with his machine gun. Petrified, we all watch as the young soldier is whipped until his flesh falls off in strips and he is thrown into the muddy river. He is forced to swim in agonizing circles while the other officers shoot bullets around him.

"Help!" he cries, flailing his arms like an octopus. The soldiers laugh at him as if they are children. For now, they have forgotten about us.

My mother watches her lover thrash, fear worrying her face. I cling to her, and pretend that her hand is not slippery with dark yellow slime.

—

After he recovers for days and nights in our hut, after they climb on top of each other, my mother confesses to the soldier that she is fearful. "Run away with me," the soldier says. He kisses her noseless face and hard crocodile cheeks. "We can be in Korea in a fortnight."

My mother laughs at him, a dull bullfrog-like sound. It echoes like a parade of imperial funeral drums. She says she is not suited for love with him.

The soldier wails as if he has been disembowelled. In his pain, perhaps he sees my mother for what she really is, something greater than or less than human. Like a child, he gently grips my mother's spider-coloured hair, begging to reclaim her love. For a moment, she acquiesces, turning her silver teeth towards him, almost hungrily, almost lovingly. My mother laughs and pulls away, smirking at his declarations of affection. Fury clouds his boyish features, and he throws her to the floor. I watch in horror as he stomps on her webbed fingers and crushes her sickled toes. Even if she did recover, she could never swim as she did before.

Without speaking, the soldier beats her until she no longer moves.

I cannot save her. I try to cradle my mother's body, but he pushes me away as though I am a sack of jasmine rice. He slings her over his shoulder and heads to the sludgy riverbank.

He guts her with a tiny pocket knife, then he stuffs her insides full of round black pebbles.

"Make yourself useful," he says, waving his pistol at me. I hurriedly collect more jagged rocks and pebbles on the beach.

"What is she?" he asks. He holds the winter-cold gun against my temple.

"She's my mother," I sob. Shaking, I take his proffered fishing needle, quickly sew shut her intestines.

I help him throw my mother's body in the deepest part of Hangzhou Bay.

Once, I would have done anything for him to stay.

The soldier cries when he realizes what he has done, and together we watch my mother's body float in the river. He speaks, passionate, about his star-crossed constellation. Seizing my hands, he assures me that he had not meant to kill her. He had a bad dream, he says. He saw an otherworldly monster.

"You're obviously a human girl," he says, shaking his head. "I don't know what I was thinking. I must be unwell."

On the soggy riverbank, we watch as my mother's long, black seaweed tresses pool behind her like a tidal wave before she sinks.

There is no funeral, no sadness for my mother, but some of the elders bemoan an ancestral curse. None of the basket-swimmers can lay their eggs.

My aunties and cousins have been crouching and sweating over their birth-holes for several days. This makes everyone foul-mouthed and sluggish—swimming with a belly full of eggs makes one sink.

"Lileng, you are so lucky," a cousin of mine grumbles. She is fourteen summers old, and this is the first time her stomach is distended. She stops pushing and rests on the muddy ground. From the river, I scoop a clay bowl of water, and she gulps it gratefully. I refill it and she asks for thirds and fourths and fifths.

"What's it like?" I ask, jealous.

My cousin sets down the bowl. She rubs her webbed hands over her massive stomach, making slow, drawn-out circles, until I realize that I am her reflection. My hands mimic hers; they rub my own flat stomach.

I touch her belly and there are hundreds of protruding eggs, hard and jagged.

"What's it like?" I whisper, longing abundant on my pink human tongue.

She finally says, "It's like being constipated."

In the moons after my mother's death, the soldier insists on becoming my protector. He brings me half-baskets of bruised tropical fruit and day-old starfish to apologize for killing my mother.

"Forgive," he says, pointing a machete at my already hard heart.

I cannot swim to market for food and have no choice but to accept the help of my mother's murderer.

Each night I bite my arm to see if my blood is bluer instead of a murderous red. I would settle for a sunset orange, which would mean a slow but sure metamorphosis. I stare at my reflection in the river and wonder if I will ever resemble my mother.

—

Stumbling to the hut one night, the soldier says that my mother has appeared to him as a gasping, staggering sea monster. He has been glimpsing the demon-ghost of my mother everywhere he goes.

"A fish and a frog," he scream-whispers. "That is what you are!"

Wherever he walks, he claims that my mother pelts the back of his head with rocks. She gurgles harsh drowning sounds at him, which make him lose his balance. He cannot eat. He cannot sleep. The young soldier's features are no longer village-handsome. He looks like dehydrated meat. The soldier says that my mother has told him that she cannot swim anymore because he filled her stomach and intestines with stones.

"I'm sorry," the soldier whispers and grips my shoulders, as if speaking to my dead mother.

But if my mother were real, why haven't I seen her? Why hasn't she visited me?

I become more afraid of the soldier as weeks go by. Especially when he begins to drink copious amounts of rice wine and tells the other officers about his frequent ghostly visitor, a fish-monster, how the women in this village do not have smooth skin like him. He shouts about curses and gloomy supernatural precedents. "Look around you!" he warns. "This is a village filled with monsters!"

When I was little, my father would say that when he looked at my mother, he could see nothing but hazy starlight. If he squinted, he could see someone faceless but cruel. It took him eleven summers before he realized the truth. It took the soldier a little more than a fortnight.

"I'm sorry that you cannot come with me, Lileng," my father said before stealing all our yuan and a sampan to the mainland. "What if you, too, become like your mother? You are stubborn like her, and that is an inauspicious start."

From my human father, I've inherited cowardice, and an insidious fear of the future. But also, an undying and unhealthy amount of hope.

I try to swim in the shallowest end of Hangzhou Bay.

As tiny children, my girl-cousins and I were taught by the oldest basket-swimmers, by our ancient turtle-like grandmothers and crippled aunties, those one-legged or finless who could no longer swim to market. I would cry and holler as the women dunked me in the river. "Lileng!" they had scolded in their water-scarred voices, "you must swim or you will die."

As I lower myself into the cold, raging water, I clutch a basket filled halfway with sand and pebbles. It seems as if my father's predictions have not come true. The water does not recognize me as one of its star-blessed sisters. My legs become paralyzed, my muscles spasm. Not one scale sprouts on my backside. The basket on my head suddenly weighs as much as the sun. It falls from my head. *Splash!*

I feel myself begin to carefully drown.

Weeping, I drag my quivering body to shore. In the midday heat, blackflies terrorize my sand-stained skin. My howling sounds distant, as if underwater.

———

By now, the soldier, my protector, has begun taking advantage of me. Drunk and fearful, he mistakes me for his beloved constellation. I lie awake, in the expanding darkness, while he clutches me to his chest. The more the other soldiers taunt him for his weakness and hallucinations, the more he torments me.

"We will run away together," he murmurs hoarsely into my ear. I detach myself. If I cry, he will hurt me more.

Nights pass. I beg my cousins and aunties to find my father who married his cousin the pig farmer. "Tell my father that Lileng needs him," I plead, but the basket-swimmers do not have hearts. Now that my mother is gone, and I have no scales or a tail, I have no rank.

I do not understand why I cannot transform. Surely I came from a speckled egg in the ground? I scratch at my dull human features, but I do not change from a girl to any kind of reptile or one of China's grey native fish.

With my small human fingernails, I dig up the last remaining eggs of the basket-swimmers and stomp on them with my bare feet. The yellow shells make a comforting crunch. Then I throw the shells and their blue yolky remains into the Qiantang River like offerings to a petty river god.

I'm no better than the Japanese soldiers. I've just killed fifteen or twenty of my mother's people.

I feel worse when I learn that my fourteen-year-old cousin, unable to lay her eggs, has just died.

—

Later, one moonless night, I am dragged to the rickety piers of the raging Qiantang River and made to strip. The young soldier insists that he needs to prove himself. I am being forced to swim to show the Japanese soldiers that I am a deceitful monster like my mother, or to be forcibly drowned.

"I cannot swim," I shout, but no one hears me. The river's vastness feels monstrous and alive.

Surrounded by my shimmering aunties and ghoul-green cousins, the commanding officer and his jeering men, the soldier holds my head down in the purple frothing water. The Execution is not swift.

"You will see," he insists, half-lunatic, half-drunk. This makes the other soldiers cheer and laugh like gibbering monkeys.

I begin to scream because unlike the basket-swimmers, I cannot breathe underwater. I am not half-fish.

Finally, the soldier lets go of my hair. I think I'm truly dead because I hear the throaty croaks of loss and horror around me. *Ribbit, ribbit, ribbit!*

Dying or dead, I float face down in the water, and I hope that my mother's ghost will appear and comfort me. But there is only the rushing sound of currents in my popping eardrums. For a while, maybe a day, I am paralyzed in a state of half death until the fish come. Grey, tiny, and sharp-toothed, they nibble on my water-damaged skin. It does not hurt after a while, but I begin to understand my purpose in life is to feed these fish.

Down, down, I descend, until I am truly buoyant, fearless.

Red-Tongued Ghosts

Since Xiang gave up haunting, she's got nothing to do. She decides to spend eternity, a tofu-coloured spectre with blistered eyebrows, hovering in front of the television and flipping through old issues of *National Geographic*. Weilin, her older sister/roommate, complains that Xiang has been hopelessly dispirited since the Tiananmen Square massacre in 1989.

"All this free time is very bad for you," Weilin says, her urine-coloured eyes blazing. Her neck hangs at a sixty-five-degree angle, and a dirty-poultry stench emanates from her skin. For sixty-odd years, out of politeness but mostly fear, Xiang has not told Weilin that she smells like burning chicken.

"The couple in room 215 are waiting for a good scare," Weilin continues, stretching her oversized jaws with her daily TMJ exercises.

Xiang puts down her magazine. "Don't you ever feel guilty about killing tourists?" she asks.

"Guilty? You're the one who got us killed," Weilin says. For emphasis, she turns off the TV by blinking—a misuse of her poltergeist powers, if you ask Xiang.

"You know I'm sorry that I got everyone killed," Xiang pleads. Her distended red eye (she's missing the left one) spits actual blood—like a busted faucet. Makes quite the mess when she's upset.

"Get off your floating ass and do something," Weilin says. She flicks her sister across her face, hard, with her elongated lizard tongue.

As the older sibling, Weilin acts as if she's the wiser diao si gui, a Red-Tongued Ghost, even though she does not like to read. Yet after more than half a century of being an undead poltergeist, her sister's truthy accusation still burns Xiang with shame. Weilin's tongue-slap always hurts—more than the perpetual rope burn around Xiang's neck, which makes her sensitive ghost skin blister and itch.

Moaning in resignation, Xiang exits the siheyuan, their family's abandoned farmhouse, and floats across the Han dynasty courtyard where the hammocked Huangshan trees hide her family's unmarked graves.

"Get over yourself!" Weilin shouts, her voice loud as monsoon rain.

The Baekdu Mountain Hot Springs, nicknamed by locals Zìshā wēnquán, the Very Hot Suicide Spring, is hidden high up the black coastal Changbai Mountains. The springs emit a harsh sulphurous smell that even the most zealous durian eaters find offensive. Yet rich tourists, mostly lovers or energetic nudists, hike from all over the world to inhale the hot springs' eggy odours. For millions of renminbi, flabby couples spend their vacations splashing in the boiling waters like overcooked lobsters, while simultaneously pinching their noses. The Baekdu Mountain Hot Springs (includes three Buddhist vegetarian meals a day) is supposed to cure all stages of psoriasis and eczemas and even minor cases of genital warts.

All of this, of course, is bullshit.

But the water is scalding enough to make your skin melt off. It is not recommended to spend more than fifteen minutes a day submerged.

Floating like an acquiescent fruit fly, Xiang passes the translated sign:

LOVER COURT GARDEN,
GENTEEL BEINGS.
20 STEP TO HOT, HOT WATER.
DO NOT COOK YOURSELF!!!

She hovers beside an arguing couple from Toronto in room 215, which faces the dusky blue azaleas in the courtyard. The husband yells: "I can't sleep. I've got the fucking runs. It's all this cabbage, I'm telling you. Why are they serving slimy cabbage every goddamn meal? And the noises—don't you hear it? The pipes keep me up all night."

"I don't hear anything," his wife says, while Xiang, on cue, emits an unearthly shriek. This used to thrill her, make her feel useful and highly accomplished in the afterlife. No creature, not even Weilin, could screech as loud as her.

"It's unnerving," the man continues. "I saw a strange woman hobbling around last night."

"It was probably the hotel maid—"

"Why was she in our room at three in the morning, looking through your underthings? I swear she took something! And did you see her face? Like cottage cheese."

"Just shut up and let's get into the water, dear. The brochure says that you're supposed to soak for ten minutes to get rid of ringworm."

"But the smell! It's like an outhouse out there!"

Normally, this would be Xiang's signal to psychologically torture the husband by knocking over a red paper lantern or overturning an exquisite bouquet of white chrysanthemums. As a Red-Tongued Ghost Maiden, Xiang used to feel that she had a duty to torment the living. Why else would she have returned from the dead with such an unappealing lizard face?

In the past, Xiang would stalk a chosen victim, howling superstitious mumbo-jumbo to make the living think they were having indulgent, psychotic breaks in a five-star tourist trap. Last year, she was a bit of a kleptomaniac, stealing jewellery and sequined thongs. Hysterical couples were the easiest to break up—all she had to do was steal ten-carat wedding rings and La Perla lingerie, sometimes swapping them with other couples' in other rooms.

It was amusing for the first forty years. Then Xiang did not understand the point.

"Why do we want the living to suffer?" she had asked her sister.

"We're deformed-looking ghosts," Weilin hissed. "What else are we supposed to do with the rest of our lives?"

Xiang has no exceptional powers, no astounding trick, except for transforming into a pasty-faced angel for twenty to thirty seconds, all the while convincing someone to somersault off a balcony. If her victims did not comply, she could just use her tongue like a lasso. That last trick was hard—she'd had to practise for a few years. The first few times Xiang tried to strangle someone with her lizard tongue, she missed and knocked over a dresser.

But Weilin can pretend to be human for forty seconds, ten more seconds than Xiang, which used to make her sister jealous.

Sighing again, Xiang watches as the couple stomps to the hot springs, still shouting obscenities at each other. With her ghostly powers, Xiang should throw a tiny bonsai tree at their heads or make someone stumble and break their kneecaps on the narrow stone pathways to the gazebo. All this so that she can expressively torment her victims (*wooooooooooooo, woooooooooooooooo!*) while they lie curled up in fetal position for days. But it all seems quite childish now. A waste of her eternity.

Maybe I am just depressed, she thinks, popping a pus-filled blister on her chin. *Mid-ghost crisis.*

When Xiang was alive and thirteen years old, all she wanted to do was leave the Baekdu Mountain and distance herself from the smelly hot springs, which were only a brisk walk from their ransacked farmhouse. She despised the daily trek through a patch of red pines and Japanese yew trees to collect drinking water for her family and their chickens.

Xiang wanted to move to Beijing and study classical literature and philosophy. If that was not possible, she'd take up a trade— maybe learn to gut fish at a factory. At the remote village school, her classmates complained that the sisters brought the smell of rot water and live poultry with them wherever they went. Chicken-Shit Sisters, the other adolescents called them, laughing at Xiang and Weilin's brown bag-shaped dresses, which were often smeared with chicken feces. *Chicken-Shit! Chicken-Shit!*

The students would spend every morning copying charcoal portraits of Chairman Mao, whose black-and-white photograph hung at the front of the classroom. After the midday meal, they'd write him letters and sentimental poems about citizen equality and ideology. The teacher once made them memorize a speech by Jiang Qing, Mao's wife and Party leader.

"Why are we doing this?" Xiang had whispered one morning. She said again in a louder voice: "What has Mao ever done for us?"

Always a relentless sentry, the teacher strode over. "The great, industrious Chairman Mao can see all," he had threatened, wielding his bamboo stick like a circus performer. "If you speak badly of him, you will be punished." He whacked Xiang five times with the stick. Her classmates laughed, tears waterfalling down their faces. Even Weilin had pretended to laugh.

"My mother and father hate Chairman Mao," Xiang announced, trying not to publicly cry. "And I do too!" This was a half truth. Her father had intended to flee to Hong Kong to escape the Communists, but could never save enough money due to his lacklustre farming skills. Her mother, satisfied to rule her children and colony of scrawny chickens, considered herself too busy for politics.

In those days, Xiang was quick to blaze in the face of injustice. Two permanent red spots glowed on her cheeks. She looked the teacher in the eye and tore up her portrait of Chairman Mao. The teacher gasped. Xiang was sent home for disrespecting her country.

When the Red Guards, a band of pimply university students in their regalia, arrived at the village school a few months later, Xiang was forced to show them her parents' house. The Red Guards set fire to their tiny farmhouse and killed their mob of squawking chickens. They clumsily disembowelled Xiang's father with a sword and forced themselves on Xiang's mother. The Red Guards tortured Xiang and Weilin, refusing to let them sleep for weeks. Xiang lost an eyeball to a hammer when she begged the student army to stop.

Xiang, Weilin, and their mother were hanged on a thousand-year-old Huangshan tree.

After death, Xiang, Weilin, and their mother immediately woke up with engorged red tongues that seemed to keep growing until they had trouble fitting them inside their mouths. They had become Angry Ghosts with broken necks, faces like over-boiled chicken. Her father had not undergone this transformation— Xiang thought it was grossly unfair.

"Why should only women become Angry Ghosts with gigantic lolling tongues?" she cried.

"Look at my tongue! It's longer than Xiang's by a foot!" Weilin had wailed.

In response to their outburst, their father had croaked three times, like a bullfrog, seeming to take offence at such honest, unfiltered statements. And their mother, furious, had spat out one thousand screaming locusts from the back of her throat. The locusts had swarmed furiously around the sisters, biting their seared skin until they cried for leniency.

In her new life as a poltergeist, Xiang had floated forlornly at first, unaware of how to navigate her weightless body. Was she supposed to turn her head to hover? What if her tongue never stopped growing? Xiang's missing eye did not grow back. She became a ghost with severely limited depth perception. *We look ridiculous*, she had thought, unable to straighten her shattered neck and dumpy hunched back by sheer willpower. It seemed that Chinese females who were murdered didn't go to Heaven or Hell; they became large human-like ghost lizards.

Xiang became angrier when she discovered that she could never leave the place where she was murdered. Women could not roam beyond five hundred feet of their graves. "I can't believe that I'm stuck here for eternity with all of you," she had said, morosely.

"This is patriarchal bullshit," she would later explain, when she forced everyone in the family to learn English by mimicking Ivy Leaguer tourists and reading progressive op-eds in the *New Yorker*.

For some reason, after Xiang's father died, he could not speak. As soon as Father opens his mouth, only dead air and flies swarm out. *Buzz, buzz, buzz!* Poor Father is like an undead flytrap. Xiang does not understand where all the flies come from.

Despite missing half his torso, he always seems to be in a cheerful mood. For nearly sixty years, Father has spent his days as a crooked shadow, right by the gloomy Huangshan trees near their old farmhouse. He is able to float wherever he pleases, unlike the women, yet he prefers to stay at his gravesite.

As usual, Xiang finds Father suspended above ground, cross-legged, and deep in prayer to Buddha. She can't help but feel a fierce outpouring of love for him. In his life as a human, Father was generally a peaceful household figure, indulging the whims of his wife and daughters. He told her stories about the Monkey King, a trickster god who could transform into seventy-two types of animals and objects. She misses these stories from her childhood. Xiang appreciates that Father, even if he could, would not verbally blame his younger daughter for his fate. When Xiang stares at Father's gentle pus-coloured corneas, she feels certain that he must have forgiven her.

To escape her sister's belligerent chatter, she spends most of her afternoons with him, watching zealous flies tumble out of his mouth. But today, in place of silent contemplation, Xiang's father hands her a piece of paper with tidy traditional Chinese characters on it, a note of instructions from Mother:

家庭会议。紧急情况。日落
FAMILY MEETING. EMERGENCY. SUNSET.

"Where is she, anyway?" Xiang asks. She dreads these orchestrated family meetings, which are usually histrionic excuses to rehash the past and blame her for their most inconvenient deaths. Father, looking sympathetic, points to the Red Bathhouse, where guests receive massages from pretty courtesan-type girls and meditate in old-fashioned steam rooms. Xiang's mother enjoys spying on young, naked men in the showers and seducing the handsomest ones. She likes to appear as a flickering apparition glowing in celestial blue light. When the men finally glimpse her true haggy lizard face, they scream, slipping and fracturing their spinal cords in the tiled shower stalls. Other times, when her victims go on solo hikes up the mountain to have a secret smoke without telling their partners, Xiang's mother, giggling, likes to push them down a sloshy trail. Sometimes the men fight back and Mother eats their faces.

"Being an Angry Ghost is slightly better than being a chicken farmer," she once told Xiang, sucking marrow from someone's chiselled jawbone. "There's not much difference between squawking chicken and screaming men."

Swatting at a fly, Xiang anxiously floats beside her mute father, careful to avoid his bad breath. She waits for her mother and her sister to appear. She wonders how she can feel so lonely, like she is being gutted from the insides, especially when her family and thousands of tourists surround her all year.

Being dead doesn't make one less sensitive, Xiang thinks sadly. She hears a squeaking, rustling sound—a tiny songbird in a yellowing magnolia bush. Flicking her tongue, she grabs the brown bird by its wings and shoves it into her mouth. She bites down with a slow, delectable crunch.

When the sun dips under a pink, hazy mountain cloud, Mother finally emerges, a voluptuous black whirlwind with a pompous-looking Weilin following closely. Both are panting like mutts, red tongues loose and wagging, dripping brown-red blood.

"Xiang is still refusing to haunt the tourists," Weilin says, sounding gassy. "I've had to triple my work. Just maimed a rude young woman who talked too much."

"The owners are bringing in psychics and ghost hunters,"

Mother announces, ignoring Weilin. "Apparently, the hot springs are now the most haunted place in all of China. They're going to try different methods to get rid of us! It's going to be a documentary."

"What channel?" Xiang asks, her apathy temporarily forgotten.

"How should I know?" Mother snaps. "We might cease to exist, maybe lose our home."

"What do we do?" Weilin asks, looking unusually pale and concerned.

"We stay hidden," Mother says, glancing at Father, who nods and belches five fuzzy flies for emphasis. They exchange glances, an unspoken cistern of communication. Surprisingly, Angry Ghosts have zero mind-reading powers. But Xiang knows what her family is thinking. If they hadn't been mob-murdered in extreme emotional states—if they had died peacefully—they would not have to worry about the post-afterlife.

All this is speculation, of course. Xiang has never met another spirit outside of her family because of the five-hundred-feet rule. She has never even met the ghosts of the hapless affluent victims that she has massacred, which would average four or five Westerners a year. She feels bad for the tourists, but comforts herself by thinking she had done them a favour by ending their overpriced vacations.

After an overly drawn-out moment, Mother says: "No more scaring or killing anyone until this is over."

"What a nightmare," Weilin wails. "What will I do instead?"

Permanent retirement! Xiang thinks, elated. She helps Mother and Weilin dump the week's bodies in the bubbling hot spring, which digests human skin and hair and teeth.

—

For an indecent sum, the unhappy couple in room 215 agrees to be featured in *The Most Haunted Hang-Outs in Asia!* documentary. A bubbly blond psychic wearing a princess tiara and ice blue tutu from California, a smiley tattooed Buddhist monk from Malaysia, and a trio of bird-thin Italian nerds with aluminum foil taped around their foreheads will take turns ridding the hot spring and guesthouse of vicious ghosts.

"I can't sleep," the man says solemnly into the camera. "I feel like someone is always watching me take a shower. Peeping Tom. You know that feeling?"

"He's just being paranoid," the woman announces. "The rooms are comfortable if a little chilly from being so high on the mountain."

Xiang rolls her good dead eye. She has been whooshing around the Lover Garden and whispering in all the psychics' ears for half an hour—all seem to be deaf to her spectral whispers. She hollers at the Buddhist monk. Nothing.

"I sense that this is a burial site for a great and bloodthirsty emperor," the blond chick gushes, tapping her sun-spotty nose. "I can, like, smell millions of children buried alive as a sacrifice for a tyrant king!" Wickedly, she grins at the camera and flashes adult braces.

The nerds with aluminum foil whisper intensely among themselves. Xiang leans in closer to hear.

She really shouldn't be so close to the living that want to exorcise her, but she can't resist. She is so close, she can feel their heartbeats. Xiang wonders what it would be like to squeeze a human heart.

When it is his turn to speak to the undead, the balding

Buddhist monk pulls a large white ceramic jar from a wooden chest. He begins to beat the jar with a tiny metal chopstick. He closes his eyes and hums for an hour and a half.

Nothing mystical happens. Nothing explodes. The misfits in the aluminum foil head-wraps *whisperwhisperwhisper*. The exorcism/ghost-ridding crap continues for another three plus hours.

Everyone is confused—even Xiang, who has spent nearly a century pondering the ambiguities of the afterlife. *The living are insane*, she decides, fascinated. *How else to explain their obsession with the undead?*

Unable to sleep, Xiang is speed-reading women's magazines. At 3 a.m., she diagnoses herself with what a 1990 issue of *Cosmopolitan* calls borderline personality disorder and clinical depression.

She's about to start rereading *National Geographic* when she glimpses a blurry face. "Aiya, you scared me," she scolds. "I thought you were a nightmare."

"Father's gone," Weilin gasps, frenetic. Her face is paler in daybreak, and her pupils look like tiny douchi on an overcooked pile of wontons.

"What do you mean?" Xiang asks.

"He just caught fire and vanished!"

Xiang swiftly follows Weilin outside. Like oversized mosquitoes, they whizz past a grinning statue of Buddha, past the Lover Court Garden to the Red Bathhouse, where Mother is howling like the north wind.

"Something is wrong!" she yells, tongue flopping from her mouth. "I was just with your father and he exploded! Where is he?"

"It must be that Buddhist monk!" Xiang says, suddenly alarmed. "It's the only explanation. Father was the kindest of us."

Xiang tells them that she was observing the psychics and the film crew yesterday—that she wasn't just reading industriously in her bedroom.

Mother begins to shriek, but stops just before a plague of black locusts can emerge from her esophagus. Now is not the time for hysterics or portentous insects.

The realization that she will never float beside her father in companionable silence stuns Xiang. Father is gone, and she's partially responsible for his second murder. For a moment, her heart pulses, as if alive, mimicking a beat.

Xiang floats back to her room. She had honestly thought that she was levelling up as a wise lady poltergeist by choosing a new path to self-fulfillment, but her thoughtlessness has gotten her family killed all over again.

The early morning film crew sets up, continuing to interview the whiny Canadian husband-and-wife duo inside room 215. Footage: six reshoots of the husband showing off the standard bamboo love bed, the silky plum sheets, and the swirly cherry blossom wallpaper. His wife is bobbing her head onscreen, but gritting her rice-white teeth off-screen.

The woman psychic waves a hefty translucent crystal, hollering: "Evil, leave this place!" The monk starts humming and drumming his jar, and the tinfoil trio glances around, seeming flabbergasted at the surrealness of it all.

"Do something!" Mother hisses. "This is your fault!"

"A ghost who doesn't kill humans doesn't deserve to live," Weilin says in disgust, using her distended tongue to smack Xiang on the head.

When Weilin and Mother begin smashing vases of dried peonies and incense sticks, Xiang thinks, *Would it be better if I did not exist?* Yesterday, a part of her had wanted to expire permanently, but now she fears the post-afterlife. Would she transform into a scaly fish-girl? A songbird? The Monkey King, who could endlessly transform? It would be terrible to die again and become an earthworm.

Watching Weilin and Mother poltergeist through the room, Xiang refuses to powerlessly expire as she did when she was murdered at the age of thirteen. She feels a ferocious migraine coming on and unexpectedly begins to flame with rage.

"Get out!" Xiang screams at the couple, the psychics, and the crew. Red ire eclipses her already limited 10/20 vision. Not since she yelled at the village's teacher during the reign of Mao Zedong has she felt this emboldened. The mortals gasp at her charbroiled face. "Monster!" they scream. "Monster!" With her red salamander tongue, she grabs a white ceramic jar and hurls it across the guestroom.

Blinking with some effort, Xiang sets six people ablaze. She never thought that she'd be able to manage such a feat with her mind. She leaves the monk for last, and as he gapes at her, she thinks of how terrible it might be to not exist. What would happen to a red-tongued maiden who was killed by a monk? Is there even an afterlife for ghosts? When she died, she had felt the wild flame that had been her life extinguish. She experienced her hotheadedness *whoooooooosh* out of her body, as if she was passing an excess amount of uncontrollable wind. She has been so freaking cold during her decades as a ghost, and so unfeeling too.

Crashing to his knees, the monk begins begging and praying and chanting in a spastic combo of Asian dialects. Xiang eats him before he can make her explode like Father.

And because she is feeling charitable, and is also too full to move, she allows the film crew to scamper away with most of their cameras and sound equipment.

"I didn't know you had it in you," Weilin says afterwards, while Mother searches through the couple's luggage for valuables.

Instead of answering her sister, Xiang glides to the debris of corpses and plucks off a hot aluminum foil hat. She puts it on her head, then crumples it into a tiny silver wad and cattle-chews it, thoughtful. Satiated, she finally burps loud and purposeful, rubbing her distended belly.

Xiang, brimming with the life force of the dead, feels grateful, a stirring in her gut, as if she almost wants to be alive. Is this a heartbeat of hope, maybe? Is this what A Purpose feels like? Something that will give her a reason to turn off the television, throw out the magazines, and leave her bedroom? Is it indigestion? It's not exactly telltale warmth or human compassion gushing through her undead veins, but she feels somehow less lifeless.

After she throws the burnt bodies into the boiling water, she might take a leisurely splash in the Very Hot Suicide Spring. She might sit under her father's tree, maybe learn to crochet or take up day trading.

Furniture

It was the Year of the Snake, the year of perpetual and extraordinary sorrow, when my father turned into a sofa. He was a foam-stuffed two-seater, the colour of medium grease. You could just tell it was him by the way the sofa sat there, forlorn and passive. The previous month he had been a man, albeit a very sad one.

"Dad?" I said to our new sofa. "How long will you stay like this for?"

There was no answer. But what did I expect, really, from a sofa?

Six months ago, my grandparents had promised us $40.99 to help my mother find a new husband. My brother Kian and I had grudgingly interviewed cooks and waiters, a few house painters, carpenters and clerks, husband-applicants who lived with their old mothers. The agreed-upon criteria was that he had to be man-shaped and manufactured in an urban part of Southeast Asia. Some of our prospective fathers, flown in from Taiwan, were toothless and chipper; others had the faces of damaged fruit. Their mothers wooed us with gluey rice cakes while the sons bragged about their affinity for hard labour.

My grandparents liked that the Investor was untainted Chinese and had educational pedigree, none of the characteristics that my father, Vietnamese, and thereby inferior, possessed. The Japanese had kicked our Chinese asses in the war, and the Koreans had disowned us centuries ago when thirteen boys and thirteen girls jumped ship after failing to find the Emperor his elixir of eternal life. The Vietnamese husband, whose people had no place in our mythology, was considered an embarrassment.

The Investor, in his suit and black vinyl shoes, was the son of an uncle of a cousin of a friend of an aunt of my rich grandparents. He had money and connections, promising to help us take my grandparents' Chinese restaurants from the status of Taco Bell to McDonald's. He brought flaccid red roses and a casket of sugar cookies. His gifts, picked up at Safeway, like a provisional afterthought, were a day old and discounted by a dollar.

As he wooed us, the Investor smirked with pity because he knew that Ah-Cy, our mother, was his. Ah-Cy, who hadn't showered in a month, showed him no preferential treatment. She laughed maniacally whenever random suitors quick-stepped through the front door. Our mother would throw her greasy hair back and holler for a six-pack and her lighter.

In our kitchen, I prepared grape juice from concentrate. "I'm going to pee in the pitcher," Kian whispered, as I cracked the ice cube trays, scraped the slushy juice with a chopstick. I had just turned thirteen, and Kian was eight years old. We were dreamy-eyed optimists who thought we could mould our futures by sabotage. Childish sin would scare away this cockroach-looking bachelor and my father would turn back into a man once again. But what we didn't want to admit was that the Investor could also change our misshapen fates.

After the Investor left, gifting us with the contents of his wallet, my grandparents congratulated us for climbing the social ladder. I even showed my father the money that we had made, and said that I was very sorry for Kian's and my betrayal; $40.99 (plus $10.25 from the Investor) was the most money I had ever seen, I said. I placed the money we had earned between the crooked sofa's cushions, and the bills and coins vanished instantly.

"Dad," I said to the yellowing sofa, "is it okay if we sit on you?"

From the very beginning, you could tell my mother was unhappy in our neighbourhood, on the outskirts of Chinatown. We lived in one of those stuccoed Seattle specials: a hideous grey cardboard that matched the overcast sky. My grandparents were our landlords and owned six of these boxes and another three condos in Arizona. When my mother wasn't working part-time at one of the family's greasy spoons, she did nothing but watch black bears gorge on the viscous juice of Japanese pears budding in our backyard. My mother, who watched West Coast rains lash into the coppice of trees; swollen ghost pears catapulting into muddy grass.

"Go outside," my mother would say whenever my brother and I returned from school, as she inhaled her cigarettes, drank from her favourite oversized mug, which was pink with a kitschy slogan, YOU ONLY HAVE ONE CHANCE TO WINE. By 9 a.m. it was always filled with more Kahlúa than espresso.

My mother was petite, with heavy, black hair, and born without eyebrows or lashes. To my father, she was quirky and ethereal; he admired her spectacular mood swings. Broken cups, a smattering of Chinese porcelain bowls, our breakfast of week-old vegetable fried rice like confetti on the kitchen floor. He didn't mind when she cried histrionic tears.

To all the neighbourhood kids, my mother was terrifying. A wrong look, a prank taken too far, would send her running at them in her housecoat. When Fat-Ass Petey Cho peed on our doorstep, she yanked him by his gangly black hair and shoved his snivelling face into his pool of urine. "Did you like that?" she asked him afterwards, almost motherly. "Was that fun for you?"

Cross-legged on the sidewalk, exiled from our house, I wrote verbose, maudlin compositions for school. Then I would doodle messy hearts over algebra equations until a neighbour-hood mother invited me in for a snack: yesterday's lo mein with still-frozen chicken nuggets mixed in. Or until my mother changed her mind around 8 p.m., when bears, clawing over our six-foot fences, pawed for sinewy rotting salmon heads in our garbage bins.

It was 45 percent my mother's fault that my father became household furnishing.

The thing was, my wealthy grandparents had bought our two-bedroom house and paid our monthly electric bills. They owned two of the biggest chains of Chinese restaurants in Seattle, and we ate our meals at their diners. In return for their generosity, my father, like everyone else in our family, was expected to do odd jobs and rotate at the various outlets. My mother waitressed and threatened to spit into the stir-fry, and I took phone orders because my girlish English, when whispering "moo-shoo pork" timidly, didn't scare away the non-Chinese. We were indentured labourers of the twenty-first century, in debt to my grandparents. My mother resented being owned and frequently complained about bargaining for her pinched-out allowance.

On weekends, my father totalled bills, counted out coins for college students on cheap dates at the Happy Smile, a greasy spoon famous for marinating its spaghetti noodles in sweetened soy sauce. On weeknights, he leisurely bussed tables and delivered ingredients to the Joyful Grin, which was a bit more upscale and sold blackened lo mein smothered in cornstarch for those with deficient taste buds. There was even a fancy seafood restaurant downtown called the Emperor's Gigantic Smile. It was booked for extravagant births, wedding and funeral banquets—for Chinese families who could afford to pay for crispy Peking duck and gingered abalone for $100/pound. When requested, Kian and I performed "The Entertainer" and "Love Story" for the customers with our choppy, unpractised hands. The Yamaha grand was shrill and buzzed on high G because my grandparents were too cheap to hire a tuner. I made quarters that weighed down my school bag, but Kian pocketed twenties. Business was booming and everyone should have been happy. After all, Hong Kong had returned to the Communists on July 1, 1997, and affluent immigrants were buying up houses in Seattle and they all wanted good, MSG-rich food.

This was our life before my father turned into a sofa.

—

It was rumoured that my father, Truong Nguyen, had been born in pieces and sloppily stitched together because his arms and legs were twisted in all the wrong places. Perhaps it was childhood polio that caused one leg to become significantly shorter than the other, contorting his slender gymnast's torso. His left arm was thin and long like an antenna on an extraterrestrial. He hid it under baggy sweatshirts, but on summer days it flapped like hanging laundry. Customers gawked. Neighbourhood kids dubbed him Le Freak, the One-Armed Bandit.

In the back kitchens of the greasy spoons, my father sold pot. He had impressive plans to begin a grow-op two blocks from our house, but after neighbours called the cops when they saw a suspicious-looking Asian man stepping out of a minivan, his start-up plants and halogen lights were seized.

Oddly enough, my grandparents always thought that Truong was a pretty man despite his crookedness and floppy arm. He had broad, high cheekbones and no facial hair. I did not look like my father. I was borderline obese, wore a troll-like scowl, as well as clunky square glasses to fix my nearsightedness. During nutrition break, cotton-candied Claudia, with her pink Miss Piggy face and pink gauzy dresses, always taunted, "Fat Face, Fat Face. Why does Mei-Chow have a fat face?"

Before falling asleep, my parents used to pass a joint between them. I'd watch them secretly from the hallway because they'd forget to close their bedroom door. My mother, pinching the roach delicately, taking tokes. They'd share whiskey in mini tea cups or cooking gin snuck from the restaurants' kitchens. Our house was choked by Mary Jane's peaty miasma, her unholy rot of cabbage. I knew if they stopped inhaling, my parents would be forced to think about how they were both slaves to my grandparents, trying to manoeuvre themselves out of this shitty familial exchange.

It was said that once you tasted the Washington Apotcalypse, you could not go back. You became stuck in a pseudo-reality of misspent youth and what you swore were better days. Sometimes, my mother and father locked the bathroom and towelled the door. I imagined them, ashy faces gawking glassy-eyed at the mirror while they smoked up and my mother hahahahaing, a sadistic braying. I imagined them under the fluorescent lights, the skin on their backs and necks blistering near the heater. The Seattle rains pounding into the feral, toffeed grass of the backyard, and oh, that wrecked and shrunken fence.

Later, the walls of my bedroom shook, and I heard them murmuring in their ragged, pre-dawn voices. I dreamed of earthquakes that would swallow up our house and the jagged bits of continent bleeding into the Pacific Ocean. I convinced myself that if we weren't dead, the west coast floods would certainly finish us off. Our house, and others, would pitch backwards, topple into a fissure of churning sulphur, water, and a squelchy mess of smashed trees.

A joint helped my mother slumber for a few hours, but it made my father shaky and inconsiderate. He would turn up the television all the way, until the infomercials became intermittent and staticky. Until the coyotes yowled as if they had queasy heartache, until the white sunlight tap-tapped my eyelids.

I could feel the enormous heaviness of it all, especially after the morning my father, believing himself to be uneducated and inferior, shot himself, not before giving Kian and me ten dollars each. It was the Year of the Snake, the year of teeth-gnashing and poor decision-making, when our lives crumbled into unimaginable bits.

You'd think that witnessing my father shoot himself over a bowl of soggy rice noodles would traumatize us for life. It would have been a different story if he had died at breakfast, but suffering from an affliction best known as endurance, he missed and blew out an eyeball on the pretty half of his face, which my grandparents later said was a terrible pity. My father didn't even look that stunned when he fell, slumping unconscious for almost seven full minutes. My mother finished her coffee before reacting, and then we could not find her cellphone to call 911.

"Why is he so selfish?" my mother had screamed, when she was a little more sober, and tried to cover my father with a kitchen rug. Kian found a soapy dishrag to stop the bleeding. My brother, with serial-killer calm, pressed down with his palms, wiped the excess blood on his Sailor Moon pyjamas, while I spoke to the emergency operator in my best restaurant hostess voice. It was July, hot and filthy; kitchen fruit flies buzzed viciously around the blood. I swatted most of them away, but some of the flies got stuck. My father's forehead looked like leftover pork.

"He's trying to leave me here with you two," my mother cried, while I gave our address to the operator.

She then saw our ten-dollar bills, and complained that she felt very left out.

Afterwards, no one talked about the incident. But we weren't invited to the year-end party at the restaurant and we weren't promoted to manager and we didn't win employee of the year. An attempted suicide in the family was shit luck. I imagined the family's holiday feast: pork fried rice, the sunny-side eggs bleeding into stringy bok choy and semi-frozen turkey that tasted like toilet paper. I was envious that my cousins would tear open gifts of iPads and red envelopes stuffed with cash, but I was glad that my father was alive.

My father, who refused to wear an eye patch to cover up his latest deformity, was despondent, spending his days lying on the carpet muttering that Kian and I had as much right to be at the party as anyone else in the family. For Christmas, we had been given a generous salary cut and two months' worth of unpaid electrical bills.

"We are lucky if my parents forgive us," my mother said, stopping to wipe my father's face as she stepped over him to answer the door. After some impassioned begging from Kian on the phone (my mother paid him $5.25), my grandparents had reluctantly agreed to visit us after Lunar New Year.

"No one want to look at an ugly man especially when he have one eye!" my grandma complained as she stomped into our house and hugged me. "He could not even die properly, but injured himself so badly that he could no longer work! Does he think we are running a charity?"

"There is nothing sadder when one must fire family," my grandpa agreed, patting my head like I was a monkey. He had been a famous opera singer in the old country of Taipei. They left within the hour.

When my grandparents stopped giving us money, my father felt he had no choice but to let the suitors in, taking their coats and hanging them facing the same way. Then he would slink to the basement, head basketed by his good hand. I suppose he felt he had nothing to offer my mother.

When the Investor moved in with us, we were given ancient Christmas ornaments and plastic flowers, old-lady potpourri and parched flora in glass jars—all on loan. Every curvy pot and each Chinese calligraphic painting was a symbol of borrowed solidarity against my father, that useless one-eyed chicken. In the mornings, the Investor strutted around the house naked, thighs jiggling as he made his rounds. My father's replacement was a pop-eyed exile of the East, of pure, insomniac amphetamine. Hahahaing whenever I averted my eyes, asking me if I would like to touch his "extra piece" as he gnashed his morning congee and eggs. When the Investor spoke, he mostly grunted and snarled prehistoric sounds. He was thin and strangely angular, and he resembled a permanently dazed pyrodactyl. It wasn't hard to believe that at the age of thirty-five (four years my mother's junior), he had never been on a date before he married her.

I always wondered why my mother felt obligated to marry this odd-looking, strangely mannered man. I wondered if my grandparents had paid him, had promised him a wedge of their greasy empire of deep-fried Chinese food or whether he just liked being a beast.

The day my mother remarried at city hall, Kian and I were

not invited. There was no honeymoon because this was a business transaction. My grandparents drank three cups of red
wine each and congratulated themselves on a "very good deal."
My father gave up and lay down on the yellow linoleum floor
in the kitchen, moaned once or twice, and then began to
replace himself with something inanimate and unsympathetic.
It was like watching a human being perform origami on himself. First, his fingernails folded deftly onto his knuckles, followed by his head and torso. His willowy legs collapsed last.

"We can sit on a sofa when we play video games!" Kian
shouted, excited at first. "Dad, you don't mind, do you?"

My father could have transformed into any household appli-
ance, like a refrigerator or a microwave oven (ours was permanently broken), but he chose to become a symbol of Chinese
extravagance.

Like most Chinese homes, ours had no real furniture because
we were too cheap to buy any. We had a plastic night table
from a garage sale, a couple folding chairs from IKEA, and a
stiff mattress in the living room for relaxing, which was more
than a lot of our Chinese friends had. When I went to their
houses, we sat on the carpeted floor drinking Coca-Cola in
mismatched plastic cups. If they were show-off Chinese, their
expensive furniture was tusselled and duct-taped into white
canvas, and we were expected to crouch on black garbage bags
as we crunched our suppers of fried salty noodles, as their parents feared the smells would saturate the carpets. These parents
believed that leather chairs and chintzy sofas should only be
exposed for overseas relatives and moneyed suitors.

Having a sofa for a father meant that we could show it/him off to our Chinese friends, whereas previously, we had been too ashamed to invite anyone over. Our sofa would kindly change its size for a select few, stretching into a comfortable six-seater when the neighbourhood kids stopped by for leftover chicken and unfizzy drinks. Even Fat-Ass Petey Cho was impressed and stopped urinating at our doorstep.

At first, our mother thought my father took up too much space. He was the kind of bulky old sofa sold at garage sales to students who couldn't afford IKEA. Becoming furniture had not fixed the imperfections brought on by an inauspicious birth on Hanoi's streets. Too often, he blocked the door to her bedroom, and she would have to clamber over him, stubbing her toes and cursing. But then she took pity and patted the sofa's lopsided armrest and asked her ex-husband if he felt better. Even the Investor tried sitting on my sofa father, but found the coiled metal springs to be pointy and unpleasing.

"Please come back," I said to our dad. Kian jumped on the sofa to see if our father would react. We were excited when one Saturday morning we woke up and he had become a mouldy-coloured armchair.

"He looks worse now," my mother said. "This grey pallor has to go."

Our father took her advice, and by mid-afternoon he'd transformed back into his usual two-seater form, settling on an unflattering turd brown.

"Why does he look like shit?" my mother asked us, and Kian and I both said that we didn't know.

—

As for myself, I thought that I was turning into a coffee table, because my limbs were becoming board-like and stiff, but I willed myself to stay a human girl. It would happen whenever the Investor came into my room when my mother was asleep, and he would slither, ophidian, under my blanket. My bed was a lumpy kid-sized mattress on the carpet.

"Dad," I sobbed, "help me, please!" and I would feel myself becoming timber. But as my bones snapped and my ligaments hardened, I thought of my little brother. Did he deserve a small side table for a big sister? I guessed that Kian could put his stack of comic books on me, and use my height to reach the tallest pantry shelf for late-night snacks and extra-spicy ramen packs.

It was only after sharing a bag of dollar-store gummy bears and playing PG-13 video games that Kian and I decided that we would just have to kill the Investor. If our father could not help us, well then, we would have to help ourselves and him. An unflinching look made Kian's eyes look grand and peculiar. Kian was a little-kid version of Attila the Hun. He was not the kind of boy who would ever consider transforming into furniture.

It was a question, a notable one, that I had been contemplating lately: Who became furniture, and why did it seem as if only weak-willed and sentimental people shed their human forms? Like late-stage capitalism, this calamity seemed to benefit real estate tycoons or people who owned houses with lots of empty rooms.

It was becoming clearer to me that happy, sociopathic people did not become furniture. Becoming furniture was an affliction reserved for the timid or incurably sad.

It would be very easy, Kian announced, as the Investor lived with us now.

We decided that on garbage day, after our mother left for work in the afternoon, Kian would crush a Costco-sized pack of Benadryl into the Investor's coffee, and when he was sleeping, we would drag him to the backyard, smother him with leftover sweet-and-sour sauce that my mom stole by the gallon from the restaurant, and leave him for the bears, who visited our backyard daily. We would duct-tape his arms and legs and his mouth so that he couldn't make any noise. Serve him up like a stringy barbecued pig that we charged $25/pound for at the restaurant.

Surely bears liked sweet-and-sour sauce as much as our Seattle customers did.

"What do you think? Is this a good plan?" I asked the sofa, and in response it immediately became a violent shade of dudely fuchsia.

It did not go well at first: my mother was late for her shift, swearing dramatically about having to do restaurant inventory. We did not know what to do when she said she had a headache and would skip.

"Dad?" I asked our sofa. "Some help would be nice."

For a moment, nothing happened. My heart rapped unhappily against my rib cage twice. Then our mother turned into a lawn chair, her bones crunching, crisp, as she folded, succinct. Our mother did not scream or wince. She wasn't that surprised, but she was frighteningly pink.

Unfortunately, the Investor did not seem to feel the effects of the Benadryl until much later. He sat on our mother the plastic lawn chair, and then yawning, he finally toppled over onto the floor. He was naked as usual, and Kian and I did not want to touch him. He kicked forlornly, and talked in his sleep. "Mei-Chow," he moaned.

Another unforeseen problem was that he was much too heavy for a thirteen-year-old girl and an eight-year-old boy to move, and we wasted twenty-six minutes trying to drag him across the linoleum floor. We rolled him in our mother's bed sheets. I said that we should tie his arms and legs together in case he woke up, but there was no duct tape or skipping rope to be found in the house. Kian checked the garage twice and asked a neighbour, who lent us Scotch tape. The Investor's eyelids twitched a few times. On his forehead, I drew a smiley face in permanent marker—the logo of our lowest-ranking greasy spoon, the Happy Smile. And we left him outside, face up, covered in sweet-and-sour sauce, because we knew the bears would come, their mouths open in vicious circles, and devour him with their fat lolling tongues.

I'd like to say that Kian and I were quite successful in our endeavour, but the Investor woke up when a black bear began chomping through half of his scalp. Unfortunately for him, he was not a weak or ridiculous person, so he did not transform into backyard furniture while he was being eaten. Fortunately for him, 911 was called by a well-meaning neighbour, but the Investor could no longer speak or remember anything.

The loss of 35 percent of his brain made him unfit for our family. My grandparents, who had found him through an uncle of a cousin of a friend of an aunt, sent our mother's new husband back to Taiwan. At this news, my father turned a celebratory shade of Lunar New Year red and became a leather L-shaped sectional. He looked like he was worth at least ten grand.

"Wow, Dad," I said. "You look nice."

Even Kian whistled.

My grandparents were always looking for cheap furniture for the Happy Smile, and so they rented a moving van and transported my mother and my father. My grandmother, sighing in her dramatic fashion, declared that flamingo pink was an ugly colour and hard for anyone to match in their homes.

At first, Kian and I were excited not to have adult supervision. We were disappointed when my grandfather promised to check in on us twice a week. Kian and I booed softly when he told us that we'd have to double our shifts at the Happy Smile if we wanted to continue living in our house. When he glimpsed our morose faces, my grandfather promised that we'd have frequent visitations with our parents/furniture during breaks. This cheered us up a bit.

"Are you happy?" I always asked my parents at the end of the day, patting my dad's upholstery. "Do you like it here?"

—

Years later, when it was high school graduation day, my grandparents took a photo of us together, minus Kian, who was on an out-of-state trip for gifted teenagers. I was in the middle, one hand touching each of my furniture parents. Both of them matched the restaurant's gaudy interior and had impressively transformed for the photo. Both were iridescent in a magenta hue.

I felt dazed as my grandmother yelled at me to smile. I convinced myself that I was happy for my furniture parents, even though I was extremely heartbroken for myself. As tears blurred my glasses and my grandfather shouted at me to straighten my graduation cap and gown, I thought that it made sense that my parents ended up this way, so that we could finally be together. A portrait of a family arranged in one room.

Colony Farm Confessions

From iPhone found on deceased Asian male,
late 20s, 5'8, 140 lb.

January 12, 04:14

Universe, ancestors, God, Buddha, anyone who will listen? I am turning thirty in a few weeks and feeling tremendously unaccomplished. I'm recording my daily happenings on my phone to make sense of the growing polyp of guilt in my slightly flabby late-twenties abdomen. Mostly, I'm just feeling shitty-sad about multiple life failures, which are starting to feel preordained. Hopefully, talking to myself will provide some distraction.

But first, I must ask, how can I truly feel anything else when I'm working at a maximum-security psych prison as Grand Babysitter and Janitor Extraordinaire to the psychotic whims of the outlawish Clydes and Ted Bundys of the world?

How can I ever be effective at Life when the only people I ever talk to are doped-up serial killers (and my refurbished iPhone 7)?

Really, I never dreamed of this. Also, I did not expect a minimum-wage job or a burgeoning stomach, if I'm being totally honest. Life is scarcely happy—like a low-budget TV movie with zero plot. I feel suicidal (okay, half joking) just thinking of this go-nowhere job. Ha!

Where do I even start when my life's mistakes began? When I ran into a banister in the second grade and knocked out my front teeth? My sophomore year at Princeton where I became too morose and tried to pay someone to write my exams?

This is my most recent mistake: Five years ago I interviewed for this shitty job, and I signed a confidentiality agreement at Colony

Farm, which is a nice name for a muddy jail estate that houses intelligent, unrehabilitatable persons lacking morals. I had to promise the director that I could handle blood, guts, and all forms of deep emotional scarring.

"This is not your normal nursing assistant job," the director had said, picking at a very large bug on her face.

"You've got something on your face," I said, before realizing the ginormous bug was a mutant mole. But the director was already filling out paperwork.

Anyway, the director just called me at 4 a.m. I'm off to work at the severely understaffed, underfunded mental hospital penitentiary now.

I must talk to myself and leave motivating voice memos every morning. Just so I have a reason to get out of bed and possibly survive until my thirtieth birthday.

January 13, 17:15

Dad and his hepatitis C–laden, cirrhosis-doused liver are really driving me apeshit. I know I keep saying this, but ever since Mom, feeling commerce-minded last year, went back to Singapore to start a cosmetic company, it's up to me, only filial Chinese son etc., to keep my aging dad alive in a big empty house with no heat because he's too cheap to pay for it. Although I do give him $750 a month for room and board, three-quarters of my measly paycheque. The man spends the money on excellent booze and cigars.

Here's a fact: Dad loves alcohol and nicotine more than he loves me, *his only son*.

January 14, 19:31

I, with my neurotic immigrant work ethic, spent a fourteen-hour shift counting and distributing doses of antipsychotic medication, mopping floors, and disinfecting minor stab wounds.

Summary of the day's events: everything was very shitty.

Patient A, let's dub Clyde 1 (of the *Bonnie and Clyde* variety), clubbed Patient B, Clyde 2, caveman style on the side of head today with an aluminum lunch tray. Clyde 2 fell down and bit off a lot of his tongue. There was blood everywhere, yikes.

It was my fault. I was distracted by a piece of gristly cafeteria meat in my teeth and trying my absolute best to dislodge it, very secretly, all morning. I barely noticed the fight until the uncanny *awoooooooooooooo* from Clyde 2 on the floor, who was clutching his mouth and rolling around like it was a fire drill. While I was picking my teeth, Clyde 1 was furiously masturbating. The head nurse was gossiping with another nurse, and she did not witness the commotion.

I dialed the prison guards, which took forever because of tax cuts and recent staff shortage. Then I had to sit on Clyde 1 when he tried to attack me with a plastic fork.

Let me be clear: this all happened in the Low-Risk Ward.

Mostly out of self-loathing and shame, after my shift I went out with P. (balding, garden gnome–shaped, barely tolerable prison security guard, not to mention twenty years my senior). At the local diner, we ate gritty pancakes and drank mimosas. Then we fooled around in his car. I didn't really want to, but I figured I should because he paid for breakfast.

"It's not your fault, Simon," P. said, when he dropped me off at home. "It's been a rough month."

I said, sighing, "Rough seven years, more like it."

January 15, 20:02

My Visa card was declined when I tried to buy a slimy nine-dollar tuna fish sandwich from the vending machine. My MasterCard was rejected. Then I forgot my debit card PIN number. So no lunch. I was mopey and constipated all day.

During my dinner break, I drank six mugs of complimentary staff coffee with sugar and two-day-old soymilk. I went for a sludgy saunter on Colony Farm's fifteen-acre grounds. It always surprises me that they don't put up a high-voltage electric shock fence around the main building, which is a generic infant-pink nineteenth-century-style farmhouse. But I guess a fence would cost taxpayers too much money.

While I was walking, it poured like a Singaporean tsunami, spitting grey water, the ponds flooding everywhere. Last year, the provincial government chopped down all the big evergreen trees and hundred-year-old oak trees because too many convicts were escaping the hospital and murdering hikers. I mean, over two hundred have escaped over the past nine years. Guess it was too much work and tax dollars finding outdoorsy dead people in the woods.

The provincial government issued a warning: *If you must hike, bring a buddy.*

They should just be honest: Bring someone you despise. Maybe a family member or ex-lover.

Colony Farm is a goddamn Apocalyptic Wasteland.

January 16, 21:09

Before my shift ended, despite practising zero eye contact, I saw an ex-favourite prisoner, seemingly normal Clyde 3. He was being escorted by P. and another prison guard. He was doped up, shuffling like a sick circus bear. A year ago, he escaped right before breakfast and killed and ate a solo hiker chick on the grounds because he mistook her for a slab of ham.

When he was caught, I strapped him into a straitjacket, and I waited for the lawyer and psychiatrist to arrive. "Why did you do that for?" I had asked him, trying not to sound too judgy and accusing. To which Clyde 3 replied: "I was just so hungry, man. I hate the oatmeal here." Nodding, I replied in a friendly but mostly neutral tone: "Yes, it's quite bland, isn't it?"

"Hey, dude, what's up?" I said, noticing Clyde 3 was waiting for a greeting, then I nodded nonstop like a cheerful, well-meaning department store Christmas elf. I know it doesn't make a difference if you're affable with a convicted psychopath, but I think they will be less likely to cannibalize you if you remain consistently pleasant.

Clyde 3, who was smiling, said, "Simon, hi! Hi! Hi! Wanna play cards tonight?"

I absolutely did not want to spend my evening with an overt cannibalistic dude even though we've had some stimulating conversations about destiny, angels and demons, pre-eating of the dead girl last year. But then I suddenly glimpsed P., looking hopeful, like he wanted to talk to me. So I very quickly said that I would play one game of Go Fish.

January 19, 15:09

Dad woke me in the afternoon after a long, chaotic night shift of wiping vomit and sponge-bathing delirious prisoners. There was an epic food-poisoning and salmonella epidemic in the Lockdown Ward for Serial Offenders. Code Brown alert. Twelve toilets were clogged. I unclogged all with feigned enthusiasm and efficiency because the cute intern was looking.

Even the director got massive diarrhea during the general meeting in the conference room. I pretended not to notice.

"Simon, Simon? I have a fucking headache!" Dad complained, pounding on my bedroom door.

"I'm off-duty now," I moaned, squashing a pillow over my head. "Call 911! For god's sake, let me sleep!"

But nonetheless, I could not say no. I could never refuse my old, boozy dad (promised Mom I'd try, you know?). So I dragged my ass up and gave him three Advil and fried up some Spam and yellow egg noodles, which he ate like a gluttonous coyote. Spam is the best hangover cure for hopeless alcoholics, I swear.

Note to my future self: give Dad minor sedatives like Benadryl after a long night shift. I would sleep in the car but I am far too poor to even afford a second-hand one. When the weather clears up, when the snow finally melts in Vancouver, I must save up for a small tent for the garage, maybe the driveway.

January 20, 17:09

A new patient has transferred from up north, Interior B.C. He's very handsome, maybe Sri Lankan? Malaysian? Indonesian ancestry? He's all symmetrical features, six-foot-two, and not like most of the Clydes at Colony Farm. Note: the Clydes here are all hairless and piglet-pudgy from the high dosage of sedatives, insulin, and anti-psychotic meds.

Anyway, this exquisite psych-prisoner is an Asian Ted Bundy. A youngish Calvin Klein model with all his hair and biceps and impeccable manners. I mean, most psychopaths are unbelievably agreeable and charismatic. But this dude is *Pride and Prejudice*. He even speaks with a posh British accent too, but I'm told it's fake.

Other catch is: he's suspected of murdering approx. fifteen to thirty women and children, including bludgeoning his best friend to death with an aluminum thermos on a Greyhound bus to Los Angeles over loss of zesty Doritos.

The prison nurses, interns, and doctors are all enamoured; they make excuses to check up on him just so's they can chat. Clydes 1 and 2, who now call themselves "soulmates" after the tray-hitting incident, are both fighting to befriend the new patient after glimpsing him once in the hallway.

According to the Colony Farm staff room gossip, the man is well versed in weather, sports, politics, philosophy, classics.

January 21, 21:25

Today I, very reluctantly, attended a dinner gathering with my snotty, ultra-bitchy friends from high school. Despite never liking one another, every few months my friends congregate at Minami, a high-end three-Michelin-star Japanese restaurant downtown on Burrard. I have skipped the last four or six times, citing my "terminal" dad as a big lie and hermit excuse. But I must save face at all costs. Especially since my friends keep bugging me via text and social media to name a convenient date for a meet-up.

I can't afford to be friends, or even acquaintances, with rich, affected Asian bankers who have pretty, bird-boned wives and vacation homes in the Maldives. I used to be exactly like them. A decade ago, I was filled with similar earthly hopes and consumed by material aspiration. Especially when I got into Princeton (pre-med Ivy League) and they didn't. But I am quite deflated now.

I cannot tell friends that I failed sophomore year at Princeton due to extreme mopeyness, which led to a temporary manic-depressive episode, by which I mean I proactively hired a poorish Harvard student on Craigslist to take my finals, which was discovered by an overtly unforgiving TA, meaning disciplinary action by the dean, resulting in Goodbye Blessed Ivy League. And after hearing the news, Mom cried and threatened suicide. I tried to finish college online at various third-rate schools, but I was too sad.

Besides, expulsion and lifelong janitorship are the ultimate no-nos for the only son of Chinese immigrants.

So I arrived at Minami very, very late. The maître d' in a silk yukata gave me a yucky look. I was wearing my holey jeans from Old Navy. I pretended to have an upset stomach and ordered the $8 herbal cleansing sencha (murky green tea) from the lush green fields of Shizuoka, instead of the main course, which was $500 rare Wagyu beef.

"So what is it you do again, Simon?" High School Friend #1 said.

"Oh you know," I said, "mostly looking after my dying dad. I'm practically his full-time nurse."

"I mean, what's your *job*?"

"Well, Dad is *dying*. Terminal cancer in his intestines, genitals, *and* lungs. Oncologist said he has less than a month to live. It's rather serious."

"Yes, but what exactly do you do for income?" High School Friend #2 prodded, slurping his seventy-dollar miso soup.

High School Friend #3, #4, and #5 looked on, nodding intensely, as if some colossal juicy secret was to be revealed. But I'm sorry to disappoint you, affluent assholes!

"Oh, my family is in shipping, remember?" I finally stammered, which was not true. This was Asian code for: we're old-money Singaporeans. We are filthy rich, flusher than A-list celebrities and the Maharajah of India, dudes. But the plodding, middle-class reality is, Dad used to be a health insurance broker and Mom worked as a dental hygienist. I could not tell Rich Asian Friends that I made minimum wage (gasp!), had not finished college, am a homosexual, and voted for Trudeau instead of Harper.

Luckily, my friends took my guinea-pig stutter for run-of-the-mill modesty.

I did not leave a tip for the fancy tea at Minami.

January 22, 12:25

Today was finally my turn to deliver the maximum dosage (900 mg of lithium, 150 mg of clozapine, 900 mg of thorazine) to the handsome new patient's holding cell. Then, I was to carefully check under the patient's tongue to see if he had swallowed them. I was nonsensically enthusiastic. It was like meeting one's favourite internet porn star in person.

Fake British Ted Bundy said, "I thank you for your kind hospitality and duty, sir."

I blushed and stuttered, "Erm . . . great!"

"Will you please tell me your name?" FBTB said.

"S-S-Simon," I said, hiccuping.

I am not sure why I was blathering on like a pre-adolescent, except for maybe the pheromones were making me dizzy. I wondered if I had regressed, psychologically, emotionally, biologically, while working among the criminally ill who are practically oversized children on pharmaceutical steroids.

Then FBTB bowed like a comely medieval knight. The bowing totally threw me off. It would have been endearing but it became very creepy when FBTB, like a nasty reptile or ravenous dog, licked my arm. Like my arm was a delicious, crunchy bone! Also, FBTB had an extremely pointed tongue.

When the lick happened, I felt a wicked stabbing in gut slash serious gas, but also a very painful radiating chemical peel on my forearm. I attributed it to static shock. I did not reprimand FBTB for the licking because I was too appalled, then I was preoccupied with looking at his face, which was blurry and too bright. It was not quite beautiful up close, like a plastic mask.

I thought I heard a buzzy voice in my head: *You taste wonderful!* Then I wondered if I was having a stroke or mild psychotic break.

I attributed my subconscious voice to my shocked alter ego. Was this a psychopath's version of sexual foreplay before committing an act of extreme violence and murder? I admit that I was absolutely stunned and confused.

FBTB, snickering like some yaoguai demon, ended the encounter by spitting a loogie in my eye. Dude SPAT big soggy one IN MY EYEBALL! It was absolutely disgusting. When I could move, I left the holding cell in a hurry.

I reported the incident to the director, who made me file an official complaint.

"To whom?" I asked. No reply.

January 23, 18:55

After work, I found Dad on the front lawn. He was slurring, naked, and half-unconscious. He was too compact, like a Volkswagen minivan, to lift by myself. So I threw my jacket over him. I must have dozed off. I woke up when Dad, exasperated, standing over me, was shaking me like I was a slot machine.

Dad sighed and said: "Simon, what the fuck are you doing sleeping outside?"

"I found you on the grass," I said.

"Bullshit," he complained. "Don't be lazy. What's to eat?"

He waddled back inside the house, and as I rolled over, I found forty dollars on the lawn. I'm excited to be able to afford takeout. No cooking tonight! Hello, small victory. Hello, forty fucking bucks!

January 24, 19:29

I had sex with P. Hate myself is an understatement. Hate is a feeling reserved for war criminals and American politicians. Not sex with an older, uglier, benevolent Troll-Man. We did it on the muddy grounds of Colony Farm, under a small, decrepit bridge, surrounded by debris and flattened pop cans. Naturally, it stormed the whole time.

I'm very embarrassed to say that I wailed like a teenage girl afterwards because of my embarrassment and overwhelming shame. P. held me for the longest time, which made me feel shittier.

Before bed, because I am feeling queasy and nostalgic, I will masturbate to an old Facebook photo of my college roommate slash crush: a long-legged tennis player and self-proclaimed Proust scholar. He may be bald now, but he's worth 3.9 billion according to Forbes for the creation of fancy skincare products.

January 25, 06:08

My arm still blazes, really hurts where FBTB tongued me. The skin is scabby and splitting, spreading like rust-coloured psoriasis. My oozing arm itches like a grisly motherfucker.

Also, the eye where his spit hit me was burning and blurry. I went to bed early because I was seeing quadruple.

January 26, 07:36

THIRTIETH BIRTHDAY!!!!!!!!!! FUCK MY LIFE.

I know I'm yelling and crying at my stupid phone but it's honestly an attempt to hype myself up since there's nothing to look forward to. Yelling while crying is a feeble attempt to get out of bed, shower, brush teeth, fake-smile, etc.

January 26, 17:13

It was a very strange birthday.

Somehow, Clyde 3 roped P. and me, Clydes 1 and 2, and some of the other orderlies and well-behaved patients into playing Game of Life (irony is not entirely lost on me) in Colony Farm's Good Behaviour Social Room. Unlike at other maximum-security psych hospitals, the director believes in monthly routine socialization when everyone is sufficiently doped up. This lets the employees be friendly and replaces staff parties, which saves money. The TV was blaring *Sesame Street*. (The inmates are prohibited from accessing violent imagery.)

When FBTB marched in with an escort and asked if he could play, Clyde 3 sort of froze in a panicky, comatose mode. I glanced around to see if anyone else noticed it, and P. smiled, shy-like, thinking I was looking at him, so I clumsily shuffled my cards.

Without waiting for a friendly invitation, FBTB plonked down in a plastic seat at the table. Clyde 3 put his hands on his forehead, like he was praying for divine intervention.

"Is everything all right?" I asked, trying to be agreeable, polite, and not alarmist. But meanwhile, I was preparing to run in case Clyde 3, who has supposedly recovered from cannibalism, decided to eat any of us.

In response, Clyde 3 started making wet choking noises. His eyeballs began to twitch. I didn't need to finish pre-med to know that something was wrong. Suddenly, Clyde 3 was yelping about his face being on fire. He knocked over the game table and threw his hands around FBTB's neck.

In an uproar, P. grabbed his truncheon and paged the other security guard for backup. I was knocked onto the tiled floor. I smashed my head very hard. I think I passed out for ten seconds and woke up with Clyde 1 sitting on my chest, giggling like an inane schoolgirl. "Serves you right," he said, poking me in the nose before the nurse and guard could drag him off.

Yes. It serves me right, indeed. Clyde 3 was sedated and dragged to Isolation. FBTB seemed unfazed. He kept smirking and wagging his elongated tongue at everyone the whole time, especially me.

When I looked in the mirror, I saw a whopping gash. My eye was swollen. The cute medical intern stitched and bandaged me up.

Afterwards, P. insisted on walking me to the staff room. He had brought me a frozen b-day cake from the convenience store. He was carrying two plastic forks, but I took the undefrosted cake and gobbled it, raccoon-like, by myself outside of the prison hospital.

There was no mention of my birthday from Dad. But I received a voicemail from Mom: "Simon, look at how far you've fallen!"

January 28, 18:25

It's the weirdest, zaniest, most wonderful and frightening thing of all. I'm either completely mad or I have acquired a paranormal gift from the most benevolent universe! I keep finding money everywhere. Crispy, beautiful stacks of it, in my pockets, on the floor, under my pillow. Even in my soiled laundry hamper. At first, I thought I must be hallucinating.

I took a batch of bills to the bank. It has been confirmed: they are not counterfeit dollars.

Despite the unnatural quality of this discovery, things are certainly improving.

For instance, P. offered me a ride home after my late-night shift, so I wouldn't have to take the bus. Before I could accept, I found $300 in my right pocket. So I thanked P. profusely, but refused his offer. I called a taxi instead, and slipped P. a hundred-dollar bill. "This is for breakfast and the cake," I said.

I did not want to owe him anything anymore, even though it's not entirely his fault that he resembles a troll, and he has been kind to me. It's amazing what a hundred dollars will do for your self-esteem.

Also, I gave Dad six hundred in spending money; then I phoned Mom, feeling euphoric, to report that I was wiring her a gift of eighteen hundred dollars. "My stocks finally took off," I said on her voicemail. "I didn't tell you because I wanted it to be a surprise."

I'm suddenly averaging $5,500 per day. At this rate, I could join the electrifying ranks of the upper-upper-middle class in six to eight months.

February 6, 6:20

I have not left any shitty-sad voice memos in a while. I'm too busy becoming an accidental millionaire.

February 7, 17:02

My arm rash lump swelling is getting worse. It looks like it's been inhabited by a colony of flesh-eating insects. I finally Googled rare parasites, poisonous spider sac under epidermis, particularly those spread by saliva, gums, and mouth cavities. Also I Googled "mysterious money showing up" and got everything from leprechauns, the Mafia, and wishful thinking, buddy.

So I booked an appointment with the doctor, but cancelled when I, agonizingly itchy and feverish all night, scratched a lump bloody, which revealed itself to be a toonie in my forearm. A toonie!

Yes, I'm not joking, but I'm freaking out like when a hyper house cat glimpses his own dumbfounded reflection for the first time. A toonie! It sounds absolutely insane and bizarre, but this is no joke. I'm not high or delusional.

I could not explain to the doctor that a toonie was hatching inside my arm like a quail egg, without being committed permanently to Colony Farm. I could not tell the doctor that it was all related to my recent good luck of finding bills wherever I go. Hopefully this is an isolated, most unfortunate incident. The internet said my immune system could produce metal objects during times of extreme duress.

Most vital question: Whom does this toonie belong to? Me?

There's no time to ponder. Dad is shouting from the hallway. How to put with the utmost filial delicacy: he has, badly, shit himself.

February 8, 16:29

I took a sick week because it appears money is coming out of my arm. Apparently I have become a full-time human ATM machine. It's very painful passing toonies from my bloodstream, through small veins and zigzagging arteries, as if my blood is solidifying metal every few hours. It's like passing an above-average-sized kidney stone. I know this is all related to FBTB, somehow, no idea how or why. I have never believed in magic or ghosts or superstitious mumbo-jumbo before.

Today, toonies began coming out of almost every orifice in my body. No nostrils yet. I could not handle a toonie tumbling out of my nose (my best feature).

Good news is, I generate spare change every time I sneeze, pass gas, or swipe right on Grindr.

Also, there's a dirty, permanent metallic taste in my mouth. All my food and water tastes like hot corroded metal. I had sharp intestinal cramps, and I thought that toonies would be emerging out of my ass-hole. But no toonies, what luck. I checked: just a walnut-sized hemorrhoid.

The other question that I should have asked when I was uncovering money on my person, but I am sadly no longer propitious, and no longer a human detector of dollar bills: Is my body stealing money, or am I generating my very own currency?

And the question that seems oddly relevant right now: Will I be able to convert Canadian to U.S. dollars to euros to pounds to pesos? What if I want to travel internationally in the future? What about my body's conversion rate?

February 9, 05:12

I woke up at 5 a.m. to an urgent call from the director. P. was missing, then found face down by cops, drowned, in knee-deep muddy pond on outskirts of Colony Farm. "It appears to be suicide or an accident," she said. There was no evidence of foul play (no convict has escaped recently), but police found quarters stuffed in his ear canals and a one-hundred-dollar bill (mine) in his wallet. I was not surprised or particularly saddened by the news.

An hour later, though, I felt quite shaken. Poor P. He did not deserve to die at Colony Farm, but maybe in the next ten or fifteen years, in front of his television set, comfortable, nursing a refrigerated six-pack.

But I was the last person to see P. alive.

The director said on the phone: "Can you come to the prison, Simon? The police want to ask you a few questions."

February 9, 18:25

After the police interview, I spent the whole day, painstakingly, grotesquely, vomiting hundreds, possibly thousands of loonies. The taxi driver and Dad were my alibis. I said that I went straight home after my shift, and everyone confirmed it. Luckily, the interview was brief. We're just waiting for an autopsy, they said. Somehow, I have an outlandish feeling that the coroner will find P., like a Thanksgiving turkey, stuffed full of dimes and nickels.

But there was a slight mishap. Clydes 1 and 2 saw me puke up coins, at least fifty dollars' worth, outside the Low-Risk Ward. Fortuitously, both are convicted lunatics, middle-aged lifers—no one will believe them. Unfortunately, when the intern was busy chatting with the orderly, they both grabbed handfuls of my unlucky loonies. "Wait!" I hollered, but they sauntered off, clutching the cursed money.

It will be a significant pay cut if I can only generate loonies instead of toonies. Maybe it's just nerves, a temporary setback. I asked the director for more sick days. She said no, we are extremely under-staffed, etc. I asked for a bigger raise, and she said yes.

February 11, 23:29

I have booked Minami for private event and ordered thirty bottles of the finest Dom Perignon for High School Banker Friends 1 through 5. "Dinner is on moi," I texted them. And feeling superior, superego inflated, I lied: "It's my 30th birthday!" Admittedly, it's not the best time for a party, due to my sometimes uncontainable, often shock-ing, vomiting of money. But I could not resist. I told myself: Think of extravagant b-day presents. Simon, think of a five-layer Italian coco-nutty cream cake from La Patisserie. Most of all, think of those long, admiring looks and whispers of *he's generous plus he looks after his dying father!*

I FaceTimed Mom to fly her to Vancouver business class. She picked up the phone for the first time this year. "I have money now," I announced, and she wept: "Simon, I always knew you weren't a loser despite your father saying so!"

February 12, 19:27

I confronted FBTB because I had to know the truth, so I switched with an on-duty nurse to bring him meds. Dull, rusty quarters (no longer shiny and new) were tumbling out of my mouth at a disturbing frequency. Twenty-five cents a minute is like $15 an hour plus my $11.75 minimum prison wage, which means I'm only making $26.75 per hour today. I could not eat breakfast. God, I have been starving this week. Choking out quarters is not just time-consuming, but it creates a very hoarse phone-sex-operator stutter.

FBTB grinned at me. "I've been expecting you," he said in a no longer faux British accent.

"What is all this?" I said, gesturing at myself.

"A gift," he said.

"Can you fix this?" I asked.

FBTB kept smiling. "Nope."

He would say no more. I persisted. So he took off his face. Underneath, he was not a man, not even a mammal. It was a cold-blooded reptile killer, a hideous old grey toad thing. He had flickering blood eyes, black warts and all. Monstrous-FBTB sniggered.

He then shoved his slimy face into mine!

I tried to scream but choked on several quarters. Afterwards, I was told that I had passed out from physical exertion. FBTB notified the security guard, and he was rewarded points for good behaviour.

February 13, 00:45

I missed work. I'm avoiding the director's multiple phone calls. Honestly, I'm much too ill, weak, and vertiginous to move from the toilet. Because all I did for the past several hours was painfully spit out and shit pennies nonstop. It has all gone downhill extremely fast—an incontinent hour of shiny dimes, then nickels, now pennies. I average $3,500 a day in pennies. Yes, I am still counting my change.

February 14, 07:10

I went to the kitchen and found Dad face down and pantless. I assumed that he was drunk and/or sleeping. I came back three hours later, and he had not moved. I turned him over and found shiny new quarters in his ears. He was clutching stacks of hundred-dollar bills—rent money that I had given him.

I cannot articulate how fearful I am. Not so much for him (he's dead) but for me. Like P., Dad touched my cursed money. *I* gave him my dollar bills. Two people are dead now, most likely because of me. Am I a ticking time bomb, carrier of a mystical disease? And most importantly, how long do I have left?

Also, I'm not too sad about Dad's death. Under normal, well-heeled circumstances (i.e., wealthy), if my stomach and esophagus were not constantly filling with metal, I would actually consider Dad dying a colossal blessing.

Only bonus: I have enough money now to keep the house.

February 15, 16:44

Expensive dinner party is tonight, but I can't cancel.

High school banker friends and wives have all confirmed. I want to recklessly, decadently, show off. $15,000-plus dinner on me.

And I can't disappoint because Mom is flying all the way from Singapore. She needs to see her only and favourite son. I can't tell her that Dad expired (magically) while I was supposed to be on nurse duty. Or that my money is cursed. I can't say hey Mom, wear gloves, a chemical suit, and a biohazard mask to dispose of your ex-husband and your dying son. Better yet, hire a professional cleanup crew.

I like to hope that I do not perish before my fancy b-day dinner. In my kaleidoscopic brain, with my best concentrated effort, I suddenly, miraculously, get better and wear a $5,000 Armani suit to the party.

I will tip a cab driver $800, maybe $850, depending on driving skill set. And driver dude or dudette, with eyeballs expanding, pupils glowing because of monetary high, will utter: *Wow, man! Holy shit! Thank you, dude! Thank you!!!*

At Minami, ignoring the maître d' who snubbed me previously, I imagine myself clapping Friends #1 through 5 on the back in manly affirmation, greeting their smiling wives with affectionate finesse, etc. We will eat spicy tuna sashimi until tummies swell with gas and then belch with the indomitable satisfaction of spending someone else's moolah. We will guzzle Dom Perignon like tap water, then make up grand and dirty lies about ourselves.

Assholes, I will loudly call them behind their backs, when they excuse themselves to go to the bathroom. If they hear me, they will say nothing because I'm the asshole paying for their suppers.

At the cake-cutting, song-singing time, Mom finally arrives from the airport, my late guest of honour. She's grinning, proud, as if she is solely responsible for this extraordinary fete. "Simon, is that really you?" she asks, looking incredulous. "How much did you spend on that beautiful suit?"

But I'm far too weak to talk now. I can't even charge my phone or run to the toilet anymore. I must shut my eyelids and lie down. Expiring at the age of thirty, like people did in medieval times, is far better than being an overworked janitor who shits nothing but pennies.

Kind Face, Cruel Heart

Six generations ago, Junjie's great-great-great-great-great-great-granduncle started a civil war that caused suffering from the wild rice terraces of Guangdong Province to the tiny carmine islands of the South China Sea. For fourteen long years, Hong Xiuquan, a stubborn and gluttonous man, led the Taiping Rebellion, but he failed to seize Shanghai and topple the illustrious Qing dynasty.

On the blood-orange eve of an ill-fated battle in Nanjing, Xiuquan and his army of coarse-faced miners, blacksmiths, and former pirates depleted their supplies of fermented soybeans and pale blue haiyan, sea salt. The men decided it was better for morale to ingest bitter-tasting vegetation than cannibalize the slowest and most dim-witted of their men. Desperate, they gathered and boiled scraggly, dew-speckled weeds that sprouted in abundance around Xiuquan's estate. After supper, many of his soldiers shat blood, while others endured violent indigestion. But Xiuquan, who was perpetually hungry, died because he consumed unquantifiable portions of the weed. His generals found him slumped on a silver chamber pot, bleeding as if he had been freshly gutted, his entire stomach caved in.

After Xiuquan's inauspicious death, the imperial army captured his loyal followers, war-grey mules, and a collection of fine British muskets. By decree of the high Tongzhi Emperor, poor Xiuquan's body was exhumed, beheaded, and burned. A royal cannon in the red Ming Palace blasted his ashes in four directions so that his traitorous soul would find no final resting place in China. Feeling merciless, the Tongzhi Emperor imprisoned Xiuquan's entire bloodline under the black sloping valleys of Mount Penglai for all eternity.

For centuries, Junjie's relatives laboured in the dusky pink underground fungi caves to find the mystical lingzhi mushroom. It was rumoured that the iridescent mushroom could provide powers of invisibility, flight, and clairvoyance. Those who consumed the fungus would possess the infinite ability to foresee China's future, receiving a hundred aristocratic titles, deeds to vermillion jade palaces, and a choice of the Emperor's sturdiest children for marriage, becoming part of China's celestial elite. Clinging to time-honoured rumour, Junjie's ancestors dug with their bare hands in the acrid bogs in search of the lingzhi. They suffocated from melon-sized tumours hatching in their lungs. They collapsed from third-degree burns, amputation, and organ removal, their bodies sinking into clay loam before being hauled up in a rusty elevator to the elusive night sky. As generations passed, the bloodline of Hong Xiuquan thinned. Junjie, his mother, and older sister Shen were the only remaining lineage.

"Kind face, cruel heart!" was a mantra screamed in primary re-education school, as concentration camp prisoners were forced to spit without mercy on black-and-white portraits of their ancestors. Their dead loved ones were said to possess kind-looking faces but rotten and immoral insides. The guards shouted that you could tell if someone would betray you by the sweetness of their facial features, which concealed a cruel, pickled heart. They claimed that the traitor Hong Xiuquan had been born with "a smiling tiger face," which meant that he was untrustworthy.

Betrayal, like boundless hunger, was in Junjie's blood.

Junjie did not know where or what exactly his father was, but his mother claimed that a wild hybrid creature, a taotie, had appeared one night screeching for food. She thought the demon to be one of the four malevolent evils, which the older prisoners whispered about as they gathered outside the gloomy concrete tunnels at the end of long shifts. Complaining in the camp was forbidden, so they would talk-story of the Si Xiong, four wicked beasts who embodied war, betrayal, lack of morals, and gluttony. The taotie was hunger personified. Prisoners warned that these foul creatures, who wandered the earth, frequented the underworld caves to incite chaos, but the taotie specifically visited Mount Penglai to feast on the prisoners' polluted flesh. "To die by one of the four evils is a death worse than being murdered by a volatile guard," the oldest in the camp warned.

None of the prisoners could actually describe the demons, but they repeated what they heard as facts. With each retelling, Junjie learned that the taotie had bulbous white lips, curved goat horns, piss-yellow tiger fangs, and three bleeding eyes, as well as a sweet baby face on its rear end.

Junjie's mother claimed that the taotie hid its cruel heart behind its human visage. After his mother, bowing and meek, had given the demon, disguised as a formidable prison sentry, her weekly ration of red onions, the taotie sat on her and swallowed her whole. His mother said that she had nearly drowned in its flatulent stomach, causing disfiguring marks to appear over her body. Junjie thought that she had actually been tortured by the camp's guards with burning pokers. But his mother swore it was all true.

"I tasted of human shit and filth," Junjie's mother announced proudly, "so he spat me back out, and within a day, you tore through my belly, fully grown and hungry." The innocent human face on the taotie's backside had been passed on to Junjie. A milky baby face that did not age but remained what the guards called "a smiling tiger cub."

Late one evening, when Junjie had turned fifteen years old, his mother reluctantly asked him for a favour. She had long ago stopped telling stories to him, choosing to believe what the prisoners said about her kind-faced, cruel-hearted son. But she needed Junjie to keep a lookout while she had sex with their camp foreman.

"He will help us," she said, combing her snarled hair with her filth-stained fingers. "The foreman will make sure that you, me, and your sister will not have to work so hard in the caves."

Junjie's pretty sister, Shen, who was seventeen and had been born of a human father, a long-deceased prisoner, had always been their mother's favourite. But Shen was spending the night at another guard's house. Junjie's mother had no choice but to trust him.

"I'll help you if I get your rations," Junjie said. Even in the squinting gloom of the bunker, his bones were visible, jutting out like twigs; his bloated gut expanding like a putrid winter melon.

When his mother left, Junjie eagerly shoved down her share of preserved vegetables and a small pile of old corn kernels with his hands. But as usual, the hunger inside him viciously scratched at his insides. Since birth, he'd had a taotie's insatiable appetite. *More*, he thought, panicking. *I need more.*

Junjie ran to the head guard. In the Re-Education Camp, guards taught the prisoners that they should be dedicated only to Emperor Xuantong of the mighty Qing dynasty. Snitching on family and friends was common. For his unfaithfulness, he was given a sliver of raw swine heart and a bowl of oily broth.

"Are you a traitor who repents?" the guard asked, rapping Junjie on the forehead.

Junjie bowed. As soon as he had finished his meal, his stomach snarled like a wild boar.

For her transgression, Junjie's mother was chained to a wooden pole and lashed twenty times with a metal cow rod. Seven prisoners were forced to take turns hitting her with their hands. Shen, her eyes as blank as candle wax, pulled out their mother's scraggly hair. When it was Junjie's turn, he refused to look at his mother, but doing his duty, slapped her three times across the face. Her body crumpled like a tree.

When Junjie's mother returned to their barracks, she was missing half of her second finger. *Like a brown, withered rat tail*, Junjie thought. Her face hardened when she looked at her son, her eyes swollen like two purple rocks.

Three thousand feet below the sour earth, upside-down towers of white stalactites hummed tunelessly. Spades of blue moss covered the rocky outcroppings like fine cloth, but gave you a terrible itch if you accidentally touched it. Grey, six-legged crickets with giant eyes scuttled and hopped, while translucent blood-red leeches and night-black snails suckled the cave walls with hunger. Junjie's mother often said that these disgusting creatures were the souls of Death Valley prisoners, all that would remain after their unpleasant deaths. Lit by ghoulish lantern light, the prisoners looked like greying hogs waiting for slaughter.

Squatting beside his bamboo basket, Junjie groped at the slime and oozing dirt to collect his daily quota—white, cloud-like ear mushrooms that only government officials could afford for virility and longevity; a handful of icy pink string truffles used to make fine, exotic poisons for trade with the West. He had never heard of anyone even glimpsing the colourful lingzhi mushroom. If a prisoner found the lingzhi mushroom, surely his entire bloodline would be freed.

What would it be like to be born outside the mushroom caves? Junjie thought as he tugged at a dense cluster of ear mushrooms. Perhaps he would have been loved by at least one person. A generous mother, a most benevolent father, and an older sister who cared for him. In a different lifetime, would he have a pet? He would very much like to raise his own baby chicken. All

Junjie knew of the outside world was from guards' gossip. He overheard that new rebel groups from Sichuan threatened the precarious rule of their beloved Qing Emperor, and China was on the brink of war with the great enemy, Japan.

A siren blared. Instinctively, Junjie dropped to the freezing ground with the other hundred prisoners on his shift.

"Which scum has been stealing from the mushroom storage?" the head guard asked. "If no one comes forward, I will randomly choose! Answer, filth!"

Silence, as thick as dung. Junjie could almost hear the wet, rumbling earth.

His sister stood. Bowing her head, she pointed at Junjie. "This is the thief! My brother has been stealing from the storage room!" She kept her eyelashes lowered, half-shut like coffin lids.

Junjie's heart sank like sodden wool.

He frequently stole mushrooms. His sister stole. His mother stole. His classmates and neighbours stole, as the nonpoisonous speckled mushrooms could be eaten raw or bartered. All the prisoners in the cave were guilty of the transgression.

The guard gripped Junjie by the neck and forced him to kneel. Junjie shivered, as though he had been dunked in a barrel of ice water. Would this be his execution?

Shen's demure gaze shifted to meet his own. He suddenly knew.

It was his sister who had stolen five spotted mushrooms the previous evening. She had boiled the pilfered mushrooms with water and rice flour. Too hungry to question his good fortune, Junjie had slurped the bitter soup.

With a closed fist, the head guard whacked Junjie on the back of his skull. Primordial flames sparked from under his lids. He fell.

When Junjie woke, his work shoes were missing. The thief had also removed Junjie's shirt but left his tattered trousers, which were stiff with urine. Junjie stumbled back to his family's barracks. His twig-like body quivered.

"Did the guard not beat you badly?" his mother asked. "Shen and I thought that you had died." She avoided looking at him, her bean-shaped eyes askance. His sister watched him carefully, though she said nothing.

"Is there any food?" Junjie asked.

His mother shook her head, but she handed him a bowl of rock salt that he rubbed into the red slashes on his head and nose. His vision blurred, and he soon collapsed on his bunk.

Sometime in the darkness, Junjie woke to the roasting scent of jasmine rice and meaty soup. Fresh rice was a rarity in camp; only the most senior guards ate it thrice weekly.

"We leave just before the workday," his mother said quietly to his sister.

"What if they catch us?" Shen asked.

"What kind of existence is this," his mother continued, her voice harsh as if she had just gargled with salt, "toiling until death? We will all die anyway. I overheard from a guard that our camp is very close to Hong Kong. If we can stay in Guangzhou and sell our bodies for a while, I am certain that we can earn enough to pay our passage. Besides, one of the guards says his family is in Guangzhou and will hide us. He will join us later."

"When they catch us, it won't be a fast execution," his sister said.

"Nothing will go wrong." His mother sounded confident. "No one knows of our plan."

Junjie understood at that moment that his mother and Shen had schemed to have him beaten, perhaps killed, by accusing him of stealing mushrooms. Now his family was plotting to leave without him. This was terrible knowledge to possess. His mother resented him for being born of a taotie, but his sister? As small children, Shen and Junjie had told silly jokes in their shared bunk, and tried to out-spit each other at the primary re-education school when they were tasked with expectorating on the portrait of their ancestor. Yet as they grew older, strange things started to happen to Shen. She claimed to be able to hear the ghosts of dead prisoners and she often recited their talk-stories. To punish her for uttering lies, their soft-faced teacher, who had once been their favourite, burned her tongue six times with red candle wax. When Shen turned twelve, she was taken to the commanding officers' barracks every night. Junjie never asked her what happened there.

Betrayal, which he had understood from birth, did not usually sting—it was no worse than a brutal beating with a horse switch. This time, though, it felt sharp, like a knife scraping his throat. *But what did you expect?* he thought. *How are you worthy of anybody's love when you were born of a monster?*

Junjie heard his sister and mother slurping, and his stomach mutinied. The rice smelled especially fragrant; the chicken gristle soup left a dreamy, euphoric impression inside his mouth. When his mother and sister retired to their bunks, he slipped outside.

—

One night every 365 days, for morale, the prisoners of Ghost Valley were allowed outside the rank mushroom caves. An old squeaky lift and pulley were used to carry up droves of the half-living, as if transporting the skeletal prisoners to the black, celestial heavens. The guards' offices and barracks were located at the unpainted entrance of the ancient elevator. Across the dimly lit stone pathway, Junjie sprinted as fast as he could, lest his mother and sister catch him.

"My sister, my mother," Junjie gasped, "they are planning an escape tonight. Prisoner 965434 and 637211. I will give you the details, but in return, I want double rations for every meal, including rice. I also want a shorter work shift."

Nodding and beaming widely, the boy guard, who could be Junjie's peer in another life, called over his superior, who looked to be the same age as Shen. Junjie had never encountered this officer before, and he was surprised when he was asked to sign a squiggly X on a paper.

"Do you have any food?" Junjie asked eagerly. In exchange for his signature, he was presented with a raw onion and a greasy pain ointment for his nose and allowed to strip the uniform off a newly dead man.

After he had eaten and dressed, Junjie was blindfolded and dragged by his unshorn hair. "But I gave you information!" he cried, as merciless hands, seemingly from all directions of a compass, pummelled him. "Kind face, cruel heart!" voices shouted accusingly.

When the blindfold was lifted, he saw his mother and sister on their knees deep inside the mushroom caves. The moss on the walls glowed a wild underwater blue, illuminating everything with a soft, milky light. His sister was flushed with otherworldly terror. His mother, glassy-eyed and impassive, stared at her severed finger. Arranged beside them, like funeral flowers, were the sweet-looking pink string mushrooms used for rare poisons. A faction of three guards surrounded them, each carrying long swords.

"Eat the mushrooms or suffer disembowelment," one of them ordered. He brandished his weapon at Junjie's closed-face mother.

"It's a pity," another said, contemplating Shen's wide, cloud-shaped eyes and soft lips. "None of the girls are as beautiful as this one."

"Nah," someone else said. "These traitors are all ugly from the soil! There's no beauty underground."

Shen's face was wild, her cheeks the shade of boiled ox brains. "How could you!" she spat at Junjie. His mother did not acknowledge him. She straightened her filthy uniform. Her head looked like it was precariously balanced on top of an empty potato sack.

"Don't be afraid, Shen," she said simply. "Your brother will be punished for his crime."

In Ghost Valley, love was an abstract concept. After all, they were only supposed to be dutiful sons and daughters of China. Yet Junjie felt stricken as he stared at his mother and sister. *I'm sorry!* he wanted to scream. *I did not think they would execute you.*

He had anticipated amputation of a foot or the removal of their ears.

The guards forced Junjie to watch Shen and his mother's execution. Blood pustules erupted on their strained maws and cheeks as they chewed. Baubles of crimson dripped from their earlobes and nostrils. It would take his mother and Shen half a workday to die.

To distract himself, Junjie began to sing a solemn tribute to the Emperor Xuantong, the only melody he knew from camp:

Solidify our golden empire,
Underneath the aegis of heaven,
All of civilization will cease to toil,
United in happiness and mirth,
As long as the Qing rules.
Our empire is emblazoned by light,
And our boundaries are vast and preserved.

"I curse you, Junjie," Shen shrilled. Her last words were cut off when the guards joined Junjie in a rousing chorus.

Junjie thought he'd be allotted his reward after the execution. His hunger clawed inside him like a diseased rodent. He approached the youthful turnip-faced guard he had bartered with. "Excuse me, sir," he said, bowing with deliberate reverence, "but when will I receive my extra portions?"

The guard laughed. "What are you talking about, donkey-shit traitor?"

"Please, I'm hungry!" he begged.

The guard, finding Junjie's cries to be irritating, assigned him the Death Shift. "This is your great reward, prisoner," he mocked.

Instead of a usual workday and a five-hour slumber in his bunker, Junjie would labour in the caves until his death. No one on the Death Shift had lived more than twelve days, except for a broad-shouldered young man who had lasted for twenty-four days before succumbing to fatal exhaustion.

Junjie wept bitterly at the news.

On the Death Shift, the wafting white and gun-yellow smoke from the bog choked his lungs. Around him, the white stalactites hummed excitedly. The prisoners avoided each other—they were no longer members of the living. And because Junjie's family was dead, he was truly alone.

The chorus of the guards rang out multiple times daily, like squabbling children: "Son of a bitch!" "Traitor!" "Human filth!" "Scum of the earth!"

Each insult, hurled with an aggressive globule of spit, bounced off Junjie like sharp pebbles. When they grew tired of abusing him, the guards talked about past dinners: grainy ox hooves and glass-coloured noodles made out of sweet yellow potatoes. How one guard's mother and grandmother would lovingly fry up translucent animal fat and serve it with a garnish of garlic and hearts of chopped ginger. Like Junjie, the camp guards had only food to live for. They spoke of feasts to be consumed outside the black mountain: slabs of corned beef, the creamy epidermis of freshly slaughtered chicken.

"Why did we ever take this cursed job where we are considered fourth-class citizens?" the guards lamented. "The food is subpar!"

"We could have worked in the paddies of Longsheng and eaten our fill of rice!"

"My cousin owns a pig farm in Hangzhou and is looking for workers. The shifts are only hard during the slaughter season, but every day, the workers feast like kings! The weather is warm, and they eat meat and fresh vegetables. Why did we choose to watch the worst scum of China?"

At their unfiltered talk, Junjie's stomach churned longingly. How astounding to be able to eat to one's satisfaction.

When the guards weren't looking, Junjie tried to sneak a cloudy white mushroom between his lips. What could the guards do? If they hacked off his hands, how could he continue to pick mushrooms? The thought caused him to giggle. Possessed by fits of animal laughter, he grinned at the other prisoners, and they gave him an even wider berth.

A few workdays later, Junjie tried stealing again. But when the guard's back was turned, he accidentally held a blushingly pink poison mushroom for too long, which blistered his fingertips. He yelped and smeared his bloody hand on his trousers. Junjie, shuddering, remembered how his sister and mother had expired.

The next night, an inexperienced sentry was assigned to the Death Shift. When the guard abandoned his watch to fornicate with a female prisoner, Junjie swiftly rubbed pink poison mushrooms on his face, arms, and wrists. To stop himself from shrieking, he chomped down on his tongue. He crumpled to the cave floor, mushroom filaments scattered in his bleeding palms, pretending that he had committed suicide.

The new guard returned, and glimpsing Junjie's cockroach-sized blisters, shouted a curse to the gods. "This piece of scum is dead! What horrible luck I have!" A more experienced guard would have stabbed Junjie's body to ascertain that the prisoner was deceased. Grunting, the guard dragged Junjie to the mound of bodies that were taken up nightly on the lift to the exterior world.

Nearly suffocating among the rotting corpses, Junjie lay immobilized, eyes shuttered, until he heard the grinding elevator halt. He wriggled to untangle himself from heavy limbs. The stench of day-old cadaver and maggots nearly made him gag, but he forced himself to take barely there breaths with his parched mouth. He counted, anxious, to fifty only, because he had not been taught what other numbers followed. He crawled behind a military transport wagon, inhaled, counted fifty more pulsing heartbeats. He waited.

Escape was possible.

The tunnel was dark metal-grey, but at its narrowing mouth, Junjie thought he could almost see an indistinct light. He treaded towards it. His heart began to *thump thump* in drumbeats. All he had to do was run across twenty hectares to his freedom. To the lush fields and rice paddies of southern China, then onwards to a faraway place called Hong Kong. As a diligent farmhand, he'd feast on warm pig stomachs and generous portions of fresh shallots every night. Distracted by the prospect of food, Junjie dropped the poisoned toadstools that he had laced between his fingers.

Where the mushrooms fell, out of the earth sprung his undead sister Shen. Her bone-yellow eyes flamed. Her fingers were charred. She laughed at him—it was a bitter, opaque sound. Blood poured from her flared nostrils.

"You're a hallucination from the poison," Junjie whispered.

Junjie took a step right, but Shen's bullish body blocked him. Swivelling his head, he glimpsed his undead mother. Her thin, rotting arms were outstretched, as though beckoning him. But she was not smiling. She was a dead-eyed spectre with maggots burrowed in a once human face. Both his sister and mother loomed over him.

Junjie understood that he had never once been loved.

Deciding that nothing living or departed would stop him, Junjie ran towards the fading light, stumbling into Shen's monstrous limbs. She shoved him backwards, refusing to let him pass, as if she was playing a game. When they were small children, she would grab his ration of old radish from his wooden bowl and hold it high, knowing that he could not reach it, making him jump over and over again until she finally grinned and let him have his breakfast.

"Go away," Junjie whispered. "You cannot be alive."

His sister's demon, as colossal as the mountain of death, hissed in response. Her shadow seemed to unwind for hectares, across the jagged walls inside Death Valley, dissolving any cracks of light from outside.

"Traitor," his sister snarled.

"I made a mistake," Junjie begged.

Shen opened her rotting mouth: "Guards! Guards! A prisoner is escaping!" His mother joined her. Death had finally given them immense power. "Guards, guards! A prisoner is escaping! Help!"

Junjie charged towards the dwindling light.

He did not slow down even when one of the guards pointed at him with his gun. "Halt!" he shrieked over the rampant howls of his sister and mother. "Get on the ground, human filth!" He did not stop as shrill, cracking shots, *one, two, three, four,* exploded into his tiny, heaving shoulders. So certain of his escape, he kept running even as his body shuddered.

In front of him, Shen and his mother transformed into malevolent beasts, a heady combination of animals he didn't recognize, all horned, clawed, and fanged red-eyed demons. The new evils, as one entity, swooped upon the guards. The men attempted to stab the monsters with their bayonets but they could not puncture their beastly skins. "Repent," his former sister and mother screamed in rasping, terrible octaves. "Repent for your crimes against us."

To his surprise, Junjie seemed to shed his own body; it was as if he were suddenly flying, watching another version of himself, his doppelgänger, face down and motionless on the cave ground.

Junjie stumbled onwards, feeling delirious. He felt thankful for a second chance as the blur of guards and screaming evils grew distant behind him. He imagined air cooling his sweaty face once he reached the mountain's summit. *What would the sky feel like on my skin at this very moment?* he thought. *Would the outside world always be as dark as the mushroom caves?*

The light in the tunnel slid towards him, full and yellow and magnificent. Laid out in front of him was a tremendous feast. A low wooden table of seared pig meat, bulbous red onions, dark orange potatoes, and large clay bowls of steaming jasmine rice. He could not believe his good fortune. With his fingers, Junjie grabbed and scooped seconds, thirds, and fourths. Never had food tasted so fresh—the onions seemed ripped directly from the soil, and the meat tasted hot and syrupy. He tore off a large piece of pig marbled with oily fat, tossed it into his open mouth.

It slid down his throat too easily. As he reached for another handful, he started choking. Ribbons of flesh pink, bone white, and crimson bulleted his vision. Then, to his dismay, he could feel rough hands yanking at him. "Not yet," Junjie said. He could feel himself being dragged downwards, being dismembered. Then gently, planted, mushrooming. His mouth filling with sour dirt. Like his ancestor, the greatest traitor of China, and all before and after him, he would be food for the mushrooms.

Sorry, Sister Eunice

We call Sister Eunice an anomaly because her rotund form is truly unrecognizable. Her earth-like circumference and squat stature would probably be the same if someone brainy were to measure her ratio of gravity to girth.

All of us nine-tail fox demons, except for Sister Eunice, are model-thin, five nine, and divinely beautiful in both fox and human form. Plus, like all huli jing, we have luxurious manes, angular features, and golden-brown eyes. We look permanently photoshopped.

Eunice's skin is potholed like a steamed rice cake. Her breath always smells like fermented dairy. The closest we've been to this sort of unpleasing odour was in the fifteenth century, when lice was rampant in the courts of the Yongle Emperor.

Even though none of us want to be Sister Eunice, we think she's hilarious. At group dinner tonight, she shows us her swollen foot and missing shoe.

"I got so drunk this morning I fell down the stairs," she says, pushing up her lenses that remind us of laboratory safety goggles. "Then I woke up on the lawn and I'd lost my Jimmy Choo."

"Oh shit, you poor thing!" we all exclaim. We do our best to tolerate Eunice because that's what good families do.

"Yep," she says, pushing her hair over her face like a shower curtain. "Fifth time this semester."

Come to think of it, Sister Eunice has a bit of a drug and alcohol problem. Actually, we all do. You would too if you were immortal, over six hundred years old and masquerading as a twenty-something-old Gen-Zer in an all-Asian sorority, Sigma Omicron Pi, at San Francisco State U.

For centuries, we huli jing have been migrating and shape-shifting into human form. We have travelled through the wild terrains of China, Korea, and Japan, destroying townships, marriages, and political careers with enthusiasm. Behind our penchant for destruction lies a manic appetite for human gris-tle. Once you've gnawed on a merchant on a ship to India or a hopeful farmer looking for a wife, it's hard to be content with a stomach half-empty with rabbit.

Fox demons are selfish creatures, meant to inhabit caves in the black forests of Xinjiang alone. We are not meant to live as pack members at an old colonial mansion, protected by the collegiate moss and the genteel veneer of an Ivy Tower. It still baffles us that we are forced to share our prey—the frat boy who reeks of beer and the stoner-loner with Dorito breath. We suppose it's just good table manners. During our biweekly group dinner, while sucking on tendons and crunching pelvic bones, we want to lunge and tear out each other's throats. But it's against house rules at Sigma Omicron Pi. *Thou shalt not kill or maim a huli jing sister until threat of extinction is over.* By des-sert time, which is always raw liver, we think about smothering each other with fluffy pink pillows. By after-dinner drinks, we wonder why we don't just throw ourselves out a window.

"So Eunice," we say instead, forcing down our instincts for mass homicide and suicide, "tell us what happened again to your shoe?"

What we don't tell Sister Eunice is that one of us stole her right Jimmy Choo after she passed out drinking a dozen rum and Cokes.

Sometimes when we're intoxicated, we waltz into campus bars and shake our immortal asses to Ariana Grande and Drake. Sister Cee-Cee will badly karaoke to Aretha Franklin, while Sister Tiffany will jam her pink fox tongue down a young visiting scholar's throat. We clutch our gin and tonics to our chests and because we are masquerading as oversexed sorority girls, we occasionally dry-hump one another when we think people are looking. As the night goes on, we loudly sob-sigh for our former lives in Asia, for days of no electricity, pre-internet, when the huli jing were influential starters and manipulators of epic wars between fiefdoms. Under the bar's strobe lights, there's a cruel, scorching hope reflected in each of our gleaming corneas. We crave a permanent return to chaos and nature. It's hard to admit that we're practically irrelevant nowadays. That human beings no longer need the huli jing to assist them in the destruction of their own species.

Anyway, last night, we had been ravenous after group dinner. Pizza, beer, and nachos are like inhaling air from a McDonald's deep fryer. It's a hot human heart and squishy liver that we're after. So after dinner, we all piled into Sister Eunice's red BMW and found a pair of studious-looking international students in front of the J. Paul Leonard Library.

"Join Sigma Omicron Pi!" we had shouted, reciting the propaganda that we had memorized and rehearsed. We preened like black-throated cranes and puffed out our chests like shiny peacocks. In pre-feudal China, commoners used to leave out bowls of goat milk and manuka honey for us on their doorsteps. If there were a famine or drought, peasants would leave out their newborn babies for us to snack on.

The students ignored us.

As huli jing, we all agree that there is zero respect for one's betters in the twenty-first century. We all agree that freethinking egalitarianism has permanently damaged impressionable young minds.

"Um, hello?" we had shouted at our human snacks. "We're talking to you?"

Still these chicks ignored us. So Sister Tiffany grabbed one of our snacks by the collar and yanked her through the passenger-side window. All would have been fine, but Sister Eunice, who had 0.914 blood alcohol content in her system (eleven lime margaritas), blacked out at the wheel and crashed her car into the doors of the J. Paul Leonard Library. No one important was hurt, thank goodness, except for the international student, who was thrown seven feet and impaled upon a flag post. Our other snack was taken to the emergency room, and doctors are iffy about her survival chances. Oh, and our poor Sister Eunice dislocated her left shoulder and cracked three ribs.

When the hospital phoned, Huixang, our benevolent leader/ emergency contact at Sigma Omicron Pi, threatened to expel us for attracting unnecessary attention. To mollify our housemother, Sister Eunice contacted the dean's office the next morning, accepting academic probation and a list of fines on account of public drunkenness and destruction of school property. Even with her upper torso injuries, she bowed in apology to our dearest Huixang and then blew her twelve air kisses as a sign of respect. Poor thing took the fall for all of us!

In the thirteenth century, Huixang (now Helen) claimed to have single-handedly toppled the Song dynasty by leading the Mongols in the Battle of Yamen in 1279, installing the Yuan dynasty. Most of us have been responsible for small massacres, muggings, arsons, and maybe one or two political assassinations, but Helen is our outlier and project manager for a reason. Helen is over a thousand years old. A huli jing can metamorphose into a human female at age fifty, and at age one hundred she becomes airbrushingly beautiful. At age one thousand, a huli jing can cause amnesia in mortals.

So when the dean arrives at Sigma Omicron Pi to present the formal letter of charges, Helen whispers sweetly into his ear and then clouts him on the head. It will take a few hours for the dean to wake up, having forgotten about fining Sigma Omicron Pi.

"What are we supposed to do with you?" Helen hisses at Eunice. "You could have exposed all your sisters. Why does trouble follow you more than anyone else in our sorority?"

"I don't know," Eunice says, her eyes watering. Up close, you can see how mismatched Eunice's eyes are. It's the right eye, yes, that never moves. It could belong to a carnival seer's— it seems to be always questioning our empty interior lives. Did we also mention that Eunice is extremely unpretty to look at, especially when she cries?

"Yes, shit certainly happens to you," we say, making our sad faces that we had spent an unholy amount of time practising when we first migrated to the States. Stoicism is not a Western trait, and Helen said that empathy in the form of exaggerated facial expressions was indispensable to our assimilation and survival.

As we wait for the dean to wake up with amnesia, Helen takes away Eunice's snacking privileges.

"It's okay," Eunice replies bravely. "It's totally fine. I understand. Totally."

"Totally!" we chorus with enthusiasm. We nod with vigour, like we've been instructed to do when hazing co-eds during Rush Week.

We walk the very confused dean to the front door. Because he is woozy and claims to like diversity, we promise that we will start a new scholarship fund for middle-class students and try our best to include other ethnicities besides East Asians at Sigma Omicron Pi.

We don't mean it. We never do.

After being banned from eating humans, Sister Eunice has been fattening herself with hazelnut truffles and eggnog lattes. The winter holidays have been hard on our complexions, but especially tough on Eunice. Her skin is flaky like deep-fried calamari. "Oh honey, no," we say, eyeing her in that pitying way. Did we comment that Eunice's corpulence is an anomaly? Huli jing are usually as thin as tree dryads.

It's not like immigration to a strange country made Eunice frumpy. No political upheaval or notable revolution deformed her in any way. Except for one or two family members being beheaded in front of her and a small incident when she was thrown from a mule-pulled buggy in the seventeenth century, Eunice has no excuse to be so ugly. None of us really knew her pre-sorority, but we assume that Eunice has always been sad and dowdy.

"I have an announcement," Eunice says at the start of our term meeting. She sips her fifth boozy eggnog and burps. It takes a while for us to shush and remember that Eunice is our sister with a drinking problem and that we love her.

"Quiet, ladies!" Helen calls out. "Eunice is going to apologize again for her drunk driving!"

But Eunice, to everyone's shock and dismay, announces that she has just been accepted to the MFA program at San Francisco State.

Her words baffle us because all huli jing major in business, finance, law, medicine, or governmental sciences to prepare for world domination. These are all proven graduate degrees that will increase our survival rate in the twenty-first century.

No one knows quite what to say.

"I'm going to do an MFA," Eunice repeats, shyly.

"What is that?" Helen finally asks, politely, but we can all see the twitchy confusion in her face. Normally our housemother is so skilled at controlling her emotions, so adept at making kindly human faces.

"It's a master's degree in poetry," Eunice says, as if this explains anything. Her beetle-sized eyes shine like eerie crystal balls. She clutches her chubby hands to her unnaturally low breasts. She sighs. At first we think Eunice is passing gas, but then we realize that the sounds are human and euphoric.

We have seen this starry look on Eunice's features once before, at a strip club. "I want to become a human being," she exclaimed after downing six Mollies and prancing around a pole. "I mean, isn't there more to life than eating undergraduates and taking over the world?" Eunice's face had burned like a lit jack-o'-lantern.

"NO NO NO!" we had protested, shaking our heads and nervously swallowing Xanax. "Killing and plotting is our life's purpose!"

To be candid, we had no clue that Sister Eunice was even literate. Her emails in simplified Mandarin, Cantonese, Korean, and even Japanese have always been garbled, mostly incoherent lines of emojis and one-word answers. Sister Eunice, a poet? Is she having a psychotic break?

Being a migrant has its difficulties, but we do our very best to fit in. English, both oral and written, has been such a pain in the ass to acquire. It took most of us fifteen something years to master the dialect and then to incorporate young-person slang without sounding like toddlers. Sister Eunice hasn't even mastered vocal fry yet. So, we ask, how can she be doing an MFA? Is it a new hybridized American slang word?

"You don't really need to be able to write," she says, blushing. "You just need a lot of feelings."

"I don't understand," Helen says. She pulls out her iPhone and slowly says: "Siri, what is M F A?"

"But how are you going to take over the world?" we ask Sister Eunice, scandalized. We flip our human hair extensions in astonishment. We try to argue away the discomfort in our spleens. There's understated horror in our words: "Eunice, how can you be so selfish?"

—

A few centuries ago, we had gathered in the black Nyingchi forests of Tibet. Helen, who had already designated herself our leader, had declared that our species was dying out like the giant panda. Due to technological advances and modernity, we had lost our high status in the East. But if we took over the West and helped large populations of greedy mortals self-destruct, we'd regain our standing. We'd disguise our huli jing human forms as an all-exclusive sorority of Type A girls. We'd eat like monsters and empresses. Because, she said, it would take a month or two before anyone found a less than stellar student among the twenty-four-hour library stacks or bones deposited in a cafeteria deep fryer. She had done an independent study on how Western Gen-Zers and their parents did not feel obligated to like one another. "They're different from us," she assured us. "No loyalty to their kind whatsoever."

"We will feast and secretly rebuild our ranks on the West Coast," Helen had said, convincingly.

But now that we're here, what have we done on a large progressive college campus? Have we avenged ourselves, seized power, affected social change, etc.? Do we, fox demons, just have mirage-like hopes, as dry and unattainable as crossing the Gobi desert? Have we toppled subpar political regimes and started multi-country wars like the good old days? Nope. Huli jing are supposed to be effective haters of humankind, not survivalist assimilating hybrids. The question remains: As an entire species, did we peak in the early nineteenth century?

Helen had made immigration to a foreign land sound so easy.

These thoughts are lost in our nihilistic haze of drinking and hard drugs. They are conflated into our nights of wild dancing at Sigma Omicron Pi fundraisers and parties.

After the first week of winter semester, Sister Eunice stuns us again at mandatory group dinner. She declares that she is having a wild affair with her famous writing professor. Her cow eyes sparkle like LED Christmas lights. A bit of meat— i.e., a geeky choral singer—is stuck between her front teeth. Did we mention that Eunice seems to be suffering from severe gastroesophageal reflux disease? Her breath always reeks of rotten fish and bleach.

And Jesus, there's even an uncanny pinkness, like a period stain, to her otherwise sallow cheeks. Love has given her an unhealthy pallor, it seems.

"It's true love, I tell you," she declares, spit landing like tropical rain on the bloodstained tablecloth. "He's my soulmate for the next ten or twelve years," Eunice says, waving her fork like a cheerleading baton. We hold our very sensitive noses in order not to sniff what must be GERD and advanced tooth decay. When has Eunice last seen a dentist? As Eunice gushes, we stare at her protruding urine-coloured teeth and we are confident that the famous writing professor is visually impaired.

How can Sister Eunice, the worst of all of us, find love before we do? Because we love Eunice, we only ask out of concern. As her sisters, we want to support her in all areas of her academic, professional, and personal life. We love her, we honestly do.

—

Eunice breaks our hearts when she tells us, to our absolute disbelief, that she will be spending two weeks in Paris during spring break. With her lover, the poet professor.

"What's in Paris?" we say, incredulous. We always go to Miami during spring break to munch on the locals.

"Well, there's pastries to eat," Eunice says as she packs her Louis Vuitton luggage set full of La Perla, which we feel she doesn't deserve.

"Really, Eunice. How could you? How can you be so selfish?" we say.

"I know, I know, you guys," Eunice concedes, looking at the floor. She looks so morose, like someone ate her secret pet parakeet, which happened just once or twice at the beginning of the semester. Then we feel obligated to pat our sister's doughy shoulder in comfort. Despite our kindness, Eunice does not cancel her trip.

For amusement, the night before her early morning flight, one of us opens Eunice's suitcase and shreds her lingerie with our extendable two-foot claws. Then we steal another of her Jimmy Choos. This kills an hour of our monotony, and then we hide her passport. She stumbles all over the house, panicking like a blindfolded mule. In her rush, Eunice breaks Helen's Ming dynasty vase, and as punishment, has to wash our housemother's gold Mercedes-Benz before leaving the country.

Eunice eventually finds her passport. Sister Tiffany put it in the freezer, next to the Saran-wrapped torso of the dead mathlete junior.

—

In Miami, on crumbly sugar-cookie beaches, in bars and rowdy nightclubs, we think of Eunice and her famous professor poet in Paris. We think of our dear Eunice as we sip mojitos and eat people.

"But what could be so wonderful about poetry?" we ask ourselves as we gulp our hug drugs like vitamin C. We are doing Buddha's work, munching our way through humanity's population.

Also, is contentment an achievable state, or is it as mythic as nirvana and an orgasm? None of us huli jing have ever experienced these human things. Perhaps happiness is as synthetic as our semipermanent eyelash extensions?

As we pose suggestively in our Stella McCartney bikinis, taking a million group selfies, we keep thinking about bovine-sized Eunice. Is she being wooed with gauche red roses at the Eiffel Tower? Is she stomping, flat-footed, becoming a cliché, along the romantic Left Bank of the River Seine? Is she stuffing her maw at the boulevards of the Champs-Élysées? Those éclairs and foie gras cannot be good for her figure. Is she better off than us? That is the only question on our minds as we dine on sun-baked flesh and slurp up bone marrow.

As we lie awake at night, our bellies swollen with human muscle, we give abundant praise and blessings to Yanluo Wang, the judge of the underworld. Did we mention that we're utterly grateful that we are nothing like poor, infatuated Eunice?

Rising before dawn, Sister Cee-Cee starts a betting pool—is the professor hideous? Most of us bet a few hundred bucks and an ounce of our designer party drug that Eunice's lover is a Quasimodo. In the hotel lobby, after ordering multiple shots of espresso, we take out our iPads and click on his faculty headshot. He is shockingly, boyishly handsome for a man in his late fifties. *What does he see in Eunice?* we wonder, miffed. Maybe he suffers from other impediments, such as mediocre personal hygiene. He can do better than our Sister Eunice. So we scour his Twitter and Instagram, and find nothing but accolades for his literary work.

Poor Eunice, we think, imagining her tripping down the stairs at her four-star Parisian hotel and breaking a doughnut-shaped ankle.

Upon our return to San Francisco, we are not shocked to find a sobbing Eunice on the porch of Sigma Omicron Pi.

"Holy shit, Eunice, your face!" we say by way of greeting.

Her face and neck are pockmarked with crystalloid pimples. The only time we've seen this sort of outbreak was in 1855, when bubonic plague broke out in villages in Yunnan Province. Eating infected peasant skin was poisonous for the huli jing. We remember the rotting pustules and black lymph nodes of our culinary past, and when we glimpse Eunice, we can't help but shudder. Should we force her to see a doctor? Is her leper-like acne contagious? Is it a hybridized form? Did she catch it from the professor?

Eunice's crying is noisy enough to wake all our huli jing demon cousins on other continents. Never mind the other eight sorority houses on Greek Row.

"I called Helen a thousand times, but she isn't picking up her phone," Eunice moans, wiping her snot on her three-seasons-ago Louis Vuitton purse.

We side-eye each other because we all know that Helen is in Brazil plotting a mini revolt with other high-ranking fox demons.

Did Eunice not get the memo? How could Eunice be so besotted with her professor lover that she could forget such an important thing? Helen is working hard to save our kind from extinction.

We let her sob-gasp, her XXL body shaking, without interrupting because it seems like she needs an audience. On closer inspection, Eunice appears to have slimmed down during her European trip. But her taste in clothing is vastly unimproved— she's still wearing her baggy San Fran State U sweatshirt and a pair of mismatched high-heeled Jimmy Choos.

"What happened to your face?" we ask, pulling sympathetic, sisterly expressions.

"Stress, I guess," she admits.

"You poor, poor thing!" we exclaim, and as she flings herself into our tanned arms, we recoil.

"I should have listened to you guys about Paris," she howls.

"You really should have," we say, trying not to chide her. We all agree to pretend that Paris never happened if she does a few chores. "Carry our bags!" we say, and she quickly complies. We say, because we are grateful beings, that she can sleep in the basement tonight.

After dinner, after seven strawberry daiquiris, Eunice, wailing, confesses that the professor invited another female student to Paris. The famous poet, who is married with five children and a reasonably attractive wife, booked adjacent hotel rooms for his trysts without telling Eunice about his second lover. Neither Eunice nor her classmate knew about one another. Furious, Eunice transformed into a nine-tailed fox and confronted the professor. She planned to eat him for a late-night snack, having already been treated to coq au vin and crème brûlée for dinner.

We gasp, because high-profile kills are frowned upon. We suppose she could have a free pass in Paris, depending on how famous the professor was, internationally, etc.

"So, just how famous *is* your ex-lover?" we ask, and Eunice says that he is a poet with just one major national award. We all agree that devouring him would have been acceptable since he has only won a Pulitzer.

Anyway, when Eunice turned into a fox, she tried to bite his neck but missed. She couldn't find the professor's carotid artery. She managed to cleanly bite off his thumb and baby finger on his writing hand. But how was she to know that he was ambidextrous? He punched her in the jaw and escaped the room, screaming that Eunice was a werewolf. "Lycanthrope!" he had hollered, as he tripped on the lobby stairs.

This is the first time that anyone has ever mistaken a huli jing for a common werewolf. We tell her that we would have been so offended if it had happened to us. We would have sent a text afterwards to correct the professor.

"You didn't get more than a mouthful of him?" we ask, astonished. "You should have swallowed at least one of his hands!"

From an animalistic and evolutionary perspective, huli jing are also supposed to know how to kill our food. Of course, Eunice is the exception. At the hotel, Le Méridien Etoile, near the Arc de Triomphe, Eunice only managed to injure herself. She shows us her missing front teeth from the scuffle and we notice the litchi-sized lump under her chin.

"Shit, Eunice," we say, horrified that a mortal, let alone a middle-aged poet, could outwit a huli jing.

—

When Helen returns, she announces that we, as a species, need to up our efforts to devour between 100 and 105 humans by the following Lunar New Year. We promise that we will do our best to mingle at Greek events. Helen recoils when she sees the hideous state of Eunice's face, but quickly recovers, asking in a mild voice if Eunice has slacked on her use of daily cosmetics.

"Oh my god, I'm so sorry, Helen," Eunice cries, bowing and scratching herself. We do our best to hide our disgust when we notice flakes of dried skin falling onto the living room's faux-fur pink rug.

It is only after six injections of corticosteroids that Eunice's skin clears up a bit and she can finally go back to classes. Her face no longer looks like it's been through a vegetable grater. And praise Buddha, her pimples no longer resemble genetically modified tomatoes.

Perhaps we are curious; perhaps we are bored. Perhaps we are on the verge of an extraordinary mental collapse or the start of a six-hundred-year-old identity crisis. But we shock ourselves when we agree to go with Eunice to a reading hosted by the English department. The writing professor is supposed to be promoting his new collection of love poetry in iambic pentameter. But thankfully, at the last minute, the dean cancels the book launch on account of a suicide within the student body.

In our weekly meeting, Eunice reports that the professor believes that he had suffered a moderate schizoid break in Paris. He can't explain the missing fingers, but to his wife and colleagues and other students, he says that a coyote or raccoon chewed them off while he was at a prestigious writing colony. He makes a joke about it in workshop, all the while ignoring

Eunice. Poor Sister Eunice got off easy. Apparently, the other classmate, the co-ed in Paris, was suffering from severe depression. When she complained about the professor seeing Eunice, he gave her an F, and she jumped out a dormitory window. Splat. Eunice says that she got a C plus for the class, which we acknowledge is a pretty decent grade.

"It's not stellar," Eunice says, wrinkling her pug-like nose. "Standards are different in creative writing. Everyone usually gets an A."

"But what did you expect?" we say. "You bit off two of the man's fingers."

According to Helen's house rules at Sigma Omicron Pi, we are allowed to transform back into our original demon fox forms only after final exams. For twenty-four to seventy-two hours, we're permitted to roam freely on campus and eat garbage along the I-5. But it appears Eunice was more upset about the affair than she let on. Without consulting anyone, she turned into a fox to stalk her professor poet, who has found another student to prey on. In fox form, she followed him from a Thai restaurant to a dessert café. While trotting after the poet, she got hit by a car, and despite her best efforts, she cannot turn back into her subpar human form.

In the living room of our sorority house, she tells us all this in pitiful fox screams. Shows us one of her badly crushed tails.

"At least you still have eight left," Sister Cee-Cee says, bringing out green Jell-O shots on a tray. "Why is everything always about you?"

But Eunice is our sister and we love her. We really do. We tell Eunice to repeat her story about getting hit by a car while crossing the road. And we gasp and clap and whoop in all the right places. We have no advice to give her, so we pour her a princely drink of gin in an unwashed cereal bowl. Eunice, always eager to please, laps it up like a newborn pup. She makes a mess on the mahogany floor.

"This is bullshit," Helen says, clucking in an irritated but motherly way. "Never in over a thousand years has a huli jing been unable to transform back into human form."

"Oh Eunice," we sigh. "It would only happen to you."

Pets, especially sizeable ones, are not allowed at Sigma Omicron Pi. We give Eunice a week to turn back into her human shape, and pray that her matronly form will be much improved. Eunice tries—she bares her teeth and looks anxiously constipated. Because we are her sisters, we massage her ratty, mucus-coloured fur and call out motivating mantras. "Just do it!" we shout. "Nike is right!" But eventually, we concede that we just can't have a wild animal in the house, and on college premises, too. We can't have anyone suspecting that we love to dine on undergraduate students. Also, if you must know, Eunice leaves her fox droppings everywhere. We even found a turd in Sister Tiffany's new Gucci bag.

We say to Eunice, we are a sought-after sorority at a well-ranked university. San Fran State may not be Ivy League, but as huli jing, we do have some standards to maintain.

It is decided by unanimous group vote that fox-shaped Eunice has got to go.

"I understand," Eunice yaps in her fox voice. Eight tails limp down.

Maybe Eunice will wander back to China, but we hear that the Pacific Northwest has some really nice trees and organic squirrels to eat.

On Eunice's last day at the house we think we should maybe bake her some cupcakes and maybe gift her with some freshly maimed entrails. But none of us have any time because there are papers to write and then there's our epic formal to plan. The theme this year is Exceptional Villains, which means that we can just go as ourselves. We talk about maybe giving Sister Eunice a map of California, hosting a barbecue with some fraternity cuties, or maybe writing a quickie sticky note.

At Eunice's goodbye party on our front lawn, we bring out quality bourbon and let her lap it from the bottle.

"We love you, Sister Eunice," we say. "We were going to make you forty pink cupcakes and buy you a good luck/sorry card."

"Oh, you guys," Eunice purrs, looking at us with those red lopsided eyes. "I'll miss you so much!"

We also say that Eunice should visit us when she becomes humanoid again. But in a way that lets her know we're just being nice and that we really don't mean it. She makes a soothing, choking noise as if to comfort us. Imagine that! As if to comfort us! Us great sisters of Sigma Omicron Pi!

As we stroke our gelled manicured fingers through Eunice's knotty fur, we wonder why her fox shape is as frumpy as her human figure. "Poor, poor Eunice," we say, and we almost mean it. We mention that we would drive her to the woods, but we're just too busy with school and party planning and glitzy world domination.

We time our goodbye to exactly six minutes because our lives are so full and chaotic, and compared with us, fox-Eunice has unlimited free time. Without glancing back, linking arms in sisterly solidarity, we march in twos and threes towards our sorority house. In the premature morning breeze, it is almost as if Sigma Omicron Pi's pink roof flag is waving at Eunice in apology.

We wonder whether Eunice will have a chance at bliss as a wild animal in America. Will the animals of the woodland love her, like we do?

And we wonder when, like Eunice, we will finally be free of our hominid forms. Back in Asia, we'd leave our dank caves twice a year to wreak disaster on unsuspecting humans. We'd coo with our foxy voices right before chomping through a jugular vein, while the salty river breeze prickled our pointy ears. In Asia, never had we been freer to feast proudly in the lush forests of Changbai. In Asia, we would never be sisters stuck under one roof.

As we head to Statistics class, we imagine Eunice, eight tails raised, wandering among the perky evergreen trees. We can picture it: under the bald Californian sun, our girl Eunice, sniffing the clean air and taking a long, excited dump in the Pacific Ocean. And yet, so many thoughts irk us. Like, for instance, is Sister Eunice really free? We just really want to know if she is less or more free than the rest of us. We're only asking because we care about her so much. Like, will she end up happier than all of us huli jing? Will she finally stop conforming to the rules and customs of this strange land?

We're so sorry, Sister Eunice. We love you, we really do.

A Bloodletting of Trees

Wearing lotus shoes the colour of fledgling suns, Yuchen and Meifan, whose feet were freshly bound, had to be hoisted upon their male relations' shoulders. *As if we are livestock*, Yuchen thought, swallowing the soupy bitterness that curdled in her throat.

"If only we could run away," she lamented to her sister, briefly forgetting that Meifan was asleep. But Yuchen was careful not to let her relatives, or the enemy, hear. Sentries with broadswords and sharpened bayonets paced anxiously by the blood-red village outposts. How long before legions of vicious Shan soldiers invaded? Where were the Emperor's promised reinforcements? After all, the township of Anding had already been occupied once at the start of the Ming-Mong Mao War a year ago, before their own soldiers forced Shan troops to retreat into the crevasses of the yellow Gaoligong Mountains. There were daily reports of starving peasants, begging for imperial assistance, who burned ink paintings of the Hongwu Emperor Zhu Yuanzhang, when no food rations from the capital arrived. Servants whispered that abandoned siheyuans in the countryside loomed like greying ghouls. In the shadeless west of Jingdong Province, there were rumours of farmers selling fresh-faced girls instead of squawking chickens.

Honour bound by blood lineage and tradition, Big Uncle and his four dutiful sons had no choice but to carry the sisters to the white forest. The funeral procession had barely marched five hundred steps from the red birch gates of their township when a farmer in a tattered loincloth stepped into their path. Yuchen was strapped to the back of her oldest cousin, a boy of seventeen with spotty, windblown features. She had admired him when they were growing up. Yuchen peeked over her cousin's shoulder.

"How much?" the pockmarked farmer asked. "For the pretty girl, and the meaty one too," he said, gesturing at Yuchen.

Yuchen was only twelve summers old, and also two seasons pregnant. She reached for her older sister's hand, but Meifan was still asleep. Her shoulders were straight, though, her neck stretched high as if at any moment she would be adorned with an empress's mianguan crown of dangling ivory pearls. As she slept, her rose-pink mouth smirked.

"These noble women are recently widowed and tainted by death," Big Uncle said, his features hardening. "How dare you interrupt their execution! You will show respect to the concubines of the late Baron of Anding."

Their husband, the Baron, had set fire to himself, his wives, his harem of child-concubines, his beloved hunting dogs, and his servants. Half a fortnight ago, hearing news of a second Shan invasion, he had bolted shut the ancestral siheyuan's doors, permitting none of his household to flee. Yuchen and Meifan had been resting in the outer hydrangea gardens when the fire started.

Newly crippled with tightly wound, petal-sized feet in their exquisite yellow lotus shoes, they were unable to walk. Yuchen had screamed at Meifan to begin crawling on her knees. "If he lives, I will kill the Baron," she promised her sister. Meifan, quietly sobbing, had lain down on the muddy road. Yuchen had no choice but to yank on her sister's twice-wound braid until she got up. While the siheyuan burned, it took the foot-crippled sisters nearly a quarter of a day to crawl to the village square, which was only thirty hectares away. Elbows raw, knees pork-coloured and goried, Yuchen had felt relief when they reached Big Uncle's house, until she remembered that their fate was bound to their husband's. In Jingdong, since the illustrious Ming dynasty, widows, whether wives or concubines, were carried into the primordial white forest to die. Yuchen and Meifan were forbidden to outlive their husband.

"I have three copper pieces," the farmer continued, refusing to bow in respect. His words were guttural, the harsh accent of the southern Yangtze. He flashed the tiny coins in his brown, square palm.

"Let our procession pass," Big Uncle ordered. Her uncle had fought in the Ming-Mong Mao War under General Mu Ying, and had a venerated machete, a dao, strapped to his box-like shoulders. He was a war hero, honourably discharged when a long spear impaled his thigh and a fragment of the enemy shaft embedded itself in his bone.

Still the farmer refused to leave the dirt road. "Please," the man begged. "My wife and infants are starving. Why should funeral rituals count in wartime? Why should these girls feed the animals instead of their fellow countrymen?"

Big Uncle grunted. He was a rigid man who believed in the empire, imperialism, and the war against the Shan. He took slow, heavy breaths, and approached the farmer as if appeasing an angry boar.

With his dao, Big Uncle quickly gutted the starving man, then ordered the youngest of his four sons to collect the three copper coins and the man's stupefied head. The fourth son also took the farmer's pointed straw hat and placed it on his own head to ward against the sun.

Yuchen winced at the farmer's headless body. Blood still shocked her. She glanced at her older sister, who had woken and was staring, almost haughtily, at the dead man. With her mouth in a cat's sneer, Meifan looked self-possessed and regal, fit to be an Emperor's First Wife. Unlike her sister, Yuchen was born soft and plump like a freshly steamed dumpling. Even their former servants took advantage of her inability to give orders.

In wartime, she knew Big Uncle could sell the man's head at a butcher's for nine copper pieces. If they found his wife and children farther down the road, Big Uncle could sell them, dead or alive, too.

A fortnight before the fire, Meifan and Yuchen had their tiny lotus feet rebroken and rebandaged at the Baron's insistence. This was the third time that their feet had been reshaped for status and beauty—once, when they were three and five years, and again when their silhouettes had displeased the matchmaker, who insisted that noble women should hack off an inch from their heels. This was at the start of the war, just before their father had been killed mid-battle, and their mother, not wanting to be a widow, hanged herself in her private rose garden. The Baron had agreed to accept them as lesser concubines as a favour to Big Uncle, who had his own wives and children to feed.

"My child-concubines have the feet of mules," the Baron had shouted at the bone doctor one afternoon. "Make their feet daintier and more beautiful by shortening a few inches!"

Yuchen and Meifan had screamed as the bone doctor, bowing and apologetic, had sawed off their big and last toes. With remorseful precision, the doctor, who served all the high-class families in this province, had then rebent and resnapped their arches, pushing their five-inch bones into smaller flower shapes. He had folded their second, third, and fourth toes like brittle origami. To prevent infection, he had scraped off their pea-sized toenails before stitching their mutilated feet into fresh cotton bandages.

Looking pleased, the Baron had presented his young concubines with matching pairs of flower-sized lotus shoes. Cut from the creamiest sun-tinted silk from Zhejiang, the shoes were cone-shaped with a sharp wedged heel, a blank tapestry for Meifan and Yuchen to personalize with intricate embroidery. The girls cried unsparingly as their rebroken feet were squeezed into their ornamental shoes. Yet they couldn't help but be astonished by this unexpected gift of finery.

That evening, the Baron demanded that the girls' severed toes be boiled in a medicinal turtle soup, claiming it would grant him eternal life. Meifan, chewing on stale cypress bark to numb the pain, had been the one who had cooked the bone soup. Unable to walk, she had instructed the servants to carry her and a tray of soup to the Baron's chambers.

"Are you alive or dead?" the Baron had shouted at Meifan, who had only nodded. When she was slow to answer, he had struck her between the eyes.

In his chambers, Meifan sat on a high wooden stool beside his canopied bed and fed him the soup while he blathered about horned demons and violent apparitions. She ignored the spectacle of her soggy toes floating in the greasy broth.

That night, she and Yuchen had prayed that their fate would irreparably change.

Grim-faced, the funeral procession marched farther from Anding, past abandoned farms and desiccated fields. Four seasons of fighting and starvation had caused many peasants to cannibalize their elderly parents and flee across the purple Guanchuan River. The townspeople also said that five thousand years ago, the white forest was cursed by an aristocrat's young, genteel wife who originally caused Anding's crops, animals, and men to die. Neighbours witnessed her drain poison, the evil gu, from complaining rattlesnakes and black scorpions that lived in tall sorghum grasses. When each of her babies arrived tiny and stillborn, the panicked husband nailed his wife to the tallest tree in the forest, still alive. It was said the woods were cursed with her feral screams.

As the white forest came into view, the spectral trees seemed to awaken in their presence. Each member of the procession heard their name whispered. The whispers grew louder as they approached.

"I cannot go into the woods," the eldest son said. He put Yuchen down, covering his ears. "It's cursed! It knows my name! It says I will die!"

Big Uncle and his oldest son argued like clashing bulls. Big

Uncle scoffed. "You will go in or you will no longer carry the family name!"

Yuchen understood as well as her cousin that the eldest son who squandered his father's legacy was as doomed as a female widow. He'd be allowed to disembowel himself with a long sword and his body parts would be pickled, used to honourably feed his family during the war. The eldest son picked up Yuchen, like a lumpy rucksack of turnips, and slung her over his back. She wiggled in discomfort.

The funeral procession, solemn-eyed and unflinching, entered the forest.

A month earlier, a phalanx of Shan soldiers had gone into the woods and disappeared. A young village girl, whom they had dragged with them, had returned, bloody and screaming. The townsfolk said the aristocrat's wife had taken pity on the poor girl and allowed her to return to the living. Big Uncle did not believe the rumours, dismissing them as old women's tales, stories uttered by gossipy servants and foolish girls to pass time.

As a child, Yuchen had been fascinated by the stories of the hairy, white coppices that could not be chopped down. Luminescent foliage that was immune to both fire and flooding. No weapon or imperial order from China's blessed emperors could destroy the haunted trees. Shamans, wise men, monks, and ancient wūpó, witches, had all been consulted, but the forest was immortal.

Sometimes, with the bored schoolgirls in the village, Yuchen would stand on the periphery of the white forest. She'd scream away her petty jealousies, which included her annoyance at Meifan's beauty, once the subject of daily conversation in Anding. Without fail, the trees would always scream back—not an echo, but a wailing, as though they were alive and being slowly dismembered. It had always been a game to Yuchen. Could she yell louder than the trees?

Later, on a dare from the older girls, she had touched the spider-like needles of a spruce. She could feel its heat, pulsing and unkind, as though it were inhaling her, luring her inside its trunk. A discomfiting warmth started to enfold her. She smelled a wet stickiness of old blood and burning sap. It was as if she was being lovingly digested. When something nipped her thumb, she shrieked, leapt back, and the tree imitated her screams, multifold. In her panic, Yuchen thought she had seen a red wet smear of a mouth on the trunk. She looked around for the other girls, but they were gone.

Yuchen craned her neck. She wanted to reassure Meifan, but her older sister had passed out again. Yuchen touched her stomach and felt nothing.

That morning, Big Uncle had given them bitter tea of black opium, which was supposed to make the girls drowsy. Yuchen had pretended to sip her sour drink. When Big Uncle had been distracted, she spat the warm liquid onto the clay floor tiles.

"What can we do if it's drugged?" Meifan had said. "We're going to die anyway."

"You don't know the future!" Yuchen had pleaded.

Shrugging, Meifan had finished her tea.

With painstaking effort, Big Uncle's two wives had knotted Yuchen's and Meifan's hair with wooden jis. They had powdered the girls' cheeks with leftover flour and dressed them in ill-fitting white cotton sangfus, the traditional hooded mourning gowns of Anding's widows. Big Uncle's first wife said that perhaps her husband would drown the girls in a creek. The second wife had packed the sisters a heavy burlap cloth—saying it would be more comfortable if he left them to starve to death or be consumed by wild animals on a blanket. "Good luck in the afterlife," they had said, touching the girls' broken feet and admiring their lotus shoes, which were an unusual shade of raw, unfiltered sunlight.

Yuchen wanted to know how Big Uncle was going to kill them. Would it be merciful as his second wife predicted? Would he just leave them and march back to his soon-to-be-occupied village?

"Will you kill us now?" she asked, but Big Uncle did not respond.

"I don't want to know, sister," Meifan mumbled, having woken but still blurry-eyed. She shuddered as the forest shook all around them. The forest screeched. *AHHHHHHHHHH! AHHHHHHHHH! AHHHHHHHHHHHH!*

"I'd rather know," Yuchen insisted.

"We are not leaving you to die in the forest," Big Uncle said. His voice was coldly detached, as if he were deliberating the sale of a prized pig or goat. "We have notified a fleet of merchants from the town of Moshale who are waiting for us four days from here. The forest is the safest and quickest path away from the fighting. There will be no Shan soldiers to stop us. The merchants have promised to sell you to bathhouses in Manchuria."

"But what about funeral tradition?" Yuchen asked, touching her stomach protectively. If a bathhouse bought Yuchen and Meifan for an exorbitant sum, the sisters would be forced to entertain men—if she were permitted to live.

As though reading her mind, her uncle continued, "They may not want your baby, Yuchen, although your feet may fetch five gold pieces."

Yuchen had heard that the Baron's head cook had traded his wife to hungry Shan soldiers to save himself and their infant son. She had known the wife well, a kindly woman who worked as a laundress in their household. She always washed Yuchen's garments first and clucked at her husband to properly feed the girls. One day, she vanished, and Yuchen and Meifan were told that they'd have to do their own washing in the river. Other servants started to disappear, along with silver accoutrements and fine blue porcelain dishes. Stories and hushed warnings moved, like creeping insects, through the Baron's household.

Yuchen shook like the trees around her. "Uncle, we will all probably die before reaching the merchants. You should just leave us here and return back to town!"

Her uncle leisurely urinated on the scaly base of a tree. Yuchen knew that she could not argue with him. His instinct to survive was greater than hers.

Her oldest cousin, who was carrying her, murmured, "I wish you luck in Manchuria, Cousin." He had always known that she had a fondness for him and would good-naturedly tease her before the war. If she had not been sold to the Baron, perhaps he would have married her as a first or second wife. He gently rearranged her on his shoulders.

Big Uncle motioned at his sons to continue their sojourn into the forest.

"We're nearly there!" the fourth son shouted, pointing to the top of a giant white pillar. The brothers stopped to look, squinting up into the grey sky. No one in Anding had ever gone farther than the pillar in the funeral clearing, but Big Uncle ordered them to hurry.

As they pushed forward, the thicket squalled. "Do not pass," a young girl's voice sang out. "You must leave now!" With his dao, Big Uncle hacked at the spindly foliage to clear a path for their procession. If he heard the warning, he seemed not to care. Superstition was for village idiots, he lectured his sons. They would be rewarded for their bravery, he coaxed them.

As the sun started its descent, the brothers talked-storied of hunting pinched-faced pheasants in springtime, their longing for spicy millet wine, and visits to Anding's eminent matchmaker pre-war. "She asked if I preferred a hard worker or a great beauty, and I said it wouldn't matter if my wife was rich," the second oldest boasted. Yuchen caught Meifan's eye and sighed. The brothers seemed to relax slightly until the trees started to whisper: "Leave if you want to live." Hesitating, they looked to Big Uncle, who seemed unaffected.

"Father must be losing his hearing," the third son teased, which earned him a clout from Big Uncle. The nervous jokes and inane talk-stories continued until the procession reached the funeral clearing. The circular meadow, larger than any nobleman's private garden in Anding, was surrounded by twelve white trees. The grass was shorn and bone white, studded by fleshy chrysanthemums peeking out from the earth like infant heads, emanating a sweet stench. The procession looked up at the giant pillar planted in the centre of the clearing. In oversized, hasty strokes of dark red calligraphy, someone had painted a warning:

IMMINENT DYING (即将死亡).

At the base of the pillar, yellow-white skeletons and insect-ridden corpses of Anding's widows lay curled up on embroidered blankets. *Like we are grand trophies to be collected and abandoned*, Yuchen thought sadly. Ornate headpieces encrusted with empress-sized rubies and emeralds adorned the skeletons of great noble birth. She touched her own simple wooden ji by reflex. Peasant women were given beige paper dolls, cracked stone mirrors, and crude wooden combs. A few were even gifted with domestic items like old brooms and tattered cleaning rags. Poor widows would need to be useful in the afterlife. *I would rather be impoverished in the afterlife than be wed to the Baron again*, Yuchen thought, shuddering.

Soldiers and thieves had attempted to steal the jewelled offerings, but it was said that unnatural deaths had befallen them. Big Uncle did not believe these tales. As his military-issue sandals of deer hide and rattan stomped over crumbly bones, he pointed out the treasures and estimated their worth to his four sons, assuring them they would be rewarded for their courage on their way back to Anding.

"It is hopeless," Meifan said to Yuchen. "We will die."

—

After their wedding to the Baron, Meifan had changed, seemingly overnight. In their shared mahogany chuáng, in the suffocating darkness, Yuchen listened to her sister's low heartbeat until orange roosters, crowing, woke them at dawn, and the servants brought them bowls of salty rice gruel and spicy oolong tea for breakfast. Like a stone coffin, Meifan had closed herself off in the Baron's house, becoming tight-lipped and resigned to her fate. She accepted punishments on her sister's behalf, but she stopped indulging in idle talk or frivolous dreams of the future.

Before they became child-concubines, Yuchen had wanted to find their oldest brother in Beijing. Big Brother had left Anding five years before the war to study urban planning in the capital. He was a gifted student, a man of maps, roads, and precision. In his letters, he had been furious when he found out that his sisters had been sold as concubines, with their feet broken and bound. *Join me,* he had told the girls. But then the letters stopped. The Baron claimed that no further correspondence had arrived from the capital.

Beijing has buildings and palaces as tall as the bluest mountains in Jingdong Province, Big Brother had written in his last letter. *The capital thrives on erudite knowledge and one's endurance for hard work. I am nearly done with my studies to be one of the Emperor Hongwu's finest urban planners, and I have befriended one of his many sons. I will soon be given a mid-ranking position at the Imperial Court to start planning new roads from the city to the far-reaching villages. How can Big Uncle have sold you to that demon? This is unfathomable! If Father were alive, he'd be ashamed to call him Older Brother. I will write to Uncle immediately to let him know that you should be sent to the capital, to my care. I shall send someone for you if I am not able to leave.*

Yuchen wondered if he was still alive. Would she finally see him again, and her mother and father, in the afterlife? Would she meet her unborn child as a spirit? Would she come to love it? She feared that the fetus was a monster, half-living, half-mad.

Sunlight was wavering into a bronzy ochre. Nothing moved around them, yet they were followed by a preternatural coldness. The brothers kept their heads lowered as they traversed around a mound of open-mouthed skeletons. Once they reached the edge of the clearing, the trees were silent, except for a faint snarling when the cousins took turns chopping through the prickly foliage.

When Yuchen woke, it was almost evening. Squinting at the salt-coloured topiary, she scanned for Meifan, who was being carried behind her. Her sister saw her looking and sat up taller. Yuchen felt a sharp relief. They were both still alive.

Yuchen was about to ask her cousin if he remembered the time they pretended to be lost in the woods when she felt herself falling with swiftness, rolling onto the brittle ground. Gripping her stomach, she felt for the baby's movements, and when she felt faint wiggling, uttered a prayer of gratitude to the lotus-hearted Guanyin, goddess of soft-eyed mercy and compassion. She thought her cousin had tripped on a wayward root or a jutting rock, perhaps twisting his ankle. But her cousin hadn't gotten up. He was sprawled on his back, hands cupping his ears. His shrieks rebounded off the spruce saplings. "*AHHHHHHHH! AHHHHHHHHH! AHHHHHHHH!*"

"Get off the ground," Big Uncle shouted at his son. "What are you doing, Oldest Son?!"

He rolled and spasmed, as if he were possessed by a malevolent yaoguai.

Big Uncle tried to make his son sit up, but the young man flailed. His son's face was as pale as the forest except for two spots on his cheek that glowed like melting flames.

"We should go back," the third son, who was carrying Meifan, said. "We can leave the girls here and take our brother to a healer."

"No!" Big Uncle said. "The merchants are waiting for us and they expect prompt delivery. We must receive our payment!"

"Perhaps someone can stay with him?" the youngest son suggested. His two older brothers blanched.

"In the woods?" the second son asked. "Are you mad? How would you find us again? It was a mistake to come!"

"Enough!" Big Uncle shouted. "Do you want your mothers and sisters and future children to starve? We must pay the Shan a tithe not to hurt us when they invade again. How do you think you were able to survive the last occupation when most of our friends and neighbours did not? Even the empire's soldiers cannot protect us without coin, my idiot sons. Each girl is worth at least fifteen gold pieces. We must fulfill our obligation or else this trip has been for naught."

"But we must help him!" the third son protested.

"We cannot continue in the dark!" the second shouted.

The fourth one, who was loyal to his father, said nothing.

Seeing that he was reaching a mutiny among his sons, Big Uncle agreed to a respite.

Yuchen and Meifan were placed hastily near their eldest cousin, who had been dragged under a canopy of tall, milky cypress trees. Yuchen tried to soothe him, but he did not recognize her anymore.

Years of misery and servitude should have taught Yuchen to conceal her emotions, but unlike her sister, she could not. She remembered the times her cousin had given her simple gifts when she visited: a bouquet of wild yellow daisies, extra slices of sweet, porous vinegar rice cake from the kitchen. She thought of how they had once walked, years ago, at the edge of the town's winding river in iridescent springtime; how excited his boyish face had been when he showed her how to skim a flat pebble across bubbling water. Now, as her cousin howled in pain, Yuchen cried with him. The baby inside her kicked without pity.

To their surprise, Big Uncle covered the sisters with the burlap blanket from his second wife. "Rest, nieces," he ordered. He patted them on the crowns of their heads, as if they were well-behaved livestock. "We have a long journey as soon as the sun rises." When he looked at his writhing son, his face grew as unyielding as the white pillar that they had passed.

Purple night descended like a dense fog. Their cousins set up traps for squirmish rabbits, but Yuchen had not seen any songbirds or chittering squirrels. They could not chop timber in the white forest no matter how hard they tried. The unpigmented wood was impenetrable to their axes. There would be nothing to make a fire, and they'd be forced to huddle together against the chill. Even with the rustling trees, the forest felt empty, like blank parchment.

No one offered the sisters any food. They were allowed a sip of water each. Yuchen watched her three cousins swallow their allotted provisions of fermented black bean bread and handfuls of dark yellow jianyan, earth salt. The fourth son hadn't finished his salt crystals. Yuchen scooped up his leftovers in her palms and offered some to Meifan, who pushed the rough grains back, claiming to possess no appetite. Famished, Yuchen winced as the bitter salt burned her parched tongue. "Water," she begged, but the three cousins ignored her.

With his breath, Big Uncle ignited a huozhezi, a large flame stick of rolled-up cotton, bamboo, and beige parchment. Flickering light illuminated their frightened, dirt-smeared faces. Grimacing as she peeled off her lotus shoes, Yuchen attempted to rub her bandaged feet, which were speckled with fresh blood. Meifan's feet were no better. Yuchen scanned the pitch-coloured soil for tangled roots, perhaps sour acorns or even a brown, shrivelled worm. A bellyful of scraggly weeds would be able to nourish the baby budding inside her, but there was nothing.

At pink daybreak, first cousin had not exhausted himself. He was still shrieking, while the others, watching their distressed brother, complained of hunger. Overnight, the trees had become livelier. They thrashed and stabbed at each other. Sharp liquid oozed from their roots and punctured trunks. It was a bloodletting of trees. Yuchen shivered. *It looks and smells like a slaughterhouse*, she thought. She had a sickening memory of the Shan soldiers who had captured all the primary-school boys during the first invasion of Anding and forced them, in pairs, to march off the town square's roof. She heard the *splats!* and smelled the hot, fetid blood again.

As the wailings grew louder, Yuchen and Meifan stopped their ears with their fingers. The sound of the trees made it seem as though they were in celebratory attendance at the Hungry Ghost Festival, marvelling at zaji stage performers imitating screaming wind demons. Before the war there had been frequent village celebrations. With Mother, Father, and Big Brother, they had watched swirling, fan-twirling dancers and classical opera singers on the stage pay tribute to their venerable ancestors. These had been joyful times, when amusement and luxuries like stacks of fresh red bean cakes and sticky rice sweets were in abundance.

The funeral party watched the ferocious trees in silence until Big Uncle snapped at them to move. As they gathered their belongings, the male cousins began to scream as loud as their oldest brother, who was still thrashing on his back. Horrified, Big Uncle urged them to hurry to the edge of the forest. He motioned at his sons to grab their spasming brother, whose lips foamed with blood and spittle, who snapped at the air like a dying horse. But it was too late. As though shot by invisible arrows, his three other sons collapsed too.

"Get up!" Big Uncle shouted. "Get up! I said, get up, my sons! Your father, Bah-bah, commands it!"

Securing his beloved dao and his sheepskin rucksack, Big Uncle began zigzagging across the white briar path. A twine grabbed his arm, but he managed to hack himself free. He sprinted sideways and fell to the ground in a convulsive fit. His eyeballs bulged from within his skull; he squealed as if he were being gutted. His kneecaps cracked slowly. "*AHHHHHHH!*" he shouted, as if imitating his poor sons. "AHHHHHHHH! AHHHHHHH!" Yuchen watched, clutching her belly, while Meifan lowered her terror-stricken face. Big Uncle cried for help. Then he too, like his four sons, began a transformation.

First, white leaves like caterpillar whiskers began sprouting from his shouting lips. Pine needles and ivory-glossed branches grew from his broad shoulders like porcupine quills. All the men's torsos and legs lengthened and thickened into impressive trunks. Their feet began swelling into ungainly roots. Their bones cracked loudly as they split, bent, twisted.

There would be five new trees in the forest: an old forbidding cypress, three slender birch trees, and one chubby spruce sapling wearing a farmer's pointed cone hat.

"Help us!" the new trees shrieked. "Have mercy on us!"

As the transformation continued, the forest grew hotter and whiter, as if it were a core of melting candle wax. The earth rumbled eagerly. The trees around the sisters shot up, expanding into a dazzling milk-white sky. The sun and the moon simultaneously eclipsed the pearly tops of the leaves. Was Yuchen imagining it? Did she see shimmery apparitions of girls, other weeping widows, standing between the screaming trees? Dead wives; displaced concubines, dressed in their finest, palest funeral daxiushans with courtly jewels around their necks; poorer widows waved translucent paper fans, beckoning at the sisters.

"I think you should go now," Meifan said to Yuchen. She smiled faintly at her sister before staring at her defiled feet. Blood had sopped through her lotus shoes, staining them the colour of a blistering sun. "I am tired of living, Small Sister."

"No, Big Sister," Yuchen said with tremendous force. Her instinct for survival had always been strong, but she could not leave without Meifan. Her loyalty to her sister was a virtue that defined her. "Come with me to Beijing! We'll have a better chance if we go together!"

"You were a good Small Sister," Meifan said, her voice heavy as a barrel filled with lard. "I don't know if you'll make it on those feet, or what will happen to your child, but you should try to find Big Brother."

Yuchen had forgotten the blistering ache that extended from her missing toes to her raw knees. She needed to find a skilled healer to stop the spread of infection and oozing discomfort. She knew Meifan was right. Despite being younger, Yuchen understood that her older sister no longer wanted to survive.

Yuchen looked at former Big Uncle and her cousins, writhing in their own executions. More and more pine needles and spiny maggot-white leaves began to sprout from their bodies. It seemed to Yuchen that they were performing a dance, punctuated by a cadence of locust-like shrieks. By now, only Big Uncle's torso was recognizable. Her once sweet cousin had become a furry birch tree with wet, winking eyes.

Yuchen looked back at Meifan, who was sitting, cross-legged, on the burlap blanket. Meifan nodded encouragingly at her. When they were small children, in the sun-brushed plum blossom courtyard of their ancestral home, they'd often picnic outside with their mother, while a servant boy fanned them. Yuchen would tug playfully at their mother's long, heavy braids, while Meifan peeled sweet litchi fruit and stared, contemplating the haughty swans and lust-calling peacocks by the emerald lotus pond. Meifan had seemed perfectly content then, and as Yuchen watched her older sister for the very last time, Meifan seemed to be almost at peace. Her thin shoulders seemed less burdened; her features, less severe. The crinkles deforming her lips and large, petal-shaped eyes were no longer visible. She looked sweet and fourteen years old again. The ghosts of the widows who had been left to die in the white forest were speaking to Meifan, comforting her in silky, rustling voices.

Yuchen's baby squirmed, like a hungry snake, inside her stomach, as if to remind her that it was time to go. She could feel a half-starved love flooding through her, for her sister, for her parents, who had been victims of their place and time, and everyone else in Anding who had suffered. Ghost-like but determined, more tortoise than girl, Yuchen began to crawl on her knees through the white, sepulchral trees. The lower bodies of her cousins and uncle had formed into sturdy, gnarled trunks, but the spiky branches that had once been their arms still thrashed with energy, as if they were attempting to pummel the heavens, dropping wide, star-shaped leaves in protest. The new trees still had their cousins' twitching eyes, fleshy gums, and gasping red lips, which moaned her name. Yuchen ignored them, whispering stubbornly to her unborn child. *You will be brave like your auntie Meifan.* Somehow, she'd find a way through the funeral forest. She did not know which direction Beijing or Manchuria lay, where the sun rose or fell, but behind her, there were only white trees and certain death.

Acknowledgments

It is a ghastly undertaking to write a book, and I am not entirely sure what possessed me to write another one. This collection has given me a variety of hives, chest pains, stomach upsets, and toothaches; it has caused neurosis, paralysis, and mild despair. But I am very lucky to have a team of talented and committed individuals behind me.

Gratitude is due to my incredible agent, Carly Watters, who is never afraid of what I email her, no matter how grisly or unsound. Thanks for your amazing belief in weirdo-me from the very beginning! Much appreciation to the wonderful Jo Ramsay and everyone at P.S. Literary. I would not get paid without you.

Deborah Sun de la Cruz for her editorial vision and thoughtful insight. Thank you for your tremendous commitment to this book. The powerhouse team at Penguin Random House Canada, publisher Nicole Winstanley, Bonnie Maitland, Dan French, Scott Sellers, Alanna McMullen, Shaun Oakey for such savvy copy edits, Emma Dolan for the beautiful, hallucinogenic cover, Brittany Larkin, Marcia Gallego, Sean Tai, and Kathleen Jones.

Many of the early versions of these stories were written in the excellent fiction workshops of Linda Svendsen, Sonya Chung, Rebecca Curtis, and Jami Attenberg. Thanks also to Jen Sookfong Lee and Madeleine Thien for your encouraging feedback.

Mom and Dad, for housing me while I wrote this book. Don't worry, I will find a steady job next year.

My students, colleagues, and amazing mentors, particularly Minelle Mahtani, Alix Ohlin, Bronwen Tate, and Kevin Chong, for inspiring me to become a better writer and teacher. To the writer-in-residence programs at the University of Manitoba, the University of the Fraser Valley, Richmond Public Library, and the Vancouver Public Library. I'm honoured to have been supported by you.

The irreplaceable Marni Berger, for reading a billion drafts and being incredibly nice about it. My dearest writing friends and sisters: Jenny Heijun Wills, Carrianne Leung, Doretta Lau, Joanna Chiu, Uzma Jalaluddin, Gina Leola Woolsey, and V.S. Chiu. How thankful I am that we can navigate this writerly hell together.